THE WAY TO HELL

ANGEL & HAINES BOOK 4

GRAHAM H MILLER

OFFICIAL WOOTENSHIRE LICENCE

Book Cover Design by ebooklaunch.com

Created with Vellum

CHAPTER ONE

Amelia Bagshaw looked up from where she was packing her school bag, immediately alert to the change in the atmosphere in the room. Her father, Thomas, looked at his phone as if it was a valued pet that had suddenly turned and bitten him. He held it at arm's length. He sat at the kitchen table, with toast and tea in front of him, perfectly angled so that he could see the television with the news on, but still keep an eye on his family. His wife, Sharon was ironing. The television was just loud enough to make conversation difficult, to dominate the room.

Sharon looked up warily as she moved a shirt to a hanger. 'What's up, babe?' It was better to show concern than keep her head down and hope.

'I'm worried about Sophie. Ever since she left home, I feel like she's drifting away. I tried ringing just now and nothing happened. It didn't even try to connect. Not even voicemail. Your daughter's phone isn't working.'

'Maybe she forgot to charge it. Don't stress about it.'

'No, that's not it. If her phone was out of charge, then it'd have gone to voicemail. Besides, I've been texting her for the best part of a week. No reply. Not one. So, when I woke up this morning I thought it was time I gave her a call. Early morning is the best time, before she gets a chance to go out or do anything.' He paused, and turned to study his wife. 'I'm worried about her. Maybe she's lost her phone or can't afford to pay the bill. I hate all this modern stuff, where you don't have a real phone number or address. Where was she living? I'm sure she told you.'

'She said she was going to stay with a friend, you know, for a couple of weeks. Then she was going to look for a job and once she'd had a bit of money coming in, she could get somewhere permanent.'

'Well? She's been gone over a month. That's more than a couple of weeks. Where's she gone?'

'I don't know. Don't worry about it, we haven't changed our address or our phone number. Even if she can't afford to pay her phone bill, or she's had her phone stolen, she always knows she can come home.' She glanced at her husband and realised she had pacified him. 'Have you tried Facebook?'

'Facebook? Yes...' He picked up his phone and peered at it closely, pecking away angrily with his finger. 'Doesn't seem like she's posted much since she left home. Nothing at all in fact.'

'What about checking her friends list?' Amelia said without looking up. When she became aware of the silence in the room and that her mother had stopped ironing, she hastily added. 'It's what my friends at school say.' She practically rolled her eyes. 'What?' She sighed. 'You know I've never been on Facebook! Without a phone, I can't, can I?' There was a silence in the kitchen. 'But my friends at school have and they're all about the drama with who's Facebook friends with who and who's blocked and who isn't.' I won't ever get the chance to even look at Facebook while I'm living here, she thought. But she knew that she'd said enough and kept the thought to herself. 'Or Instagram, or SnapChat,' she suggested. 'There's loads of them out there.'

'Yes! Of course!' Thomas just started tapping away at his phone and muttered under his breath while doing so. All Amelia could hear were occasional words, 'who the hell's that?' and 'blocked'.

Amelia looked around and realised that while he was busy looking for her sister, for once the attention wasn't on her. 'Guess I'll get ready for school then,' she said quietly. She gathered up her bag, coat and blazer and left before anything else happened.

THAT LUNCHTIME, Amelia walked over to her best friend Sara.

'Hey Amelia, has your dad changed his mind yet?' Sara said as she looked up from the tree stump where she was sitting, bent over her phone.

'Changed his mind? About what?' Amelia tried to figure out which of her dad's rules Sara was talking about.

'I mean, do you have a phone?'

'Nah, that ain't happening in my lifetime.'

'How about...' Sara pulled a phone out of her bag. 'Did you want my old one? I mean, it's rubbish, low memory, totally like three years out of date. But I charged it up, reset it and it still works. I've got a charger and I've put an old Pay As You Go SIM in it that has some credit left on it. But you won't need much if you can get it onto the home Wi-Fi.'

Emotions swirled through Amelia. Hope, that someone might do something nice, but mixed with fears. What if this was a joke? Worse, what if her father found out? Nervously she asked, 'That's for me?'

When Sara nodded, Amelia started to believe. Obviously she'd have to make plans. She couldn't go home with a phone. Her father made sure that she was never to have a phone. In his head it was a gateway to a horrifying world of pornography, grooming and drugs for sale.

But on the other hand, she ached for it. It would remove the barriers that existed between her and her friends. For a brief moment she allowed herself to imagine what it would be like. She could play games, join in with her friends, have messaged conversations late into the night. Conversations that her parents would not be able to overhear.

And then reality intervened. She looked around nervously at the playground. It was an overcast but dull day with a cold edge to weather. They were stuck between the Halloween half term and Christmas. It wasn't close enough to Christmas to be exciting, just the dull grind through another school year.

Amelia's heart sank when she saw her father coming out of the school buildings and scanning the playground. That really was a disadvantage. There ought to be a law against parents being teachers at the same school as their children.

Without thinking, she dropped the phone into her pocket. She even liked the way that it felt as it slid down the fabric of her blazer and made a thunk as it settled in her pocket.

'Do you think he saw?'

'Who? Mr Bagshaw?'

Amelia rolled her eyes the way she always did when her friends treated her father just like any other teacher.

'Come on, let's go down The Backs and I'll show you how it works.' This was an area down the back of the playing field where there was some scrub land. Teachers would occasionally wander down and keep an eye out, but generally it was too far from the buildings for the teachers to venture close. It was an unspoken rule that they'd watch from a distance, which made it more suitable for private conversations than anywhere else on the school grounds.

For the next ten minutes, Amelia and Sara were blissfully happy. Sara showed her all the features of the phone, while apologising for how basic it was. But Amelia didn't care. It was something to call her own, something that hadn't been provided by her parents, and that in itself was precious.

'What's this app? StringCan?'

'It's some weird messaging thing. I installed it because there was all that fuss last year. All the olds and parents got scared by it so I thought I'd have a look. Never really got the hang of it.'

'Why not?'

'It's meant to connect people who haven't met. You can set up your profile and then look for people based on lots of attributes, like what music or sports teams they're into. Or you can put in a mobile number and it'll text them a link to install the app.'

'What got everyone all worked up about it then?'

'Well, they figured you could use the system to identify children and then all the perverts would use it for grooming. They released an update so that all the child accounts got flagged up with a little icon. That's when most people stopped using it.'

'Oh right.' Amelia was already scrolling through the other apps, looking for something new. Finally, she powered it off and weighed it in her hand for a second or two. She looked at it as if it was a time bomb. 'Listen, Sara, I know it's awkward and all, but can you keep this over the weekend?' It was a Friday and Amelia was tempted to break the monotony of a weekend at home with the new phone. But she knew this was such a large violation of her father's rules that she'd have to be very careful. 'It's not that I'm not grateful, really I am. I just need to take a few days to find a safe place to hide it in my room.'

'Your parents are proper freaks, you know that?'

'Tell me about it. But what can you do?'

CHAPTER TWO

DC Emma Angel had spent long, dull weeks at home. Her boss, DI Slater had reported her to Professional Standards and taken her badge, radio and security pass. She had presumed there was an investigation underway into her conduct but she hadn't been notified of any progress that might be happening.

However, her payslip had arrived, together with a message informing her that she was suspended on full pay. Finally, she received a terse phone call informing her that she was required to attend a meeting at Bradwick police station, followed up with a letter confirming the date and time. The one ray of hope was that the letter described it as a back to work meeting. As it was scheduled for eight on Monday morning, she hoped that it was a sign she'd start back that day. She just didn't know if she'd have a reprimand on her record, or extra supervision.

The days dragged past until it was finally time to present herself and learn her fate. She arrived at the station and went through the somewhat strange experience of signing herself in as a visitor to the place where she'd been working for years.

When she let herself into the conference room however, she got a shock. There at the head of the table sat Michelle Jones, the Detective Sergeant from Professional Standards who'd overseen the operation that led to Rob Haines' downfall. As usual, Michelle was looking immaculate, her perfectly manicured hands resting on the piece of paper she was reading, while her laptop was set off to one side. With her flawless complexion and hair, she might have been posing for a magazine article about how to be professional and stylish at work.

Away from the magnetic pull of Michelle there were two other officers in the room, both men wearing near identical charcoal suits. The older one looked up as Emma entered, smiled warmly, and gestured to a chair. 'Ah, DC Angel, do please, come in and have a seat.'

Emma sat down and looked over at Michelle Jones. 'Do I need to get a police fed rep in?'

'No, no, I don't think that'd be necessary,' the older man said, before catching himself. 'I mean, it is your right, if you feel that some external advice would be useful. But I think you've jumped to some assumptions. I'm DI Simpson, from Professional Standards and this is my colleague, DS Breznowski.'

'So, DS Jones isn't part of the investigation then?' Emma said slowly.

'No, *DI Jones* is here in a different capacity.' Simpson paused and took a deep breath. 'I am aware that the two of you have history but if you'll indulge me, I want to start at the beginning. We have conducted an in-depth inquiry into the handling of the recent spree killer case, in particular looking at the suitability of Gordon Bell as a suspect and the way that alternative suspects were investigated.

'As part of this process, we carried out interviews with DI Slater, as well as the rest of the team. As I'm sure you're aware, Slater was due to retire before he was brought back to head up the CID team. As a result of these discussions, we've decided that it was a regrettable lapse in judgement on the part of DI Slater not to listen to your concerns and investigate alternative theories of the crime. Bearing this in mind, he has chosen to take his retirement, effective immediately.'

A silence fell on the room. Emma realised that everyone else already knew that Slater had left, and she was the last to know. But she felt her shoulders relax. Now that it was over, she recognised how much of her working day had been taken up with fighting against her boss and worrying what he might do next. It was all over. An emptiness settled over her, an awareness that her future was now blank, open and unknowable.

Simpson looked uncomfortable. 'The Service would like to acknowledge that you saved us from a lot of embarrassment in the future. This case could easily have been undone in five or ten years' time, which would have caused a lot of damage.' He slid and envelope across the table. 'Your badge and pass. The official record of the investigation will show that you are exonerated of all blame in what happened.'

Slowly the pieces started to fit together for Emma. She was back in CID, with a clean record. Michelle Jones had been promoted to Inspector but hadn't made any contribution to the disciplinary process.

'So, that brings us to the present. With Kevin Slater now retired, there was a vacancy at the top. We offered it to DS Chisholm, but he chose retirement as well. Michelle has passed her inspector's exam and was waiting for a posting. So, DI Jones is now your new boss, head of CID. It's not only your first day back, but DI Jones is taking up her new posting starting today as well.'

Michelle Jones inclined her head in a nod of thanks to

Simpson. 'Thank you for that summary. I'm looking forward to the challenge of running CID. Hopefully we can get things on a more stable footing than it has been in the past. And, Emma,' she turned the full force of her smile on Emma, 'I hope we can put the past behind us. I think you've shown that you're a conscientious officer and I'm looking forward to working with you.'

Emma didn't really know what to say. She knew from experience that bad mouthing your previous boss was not the done thing, but she struggled to find good things to say about Michelle Jones following their previous encounter. 'I'm all for a completely new start. Let's turn the page and write something new.'

Michelle nodded, possibly accepting that there was nothing else that her DC could really say.

'Well, I think that's all that really needs to be said,' DI Simpson said, looking around the table.

Michelle stood up. 'If there aren't any more questions, then you can come with me and get straight back to work, DC Angel.'

DC Emma Angel rose to her feet, relieved the meeting was over.

AS SHE FOLLOWED her through the corridors and back to the CID open plan area, Emma wondered what it'd be like in the office with Michelle Jones as a boss. Her previous bosses had been challenging in their own way. Rob Haines was now one of her best friends, but he had been difficult to work for. She'd never really decided if he was doing the right thing or not. Then there was DI Kevin Slater, who was nothing short of a nightmare. He'd had a vendetta against her from the outset.

DI Jones went to her office and Emma sat at her desk, logged on and groaned at the number of emails and alerts that had accumulated in her absence. She knew that Brian Chisholm wouldn't be around any longer, but she was strangely glad to see that Suse Berman was at her desk. And Nick Dent still looked young and fresh faced. She was glad that there was some sense of continuity, even if the atmosphere felt strange and different.

'So, you outlived old Spreadsheet Slater, then?' Suse said. For her it was a warm welcome.

'You give me too much credit,' Emma said, smiling. 'It's not a great achievement, he had one foot out the door as soon as he arrived.'

'What kind of retired policeman do you think he'll be?' Nick Dent asked. 'I mean knowing Slater, it'll either be a country cottage with roses around the door or running his own pub.'

Emma really missed Brian Chisholm's input. He'd have had something to say about pubs run by retired coppers. And it'd probably be politically incorrect too.

'Oh God, if he ran a pub, he'd be the worst sort of landlord,' Emma said without thinking. 'The one who marks all the bottles and counts the tips. He'd know exactly how long drinking up time was as well. Everything would be on a spreadsheet.' She shook her head.

When the laughter had died down a bit, Suse got serious. 'Anyway, the main thing is, we owe you a vote of thanks. It was all shaping up to be a complete mess. I still say that if Gordon Bell had gone down for it, we'd have been on a Channel Four documentary in ten years' time. With dodgy actors from daytime TV playing us in reconstructions. And they'd have proved him innocent.'

The conversation was brought to an end when DI Jones left her office, walked to the front of the desks and clapped her hands. 'Right. For those who don't know me, I'm Detective Inspector Michelle Jones and I've just been transferred to be the head of CID. DI Slater has retired and I've taken his place. He was just a caretaker, with a few months left to go and now he's gone. But I can assure you that I'm here to run the department, fully committed. This is where I want to be and I fully intend to make a go of it. I know that in the past there's been a fair amount of disruption in this department.' She looked around the room, catching Emma's eye.

It was Emma's chance to say something, but she chose to keep quiet. She could see nothing to be gained from speaking now. Again, she found herself wishing Chisholm was still here. She couldn't imagine that he had avoided Professional Standards for his entire career.

'I have further news,' Michelle was still speaking. 'We're getting a couple of trainee detective constables joining us. It'll be a chance for them to get some more experience working with us, and will help plug the resource gap left by DS Chisholm's retirement. First up to have a chance at seeing what life here is like in CID is John Fletcher.' She looked around expectantly, then shrugged. 'Well, the first lesson that we'll teach him is how to be punctual.'

She was interrupted when the phone rang. Without anyone asking, Nick Dent got up from the desk where he was perched and went to answer it. 'Anyway,' Michelle continued, 'we're going to leave the past where it belongs – in the past. Hold on.' She turned to where Nick was trying to attract her attention while wrapping up his conversation on the phone.

When he finished, she had a brief whispered conversation with him and then brought him to the front of the office.

'We've got a dead drug dealer,' Nick Dent said simply. 'Over on the edge of the Seaview. He was parked up outside a row of shops. One of the shopkeepers came across the body this morning when they came in to start work. He was lying next to his car. Stabbed.'

'How do we know he was a drug dealer?' Michelle asked.

'I spoke to the PCSOs who were first on scene. Apparently that car park has no CCTV, so at night once all the shops are shut, the dealers can park up there. Given that we have a young male found stabbed next to an expensive SUV...' Nick didn't finish the sentence but shrugged instead. 'I could be wrong, but you know, first impressions and all that...'

'Right then,' Michelle said. 'It looks like my introduction speech is over. Suse, would you head over there, make an initial assessment? Take Emma with you. If it looks straightforward, stay there and process, liaise with the coroner, undertaker, evidence and search teams. You know the drill. Anything funny, give me a ring and I'll be down there. Meanwhile the rest of us will set up an investigation. Do we have a name yet?'

Nick Dent looked down at his notepad. 'Car's registered to a William Hawsley. He's had a few cautions for possession. The PCSO who made the initial contact checked against a photo from the DVLA and it looks likely that the body is the owner. Obviously it'll need checking against fingerprints, and a formal identification from next of kin, but it looks likely.'

'Right then. Everyone else, I want to know everything there is to know about Hawsley,' Michelle said. 'Emma and Suse, stay in touch. Let's get to work!'

The door to the office opened and a young man walked in.

White, short dark hair gelled up, and wearing a shiny suit and tie. Suse looked up, 'John Fletcher?'

'Yes,' he said.

'You're late,' Michelle said sharply. 'I've no time to lecture you on the importance of time keeping. You're here to get some experience, so you can go with DS Berman and DC Angel to view the crime scene. Watch what they do, learn what you can, touch nothing and keep your mouth shut.'

CHAPTER THREE

The three officers pulled up in a car park outside a small row of shops, set back from a main road that led to the seafront. Nearly all the spaces were taken, and they had to walk over to where a corner had been taped off.

The sun was low in the sky and the shadows still had frost in them. Emma looked at the ground to see where it was safe to walk. There was a chill in the air and all of them pulled their coats tighter as they walked to the small row of shops.

In the centre of the cordon of police tape, a white SUV sat alone. As they approached the constable who was guarding the scene, the three CID officers signed in on a clipboard and were helped through the tape.

The closer they got to the scene, the worse the smell became. Usually the cold kept the smell of death down but here it was strong enough to overcome that effect. Emma was used to the coppery smell of blood, but there was a rank toilet smell overlaid with something else, equally bad.

The car park was surrounded with a low brick wall. The suspect car was parked as far away from the entrance as possible, tucked into a corner. On the far side of the vehicle was a footpath that led along the edge of the car park, through a gap in the wall and on to the shops. It was on this path that the body lay, face up, parallel to the car that he'd owned in life.

'What the hell is that smell?' Emma said.

'Yeah, I know,' John said. 'I mean, these car parks are never very nice places but that's worse.'

'Good morning,' Dani Price, the pathologist said, standing up from where she was crouched over the body. 'That smell is because he's been gutted like a fish. It's like when you're sick, everything that should be inside suddenly arrives outside, along with the smell. I've seen plenty of stabbings, but he looks like he's been ripped open, right through the intestinal wall.'

'Ewww,' Emma said. 'Is that what killed him?'

'Probably. I'll know more when we get him onto the table.'

Suse nodded, then asked, 'Could he have gone far, once he was stabbed?'

'No more than a few steps, he would've collapsed fairly quickly. There's a whole host of organs and blood vessels in there, so his blood pressure would've dropped like a stone, along with the pain, and the damage to his core muscles. In short, he didn't stand a chance. He would've bled out in a matter of minutes.'

Suse turned to John. 'Looking at the puddle of blood, he was most likely killed here, outside his vehicle.' She leaned in to look inside the car. 'No blood in there at all. So, he was standing by his car, maybe waiting for someone or chatting on his phone, when he was killed?'

Emma looked around outside the car, then pointed her toe at something on the ground. 'Looks like half a joint,' she said. 'We'll have to get it tested, but that looks fresh. And it's half-finished, so he was probably smoking a blunt and got surprised.' She pulled on a single glove, retrieved the half cigarette, and dropped it into an evidence bag. 'We can check DNA and see if it's either his or his killer's.'

John nodded. 'Most likely his. He wouldn't want to get his flashy car all smelling of dope smoke.' He took a good look at the victim's face. 'He looks young. How old was he?'

'If the identification is right,' Emma said, 'this is William Hawsley, also known as Bill, and he was twenty years old.' She looked down at his face, now pallid, his previously full lips now an unnatural blue. He had longish ginger hair that curled back from his face. She was struck by how young he looked. He was only a handful of years younger than her. She was shaken because of the way she'd grown up. When she was old enough to see what was going on, she realised that some of the family and friends she knew would go to festivals with drugs and sell them there to recoup their costs. This young man reminded her of those days. In her head there was a world of difference between that and this young man selling drugs from a car park. But she was aware that in the eyes of the law, they were the same.

She could see the adult face starting to come through the victim's features. She could see that he might have grown up to be a tall, well-built man, probably with a receding hairline and jowly face. Except now he never would.

'Wow! Dealing drugs obviously pays.' They both looked at John who was walking around the SUV that loomed over them. It was white, shiny and nearly new. The door was still ajar and they could see leather seats and an array of buttons and technology. 'Yep,' John said drily, 'looks like we're in the wrong job. That's one fancy car for someone who's just stopped being a teenager.'

'Yeah, but he paid for it, didn't he?' Suse said. 'He

might've got rich quickly but he also got killed for it.' The two detectives looked at each other and nodded.

'What else do we know about the victim?' John broke the silence.

'We'll have to wait until we get back to the office,' Emma said. 'While we're here, the rest of the team back there are working up all the information. Hopefully we'll have a next-of-kin and some idea of who his enemies were.'

'To be honest,' John said earnestly, 'he was hanging about here where the kids come to buy their sweets and selling drugs. Does it matter who his enemies were? I mean, someone's done us a favour.'

'Hey! We'll have less of that,' Emma said sharply. 'We were all idiots when we were teenagers. Yes, there's a chance, quite a good one, that he would have grown up to be a criminal that we would have locked up over and over again. But maybe he'd have beaten the odds. I know there are some people who get out of prison and hook up with charities. Finish their education. Those people go on to become advisers to shine a light further back down the path, help other people out of addiction and crime.' She stopped to take a breath. 'Either way, he never got that chance, he's never going to make the choice and that's where the crime is. Somewhere he's got a mother, probably friends, a family. Someone somewhere will be wondering where he is and when he's coming home.

'We're going to treat this victim exactly the same way as if he was the Mayor of Bradwick, are we clear? We're going to work this crime scene, just the same, no matter who the victim is or what you feel about him.'

John looked down at his shoes. 'Yes, sorry. I've spent too long arresting the same people, turfing them out on the streets and then picking them up a week later. I guess I've just got cynical.'

'Well, I've said my piece. Let's process the scene,' Emma said briskly. 'You check his pockets and I'll search the car.'

It's not often I outrank someone, Emma thought, so I'll enjoy it. The job was the job, so John got his gloves on and carefully started working through the pockets in the jeans and jacket that the victim was wearing. Emma meanwhile leaned into the car and started opening the glove box and checking in all the pockets and cubby holes in the front. She didn't get far before she climbed out and said, 'Suse, I think we've got a problem.'

The trainee detective constable straightened up from the body and said, 'I was about to say that. What have you got?'

Emma held up several plastic bags. Some held small wraps of drugs, others were full of pills and a few held wads of dark green leaves.

In reply, John held up several fat rolls of notes that he'd found. 'There must be thousands of pounds here. If it wasn't robbery, then what was it?'

'Not a turf war either,' Emma said. 'I mean this would be a good startup if you wanted to take over. I've never seen a battle over territory where they leave all the good stuff behind. Drug dealers are, by their very nature, lazy and greedy.' She thought for a moment, choosing her words carefully. 'Maybe you're not the only one who thinks he was a waste of space; maybe we have a vigilante in town.'

John didn't answer directly. 'Is there anything else we need to do here, or shall we head back to the station?'

They both turned to look at Suse who'd been chatting with the PCSOs and talking on her phone.

'I think we can head back to base. John, fetch the camera from the car, let's get our own photos. Emma, can you bag up the evidence please? I think we've seen enough here. Something smells bad about this, and I don't mean the fact that Bill's insides are on the outside. Let's get this up on a board and start digging into his life. Someone disliked him enough to kill him slowly and painfully.'

CHAPTER FOUR

Sharon Bagshaw shouted up the stairs. 'Amelia! Get down here now! You won't have time for breakfast if you don't get up soon.'

'What does she normally have?' her husband Tom asked. 'I can make it before I head out?'

'It's all right, I can cope,' Sharon said. 'Don't you have to be in early?'

'I'm sure they can cope without me for another few minutes.' Sharon looked disbelievingly at her husband. 'Seriously, I want to help.'

'She has a bowl of muesli,' Sharon said. 'Something about white toast and marmalade having too many refined carbs first thing in the morning. I don't really understand it.'

'That's easy, at least!' He started opening cupboards, looking for bowls and cereal. 'Have you got any further in working out how to get in touch with Sophie? I've tried getting in touch with her friends online but no one seems to know anything at all.'

'You know,' Sharon said thoughtfully, 'it could be good

news.' He husband stopped his searching and frowned at her. 'I mean, if anything had happened to her, then surely one of her friends would've posted something like "hope you get well soon" or "you'll find a job" type of thing?'

He filled a bowl with muesli and went to the fridge. 'I'm not worried exactly. But she's been living with us for her whole life and moved out only a month or so ago. The family doesn't feel right if she's not here. I should be able to look after my girls and I can't do that if they're not here.'

Amelia ran into the room, blouse untucked. 'Oh, wow! Muesli! Thanks Mum!'

'It wasn't me, you should thank your father.'

A sudden silence fell across the room. Both women looked nervously at Thomas. Unaware of the atmosphere in the room, he smiled broadly. 'It was no bother! You're welcome. Now I've got to get to work.' With that he breezed out of the house, the door shutting gently behind him.

Amelia looked at her mother, a frown on her face. 'What was that all about then?'

Sharon stayed at the sink with her back to her daughter. 'I don't know what you mean.' Her tone sounded final, but Amelia was having none of it.

'You do know what I mean,' she said angrily. 'Half the time we're walking on eggshells, never sure what he's going to do next. Then all of a sudden it's like he's walked out of some crappy sitcom and he's all smiley and happy.'

'Can't you just be happy, for once?' Sharon snapped.

Amelia caught herself. She knew that today Sara would bring in the phone and she'd be able to have it at home. 'Sorry, Mum,' she said in a tone that she hoped was a bit rueful. 'Just woke up a bit late and now I feel all rushed. I didn't mean anything by it. It's just nice to see Dad in a good mood.'

Sharon smiled. 'Well, you might be right, it doesn't happen that often. How about we just make the most of it and don't rock the boat?'

Amelia nodded. 'I'll try to be good at school,' she said. And if I get my way, I'll avoid him altogether, she thought.

CHAPTER FIVE

When Emma, Suse and John arrived back at the office, the rest of the team already had the crime board set up and photos of Bill Hawsley attached to it, along with his basic biography and details of the crime scene. Everyone was at their desk and working away busily. Emma turned to John Fletcher. 'You see, the first twenty-four hours are the best time to solve a crime.'

'Fletcher. My office. Now.' Michelle Jones stuck her head out of her office door, shouted at the new detective and was already sitting back behind her desk by the time he started moving.

'Let's get as much into the computers as we can,' Suse said. She didn't need to add, 'Before the boss finishes shouting at John and looks for another target'. Everyone was studiously trying to look busy and avoid the anger of the new boss.

The rest of the day passed uneventfully, with the team working hard to build a picture of William Hawsley. Some of it was conjecture, but he had been unremarkable at school, rumoured to be a bit of a bully. He'd left before his exams as he'd already started dealing by then and simply took it up full time when he couldn't be bothered with education anymore. He was suspected of shoplifting and fencing stolen goods in return for drugs. He was certainly a known figure, and even though he was only twenty, he had already generated a substantial file.

But even with all that information, Emma still couldn't see this as the beginning of a turf war over drugs. There was no way that a rival gang would leave that much money and product lying around waiting to be picked up. And as suspected with the time and location of the murder, neither the CCTV nor the door to door turned up any leads or sightings at all. So it was highly unlikely that the killer had been disturbed.

The reports from scene of crime confirmed their initial suspicions. Bill had been outside his car, probably smoking a joint, when he was attacked. It seemed that the attacker stabbed him, then made away without disturbing the rest of the scene.

All of which added up to the fact that there was no clear suspect emerging from the evidence as it was entered onto the computers. The other big motivation for murder hadn't panned out either. At twenty, Bill was playing the field but didn't seem to have any fixed or serious relationships. Emma supposed that sooner or later they might find that he'd been involved with a married woman, but again, it didn't feel right to her.

As the day was winding down to the point where most people would normally be considering going home, Michelle Jones came over to talk to Emma.

'We've had word from Dani that she's moved our victim up to the front of the queue. She's just completed the post-mortem. Usually she'd email the report over straight away, but she says she's got some new evidence. Can you go down to the lab and see what she's got? Bag it, tag it and put it into the system. We'll all still be here when you get back.'

EMMA, like most police officers, didn't like going to the pathology lab. It was right down in the hospital basement, and now, deep into winter, it was dark outside even though it was still only early evening. The hospital administration had recently re-decorated the space so that it was now bright and airy with a nice relative's room and a viewing suite. That makeover hadn't reached the working areas though, which were still stainless steel and tile. And none of it hid the smell or the fact that it was the last place that a patient would visit in the hospital.

Emma found Dani in the autopsy room, just closing up Bill Hawsley. When she'd visited her first post-mortem, Emma had wondered how she'd cope. She'd heard the stories of rookie cops who fainted or threw up. But she found that she was able to maintain a level of detachment. Without going too far down the path of her parents' beliefs and her upbringing, she did believe that once a soul had departed, the body that was left was just an empty vessel. And, in her job, it was a source of evidence.

It didn't mean that she was completely detached though. The body brought home the fact that there had been a living person who'd been killed. She could see the potential of who they would've been. And the autopsy also revealed the violence that had been done to them. It was impossible to ignore the pain and fear they felt when it was laid out on the table.

'Right, so I can get the questions you always ask out of the way before you even get a chance,' Dani said with a smile.

'There was a frost last night, so I had to get the calculator out, but I can give you a time of death. Between midnight and two this morning.'

Emma groaned.

'What's wrong? Doesn't that fit?'

'Oh no, it fits perfectly. You saw where the body was found. He was between his car and the row of shops, with no CCTV. Now you tell me it was between midnight and two? There would've been no one around on a cold night and practically zero chance of any car going past with a dash cam.'

'And even if they were, he'd have been hidden from the road.'

'Tell me you've got something better on the cause of death.'

'A lot better. There's no mystery here, massive blood loss would've caused his pressure to drop through the floor leading to cardiac arrest. No surprises there.' Dani indicated the body. 'Let me walk you through it. So, this guy was stabbed low down on the left,' she pointed to where she'd closed his side, 'with something long and sharp.' Dani was entirely professional, going through the injuries in order. 'Then the assailant dragged the knife across the abdomen. The knife was long and sharp, it cut the left kidney, through the colon and small intestine before getting the descending colon on the other side. Guy had no chance.'

Emma half listened as Dani detailed the damage to his muscle wall and the fact that he would've died a slow, lonely death due to blood loss. But a part of her brain was looking at the figure on the table and thinking that it could have been her a few months ago. She'd been surprised by a suspect, Greg Watts, who had a hidden screwdriver in his left hand. While she'd been distracted by a rock in his right, he'd stabbed her with his left, nearly killing her.

Emma felt queasy for the first time ever at an autopsy. She felt slightly dizzy and took a step to maintain her balance, reaching out one hand to the edge of the table.

Dani stopped what she was saying and looked over at Emma, who had gone quiet. 'Are you all right, Emma? I mean, I know there are some officers who it's best to meet in the lab and others who can handle a dead body. I always thought you were one of the latter type. Oh my God, you've gone pale, as well. When did you last eat?'

'I had breakfast, and well, biscuits with coffee during the day.'

'And breakfast was when, exactly?'

'About seven, give or take. I had to be in early for back to work meeting, then they found the body and it all kicked off.'

Dani frowned at her. 'I bought a sandwich to eat later, before I drove home,' she said. 'You can sit in my office and eat it, I'll make you a cup of tea.'

'I can't do that! I'm not taking your sandwich.'

'You can,' Dani said firmly. 'We're in a hospital, and I'm friendly with some of the nurses. You have something to eat and a cup of tea, or I'm phoning them up and saying you nearly fainted. I'm sure they'll have time to give you a proper check-up.'

The two women stared at each other, but the moment was broken when Emma's stomach rumbled. She laughed. 'Betrayed by my own body,' she said.

When they were sitting in Dani's office, and Emma was eating, the pathologist said, 'I'm sorry if I came on a bit strong. But I am medically trained even if I spend all my time down here. You did go really pale, and I saw you sway and hold onto the table. Last thing I need is you fainting and hitting your head.'

'I'm usually fine with autopsies. It's just when you said

the words, you know, the description of the injury. It was the phrase "long and sharp" followed by the damage to the kidney. Exactly the same words I heard when I woke up in hospital after I got stabbed by Greg Watts.'

'Oh! No, I'm sorry. I didn't think. I mean I know what happened to you. But I didn't connect it up.' She was appalled.

'It's OK,' Emma said. She paused, then asked, 'Dani, how close did I come? To dying, I mean?'

'There's no way to measure it. And, I wasn't your doctor, so I haven't seen your chart.' She stopped to think. 'You had a couple of advantages over William Hawsley. You had a simple puncture wound, whereas this victim was sliced open so the wound was much bigger. You couldn't do that with a screw-driver.' She looked up to check Emma was okay. 'The other thing is that you had access to your phone and an ambulance three streets away. Hawsley didn't have a chance to call for help.'

'We found his phone in the car park, with a cracked screen. I figure it was taken out of his hand and thrown over the car.'

Dani nodded. 'And even if he had managed it, he was hidden and it was a Sunday night. It's unlikely even if he made the call that emergency services would've found him in time to save him.' She shook her head. 'Like I said, you were very lucky. This one wasn't.'

'It's OK, Dani. And thank you for talking to me honestly. It's good to know how lucky I got.' She had finished her food and drink. 'I'm fine now. And Greg Watts is behind bars and I'm still here.'

Dani nodded, relieved to be past the awkwardness. Both of them moved back through to the post mortem suite. 'Any-way, the reason I called you down rather than just email the report is that there was a foreign body in the wound tract. It was inserted there post-mortem. Just after he was killed.'

'Foreign body? What is it?'

Dani held up an evidence bag with a shiny silver coin in it, larger than any currency that Emma had seen. 'What the hell is that? Some sort of commemorative crown or something?'

'It's something to do with football,' Dani said, sounding as baffled as Emma. 'FA Cup 1972.' She handed it across.

'So,' Emma said, 'he was stabbed just to insert a coin?'

'No, wouldn't have said so. I mean, the injuries would've been fatal, anyone would know that. And anyway, putting something that large in the abdomen would cause all sorts of complications. No idea who did this or why they did, but there was only going to be one outcome.'

Emma nodded. 'Someone wanted him to die and wanted it to happen slowly and painfully.'

'Got it in one.'

'But they left something behind. It's definitely a good lead. I'd better get back to the office and put this on the computer.'

'Well, don't work too late, and make sure you have a proper dinner.'

'I'll log this into evidence and then I'm seeing Rob Haines so I should be eating properly. Thank you for everything.'

CHAPTER SIX

'Amelia, come in here please.' Amelia tried to decipher her father's tone of voice. It was worryingly neutral. Even with her finely honed skills, she couldn't tell if she was in trouble or not. That was the problem with having a teacher as a parent – they could control their tone of voice instinctively.

'Yeah, what's up?' She came into the kitchen and leant against the worktop facing her father at the kitchen table.

'I saw you today, in the playground, with your friend. Anything you want to tell me?'

A trap. What had he seen, and what should she admit to? 'Nothing really. I was just hanging out and chatting.'

'I thought I saw you with a phone. You know, head down and tap-tap-tapping away. Like a bloody chicken looking for grain, you looked like all the other brain-dead pupils. You're better than that, I know you are. Rot your brain, they do.'

Amelia wanted to point out that he had a phone in his pocket, that most of the time he had his head down hammering away on it. Occasionally he got angry with it, or laughed at things that no one else could see. But she knew better. Now was not the time for answering back. 'Yeah, Sara showed me something on it.'

'Sara?'

'Yes, Sara Frost. You know her, you've met her parents even.' Please, she thought, please remember. She's my one friend and you approve of her.

'Oh, yeah, I remember. The chubby one? Yeah so, why did she give you her phone?'

'She didn't give it to me.' Chubby? Really? She didn't know that her dad looked at her friends that critically. 'No, she was just showing me something on her phone.'

'Something? What? Are you sexting? Swapping explicit photographs? I've heard all about that you know. I read the papers. I work in a school and I've been on the training courses. I know you're only thirteen, but I've had to deal with kids much younger than that involved with all this.'

'Dad! Please! No! Eww! It's nothing like that.' She paused and took a deep breath. She needed all her resources to figure out how to handle her father. She'd come straight home and dumped her bag in her room. She knew that the phone was there, nestled in the pages of an exercise book. She had been about to hide it when her Dad had called her down. 'Listen, Dad, it's difficult being thirteen without a phone. You know, Justin Timberlake was only famous because of YouTube, and you know Psy and all that. But that's old, from years ago. Now it's all TikTok and memes.' There was a pause as she evaluated how far to push it. 'I feel like I can't even understand half the conversations my friends have, the things they talk about. It's like I've moved to a foreign country and haven't seen any of the last year's worth of TV shows or heard any of the pop music.'

'Baby. I know it's hard right now. And you probably hate me for it. But you have to understand that I'm protecting you.

It's what I do as a father. It's my job. And when you're older and your brain has stopped developing, you can have a phone then. And, do you want to know something else? You'll be streets ahead of everyone else your age. You'll be able to concentrate, to read a book all the way through. You'll be able to work things out for yourself, while everyone around you will have had their brains turned to mush. Most people of your generation can't think for themselves, they just look stuff up on their phones and it tells them what to believe.'

'I know, Dad.' She paused again. 'But is it OK if Sara shows me things? Just now and again, in break times. Short things, or just pictures. Just to keep me up to date.'

He paused, sat at the table as if he were a king on his throne weighing up some matter one of his subjects had brought before him. Eventually he nodded. 'Okay then. One day you'll understand.'

Amelia nodded quietly. She thought she'd got away with it, so she slipped away and went up to her room. She looked around and wondered where she might hide her phone and if it had been a bad idea to bring it home. But the thought of having a connection to her friends was a powerful one. At weekends or late at night, she could pick up messages and chat to her friends. She'd still be in touch over the school holidays. Even if no one else was awake when it was safe to get her phone out, she'd be able to catch up on past conversations. She'd be included, part of the clique.

She pulled open her underwear drawer and peered at it carefully. She'd long suspected that her parents searched her room, so over the weekend she'd set up a series of checks to see how far they'd go. Although it looked like it was in a mess, she had four pairs of underwear that were really uncomfortable and she never really wore them unless nothing else was clean. On Friday night, she had placed one in each corner of the drawer, while leaving the rest looking like she just chucked them in there. Very carefully, she inspected the contents of her underwear drawer, looking for the bad pairs. They were everywhere, two next to each other and only one in a corner.

So, she thought, my underwear drawer isn't safe. She pulled open another drawer in her dresser and moved through a mess of pens, pencils, rulers and other rubbish from school. Towards the back was a box of tampons. The ultimate thing to repel her parents, especially her father.

She opened the top and looked at the space. She reckoned she could shake them all out, slide the phone into the bottom and then hide it under the remaining tampons. And the top had a little tag she could fold in which might help her know if anyone messed with her stuff.

She knew that she couldn't be caught with a phone at home. She had no idea what punishment her father would dream up. But it would be beyond imagining. On the other hand, the possibility of escape, even only virtually through her phone, was a powerful attraction.

CHAPTER SEVEN

'ROB, what do you want to do for Christmas this year?'

Rob looked up from where he was scrolling through his phone while a football match played on the television. He frowned at his wife. 'Same as usual, have the girls over for a few days, watch rubbish television, drink too much, eat too much and consume several tins of chocolates until only the toffee pennies are left at the bottom.'

'I quite like them actually,' Jem said distractedly. 'Anyway, we've got the chance to do something different this year. Something we haven't done for over twenty years.'

'What's up?' Rob was suddenly alert to a change in his routine.

'Abby and Mitch have decided to spend Christmas with his family this year.'

'They just decided to go to someone else's house for Christmas without discussing it with us?'

Jem sighed. 'It's much more complicated than that. Remember, Mitch's father died back in January and this is his mother's first Christmas without him. Mitch is an only child as well, so he's had to be there a lot already to support his mother. And it's Abby's first Christmas with him. Apparently, Mitch's family loved Christmas and had all these traditions around it, mostly with just the three of them. So, now that his father's gone, they've decided to start again with Abby and Mitch and make new traditions.'

Rob grumbled quietly to himself. His good nature meant he couldn't complain openly about his daughter choosing to be with her new man, and he was proud of how she'd supported him over the last few months. But he still wasn't happy about it. 'OK, so you, me and Charlie. We'll have a great time and then in the new year we'll all get together. Maybe if Abby and Mitch are still together, next year might be time to meet his mother. We might even be able to do Christmas over there?' He caught sight of Jem's expression. 'What happened to Charlie? She not coming for Christmas either?'

Jem nodded. 'Aaron surprised Charlie with a trip to Lapland. Well, Norway technically. But it's the full Christmas experience. Snow, reindeer, the whole thing.' Her eyes shone.

'Charlie always loved Christmas. The magic of it. Why did they have to arrange it both on the same year though?'

'They didn't arrange anything at all. Abby and Mitch made their decision after talking with his Mum. But at the same time, Aaron had already bought the tickets and was going to keep it a surprise. Each of them assumed that the other would be here for actual Christmas Day. I've spent most of the last week on the phone with both of them trying to square the circle but I don't think it can be done.'

Rob took a deep breath. 'I suppose so. I can't really blame either of them. It's just a bit of a shock that they won't be home for Christmas.' He shook his head. 'It seems like the two little girls with the stockings and the tree and presents and everything was just a year or two ago. And now they've not only left home, but they have their own lives and they'll be starting families.'

Jem laid her hand on his arm. 'But you know it's the point, don't you?' He frowned at her. 'I mean of having children, that you can see them leave the nest, spread their wings. It means we've done a good job raising some good people. Seeing them leave and start their own lives.'

'Not that good if they don't even want to come and visit their parents for Christmas.'

'Oh! Don't sulk. We can have a quiet time at home. Your aunt always throws a huge party on Christmas Eve, we can still go to that. Have a nice Christmas meal, just the two of us.'

'I've always pitied those people who buy turkey crowns or those Christmas ready meals. It should be time to roast a whole huge bird with all the trimmings and squeeze everyone in around the table. Not get some small thing for two.'

'Well, I started off trying to persuade them and then I worked with them to see if I could fix it. There's nothing anywhere that can move. Mitch has already told his mum that they'll be there to help her over the most difficult day since her husband died. I mean, there's no way they can back out now. And Aaron has already paid for the holiday in full and won't get anything back if he cancels. He can't change it to another date as it was booked out months ago. Really, there is nothing that any of us can do. I've just decided to make the best of it. You can either try to talk them round yourself or just accept it. We've still got weeks to go so we can make other plans. If you want to, that is.'

Rob shook his head. 'I'm not a monster. I understand that Abby is doing a very good thing. It's not going to be a barrel of laughs spending Christmas with a grieving widow. She's doing it for all the right reasons. And Aaron is doing a lovely thing for Charlie, and I know they're struggling for money. It wouldn't be fair to ask them to cancel just because we're feeling a bit lonely.' He paused and watched the match without really seeing what was on the screen. 'No, we'll make this work. somehow. Like you said, just accept that life is moving on.'

'And you're all right with that?'

'Kind of. I've left the job that meant everything to me. I thought I might be able to mentor new officers coming up, pass on some of my wisdom.'

Jem took his hand. 'I know. It's hard. You've lost so much over the last year...' There was a quiet moment where nothing was said. Then Jem picked up her mood. 'Come on. We'll go over to your aunt's on Christmas Eve, book a taxi so we can drink if we want to. Then when the day itself rolls around, we can sleep in as late as we want, watch crap on TV, drink ourselves stupid and eat whenever we feel like it. It'll be good. We won't accept any invitations and just spend the entire day being selfish!'

Rob nodded. 'Now you're talking! There's always so much pressure on Christmas. We can potter around over the holidays and see your family and mine. And obviously the girls won't be avoiding us completely, so we can see them. I think it might work out OK.' He sounded upbeat, but he could feel the shift in his life. Another certainty was dropping away. Another step was being taken into a strange and unknown world.

'Anyway, listen, Emma will be here soon and we haven't ordered the takeaway yet. Chinese?'

'Yeah, sounds great.' Rob tried to change his mindset ready for his visitor.

EMMA WRAPPED up work nearly twelve hours after she'd walked into the station to find out if she still had a job. She'd been texting Rob as she worked so he knew that she'd be late for her dinner appointment at his house.

She was exhausted and knew that Rob wouldn't be happy to learn who had replaced Slater in the CID. But she knew that he had his network and would get the information sooner or later. Better that he heard it from her, no matter how awkward it made the evening.

'Hi Emma,' Jem said when she opened the door. 'Where's that lovely boyfriend of yours?'

'Pete's been sent away on a training course. Three days residential. When he found out that it was my interview today, he offered to change the date. But I know he took months to get the authorisation for it. We've been texting each other all day.'

Jem nodded. 'What's he learning about?'

'Don't ask me! He said something about new software to forensically analyse electronic devices. And then to preserve the chain of evidence.' She frowned. 'Still can't remember what it's called and I probably haven't got the details right.'

Jem laughed and led Emma into the dining room. The Chinese takeaway had just arrived, but as soon as the food was served, Rob asked, 'So, what's the big news? I know you're on day one of a murder case, but can you bring me up to speed on the departmental changes first? I heard a whisper that Slater's finally taken his retirement. Pushed rather than jumped, apparently.'

'Nothing gets past you, does it?' Emma paused, then ploughed straight ahead. 'You already know that I've got my job back.'

'And there's no fall out from you going off the reservation and finding the real killer?'

'No. Quite the opposite. Slater copped it. They carried out an investigation and decided that he failed to follow through on alternative theories of the crime.'

'Oh, let me guess, my sources are right,' Rob said. 'They didn't actually sack him but they let him retire with all his pension rights and everything else?'

'Go it in one. He was about ready to retire when he took over. And he said he was only taking over to steady the ship before a new boss arrived. So, he's out. New boss started today.'

'New boss? Not promoted one of the lads then?'

'Yeah.' There was an awkward pause that stretched out as Emma tried to work out how to tell him.

'Wow, it must be bad,' Rob said. 'For you not to say straight out. How are they going to find someone worse than Slater?'

'It's Michelle Jones. She's been promoted to DI.'

There was a long silence.

'I know she tried to bring you down,' Emma said carefully. 'But I do have a feeling that I could work with her. She can't be as bad as Slater.'

Rob clutched a hand to his breast. 'Even though she's my sworn enemy?' he said in a mock dramatic tone. 'You think you could work with her?'

'Oh, come on, stop hamming it up! She's not that bad. She had a job to do when she was tasked with investigating you and she did it as fairly as she was able to.'

Rob nodded grudgingly. 'Still, anyone who'd actually take a job in Professional Standards, I'm not sure I could ever work for them. You know, spying on other officers.'

'You forget though,' Emma argued, 'that's why I joined. I wanted to change the culture. Not every police officer is right. And someone has to weed out the wrong 'uns.'

'Listen you two,' Jem interrupted. 'I know you could argue this subject back and forth all night long if I let you.' She paused and looked at her husband. 'Rob, you did the wrong thing for the right reasons.' She turned her head. 'Emma, you are fiercely loyal, both to your ideal of what the police should be, and to your friends. Now, I love both of you, so would you just drop it.'

They both nodded at each other. 'She'll be a sight better than Slater, I suppose,' Rob said grudgingly.

Emma just nodded, unable to believe that she'd got a concession out of her former boss. She didn't trust herself to say anything else.

After she'd served herself a second helping of food, Rob asked her. 'What's the deal with the new murder? Is it going to be one of those open and shut cases where you catch the ex-husband standing over the body with a knife?'

'It's still quite early but I don't think so. At the moment we have a grand total of zero suspects. Or, possibly half the drug taking population of Bradwick. It's hard to tell.'

She quickly assessed how far she trusted Rob, and what she could safely tell him. But then she realised he would never harm her career and he had other sources of information, so she filled him in on the day's events and what little they knew.

Rob pursed his lips and thought for a moment. 'You're right about one thing. At first glance, it sounds like a classic drug problem. Young guy trying to carve himself out a niche. Been dealing for five years, gets himself a flash motor and tries to move up a level or two. He's bound to bump into some nasty characters who don't want the competition. I mean, it sounds like a bit of overkill, usually a good beating would be the first warning.'

'But, there's the money and the drugs.'

'Indeed, that is the problem, right there. If he'd pissed

someone off, then a good beating and removal of all drugs and money would send a message. And set the new business back a fair way.' He took a drink from his beer bottle. 'So, something personal. Have a look for ex or current husbands, or people he's stolen a lot of money from.'

Emma stifled a yawn and then apologised. 'Yeah, that's about as far as we got. I'm sorry, I've got to go home. New boss, new murder, I'd better be in early tomorrow.'

CHAPTER EIGHT

'RIGHT EVERYONE, let's get the basics down first,' Michelle said as she walked to the front of the room. Emma had just arrived in the office. 'This is William Hawsley, also known as Bill.' She tapped his photo that was stuck up on the whiteboard with his name and the word "victim" underneath. 'Let's not have the elephant in the room, he was more the sort of guy we'd be usually arresting rather than protecting. But the fact is that he was stabbed and left to die in the gutter. And no matter how many drugs he sold, or stolen goods he traded, he didn't deserve to die like that. No one does.

'This was someone's son, a grandson, and he had friends, associates and a family. And they're all counting on us to find out who killed him. So we'll have no attitude, no "maybe it's for the best", none of that. We'll process this, find his associates and his enemies, and find whoever killed him, just the same as we would for anyone else.'

There were nods and murmurs around the room.

'Now, we've cleared the air, let's get on. Our victim was only twenty years old, which is no age. We know he was a drug dealer, and he probably parked up in that car park because all the shops shut at six and there are no CCTV cameras. So it's perfect for dealing. Unfortunately, that also makes it perfect for our killer. He could've driven along the main road, and stopped off, so we need to check the cameras along here.' Michelle pointed to a map. 'Or, he could live on the estate. There are several pedestrian routes into the car park that bypass the main road all together and link to residential roads with no CCTV on them. Ideal for his customers but it also makes it hard for us to track his killer.'

'Do you think this was a drug feud? A fight over territory?' Suse asked.

'It's a possibility, but not a likely one. One of our jobs will be to establish whether that was his usual patch or if he's just moved there. Emma, you've been to the scene and found something that makes you think it wasn't a turf war?'

'An initial search of the body, and his car, found both money and drugs,' Emma said. 'I think that makes it very unlikely that this was a rival drug gang. No dealer would pass up some free money and product. It also rules out a simple robbery.'

Michelle nodded. 'That makes sense. So someone is sending a message.' She looked around the room. At the moment, it was only CID gathered, although soon uniformed officers and civilian staff would be joining them. 'What I'm going to tell you next stays within these four walls. It could be the one thing that helps us find our killer. It'll certainly help in weeding out the nutters and serial confessors from the mix. Dani Price, the pathologist retrieved a coin from deep inside the wound. Whoever stabbed him must have placed it there.'

There were mutters around the room.

Emma said, 'It was really deep in there. We were first on scene and we didn't see anything.'

'Yes, it was pushed right inside the abdomen. Photos of the coin, both sides, on the computer. It's not legal currency, it's some sort of promotional football coin. Emma, I want you to stay with this lead. I want to know everything about it, where it came from, how many there are, who owns them. Most especially has anyone local made any purchases recently? But listen, this could be the key, so we'll keep it within CID for the moment.

'Moving on, we'll get uniform involved to canvass the area. And we need to get the CCTV data here so we can begin to go through it. Let's build up a detailed picture of Bill Hawsley's last twenty-four hours. I want to know where he was living, when he went to that carpark, all the details. And we need to find out how the killer approached the scene and which direction they left in. On top of that, we'll do our best to build up a picture of our victim's network. Obviously this is going to be hard to do as he was a drug dealer, so people aren't going to want to talk to us. Fletcher, can you hit up the social media? Start with his profiles and see how far you can spread out into his network. Try to pick up on the chatter as well, see what people are saying out there.'

'Right you are, boss.' There was a brief pause. 'You just give the social media stuff to the youngest member? Like, I'm a gen-Z so I can understand it?'

'I gave you the job because I'm your DI, which makes me your boss. So I divide up the jobs according to who I think would be best at it. And your job is to do what I say.'

John looked around as if to say, what? I was only joking. But no one met his eye.

At this point, the CID department were joined by the rest of the people assigned to the enquiry – uniformed and civilian officers. Jobs were handed out, and tasks were written up on the board.

When the meeting broke up, Emma went back her desk and decided to start with Google. She soon learned that 1972 was the centenary of the FA cup, and Esso petrol stations handed out coins as part of a promotion. There were thirty-one coins, thirty silver coins featuring each team that competed, plus an extra, larger, bronze coin commemorating the Leeds win over Arsenal in the 1972 Centenary Final.

Her excitement was short lived as she moved over to the auction and collection websites and found out that they were common and consequently cheap. It seemed that for under fifty pounds you could get a complete set in a folder. The coin that had been found was a West Ham one, but there didn't appear to be any significance to that either.

There was something about the seventies that made her think of Rob so she decided to give him a ring.

'What do you know about petrol station football coins?' she asked when he answered.

'Not a lot.' There was a pause as he thought. 'I think they're a bit before your time. What was it? Early nineties? I don't think I was even a young constable at the time. Of course, if they'd done them when I was in CID, then I'd have collected several sets with all the driving around. They're probably worth quite a bit now.'

'You'd think so, but no. I've just been looking on eBay there's lots on there and quite cheap too. Anyway, we've found one at a crime scene.' Emma mentally reviewed what she'd said and decided how far she should go, and how far she trusted Rob. Even though he'd left the force, she would trust him with her life or career. 'But it's not from the nineties, it's one of the 1972 coins. I've had a bit of a dig around the internet and they made them for several years, the 1990 set was the most recent so you were right about that.'

'Ah, well, sounds like you know more than me then.' He paused for a moment. '1972? That's nearly fifty years ago. It's doubtful that whoever left it at the scene was the same person who collected it from the petrol station.'

'Yeah, it's just another mystery piled on top of a lot of others,' Emma said with resignation in her voice. 'Listen, this coin thing is being kept from the press, you know, to weed out the usual attention seekers, psychics and other people.'

'Yep. Not a problem.' He paused for a moment. 'They're the sort of thing you'd find if your parents died and you cleared out their house. Especially being that age. Someone could've collected them at the time, tucked them away at the back of the cupboard, and now they could be into their seventies or eighties. Then the children either have the funeral or put them into a home, and have to clear out the house.'

'I can see that happening.' She sighed. 'I'll file it away as something that we can try against any suspects that come up. But our killer could've just as easily bought a set or just one coin in a boot fair. Or had one given to them by a friend. Anyway, thank you for last night and for the input.'

Emma ended the call. She went back to the photo on her computer. She knew why she'd phoned Rob. Even though he wasn't really old enough for it to be his decade, Rob loved all things seventies, from Roger Moore James Bond films to The Sweeney. She thought that he hankered after a simpler time when men could have hairy chests and slide big cars around corners while nicking villains.

Rob didn't seem to be overly bothered about collecting football coins. Somehow he'd missed out on the obsessive collecting gene. But one thing was becoming clearer. The link between cars, football and the seventies meant that she was thinking that a man was the attacker. She knew she shouldn't be stereotyping by gender, but she simply couldn't imagine a woman carrying out such a violent attack and then putting something collectable in the wound. She was prepared to accept that she was wrong, but she had to start somewhere to figure out who was responsible.

CHAPTER NINE

Rob arrived at his office on Tuesday morning still turning Jem's news about Christmas in his head. He had never really thought about Christmas in the past, it was just something that came around every year. Holidays just happened, following one after another. Of course, when he'd been in the police the whole period from Halloween until past the new year was always hectic. More parties combined with ever shortening days and worse weather meant there was more crime and more accidents. From domestic violence and pub fights to suicides, it was a busy time of year. But it was also nice in the station. Tinsel and decorations went up. In hindsight they looked a bit naff, but at the time they lifted the mood. And people went down the pub more than usual and there were work Christmas dinners. Even someone bringing in a pack of corner shop mince pies lifted the day.

It suddenly hit him hard. They were in the run up to Christmas right now. In his semi-retired, running a private detective agency, life, he hadn't noticed. The closest he'd come was noticing that the receptionist had a small Christmas tree on her desk. But it still wasn't the same as being on the job. And it never would be.

He wouldn't be going back to the station. Not back to work. No more slightly tatty decorations and boozy lunches. Obviously he knew that he was no longer working as a police officer but moments like this drove the message home. After so many years, leaving the job was akin to a bereavement, and he felt as if he was grieving. And in the first year, he was bound to keep tripping over these milestones.

He could ring round a few friends and get an invite to the CID Christmas meal. Actually, he wouldn't have to try that hard, he could go with Emma. But the moment he'd had the thought, he rejected it. There was no one in CID he knew apart from Emma. The whole night would be strangers telling each other stories about people he didn't know working on cases he hadn't been involved in. And all done while they got progressively more drunk. He hadn't returned to his pre-head injury level of drinking, and had no desire to now.

Rob consoled himself by looking at where he was now. Everything was better than it was in the police – the office itself, the coffee, even the receptionist. It looked better and it was more comfortable. And yet he wasn't entirely satisfied.

He thought over the conversation with Emma last night. He wished he was still involved with the investigation. He missed the late nights and the early starts along with the satisfaction of solving a crime. He even, in a strange way, missed the awful police station coffee.

He needed to stop wallowing and get on with work. He powered up his work mobile phone and saw that he had a text message. He frowned as clients usually phoned and left a voice mail. He tapped the notification.

Please help me. Connect with me on StringCan now.

It was a tempting message – it played into exactly why he had chosen both of his careers, this one and working for the police. His thumb moved over the link, then moved back again. Clicking on random links was a bad idea, especially from unknown mobile numbers. But there again, someone, somewhere might need his help. No, he wouldn't be stupid. He'd do the right thing and delete it. Although he didn't do that either. He had a better idea.

He switched to his personal mobile to call his daughter. Abby was always the one in the family who was better at technology. And he'd feel better for talking to her. He'd feel like she wasn't slipping way.

'Hi Abby, it's Dad.'

'Dad! Has Mum spoken to you yet? I bet she has. Listen, before you get on my case, let me say something. Mitch has had a really tough year, since his father died. And he's done so much to support his mum throughout all of this, but Christmas is going to be tough. On him and on Marjorie. And I just want to be there to support both of them. Is that so bad?'

'No, Abby, it's not bad. I won't pretend that I'm fine with it. But I do understand it. We've obviously brought you up well, and I'm so proud that you're doing the right thing and supporting your boyfriend and his family.'

'So, you're not phoning up to guilt me into coming back for Christmas?' She breathed out a big sigh. 'In that case, what's up?'

'Have you heard about this new app, StringCan?'

'Oh yeah. Although it's hardly new. There was a big fuss last year, all over the papers and on daytime TV. For a few months it was the latest thing that's worrying all the middle-class, middle-aged parents up and down the country.'

'People like me, you mean?'

Abby laughed. 'Yeah, I suppose so. What's got you so worried about it?'

'It's come up on my phone. My work phone. I got a weird text message asking me to connect through it.'

'Yeah, that figures. One part of it is that you can connect with anyone as long as you know their phone number. That's what scares people. Who's trying to get in touch with you?'

'I don't know. I listened to you kids and don't click on random links.'

'Well that's good. The link can be clicked on, but you have to be careful. Once the page has loaded up, don't enter any data on it. The first thing you have to do is to check that it has a green padlock to the left of the link.'

'Green padlock. Got it. Hold on, I'll put you on speaker and get my work phone out.'

Rob carefully clicked on the link in the text message and watched as the StringCan page loaded.

'Yeah, it's someone with a weird username. BaggyAmy? There's a warning come up that it's a female under eighteen but that's all I know.'

'Yeah, I remember now. they changed that on an update after all the fuss. Now anyone's profile has to show if they're over or under eighteen. Meant to make it safer.'

'Safer?'

'Well, yeah. It had a reputation as a hunting ground for paedophiles. You know, send out hundreds of requests and then start grooming anyone who's stupid enough to reply. Now they have nowhere to hide. They can't pretend they didn't know.' She sounded a bit resigned.

'I can see that, the standard defence is to claim ignorance.' There was a brief pause. 'So, what do you think I should do?'

'With this girl? Why do you want to get in touch? It seems

to be a lose-lose situation for you. How do you know it's not someone doing white hat cat fishing?'

'Abby, can you say that again, but in English this time?' Rob hated feeling old.

'Sorry. I mean it could be someone pretending to be a young girl in the hope that a paedophile will start grooming them, then they can lure them out for a meeting and entrap them.'

'Oh, you mean like vigilantes?' Rob thought for a moment. 'Well, if she tries to talk to me about anything grown up, sex or anything even remotely dodgy, I can shut her down. I'll keep an eye out for anything approaching a fishing trip.' He was almost speaking to himself.

'I still can't see any good coming out of this,' Abby said, obviously concerned. 'Listen Dad, be careful OK? I've got to get on so I'll talk to you soon. And we'll sort out a date to meet up before Christmas and also sometime in the new year. I promise.'

With that she hung up and left Rob looking at his phone screen. He mentally compiled a list of pros and cons. He could avoid being tricked quite easily as he wouldn't be attempting to groom anyone. He wouldn't agree to meet in person and he would avoid any remotely dodgy or personal subjects. On the pro side of his list, he added the fact that he'd be able to help. It would provide a respite from his day-to-day grind of employment checks and cheating spouses. And now it was clear that his daughters didn't need him, maybe he could help someone else, put into practice what he'd learnt.

In the job it had always struck him that there were differences in upbringing between victims and criminals. It was a massive oversimplification to say that someone with a difficult upbringing would go on to be a criminal. But over the years in the police he could definitely see a pattern. And if he could be the one influence that moved someone away from a difficult situation and get her on the right road, well, it was an obligation. It would be far better than leaving her to be arrested and processed through the whole criminal justice system.

For the next fifteen minutes, he flicked between a help file on his laptop and his phone as he struggled to set up a new account with his details and a new password. He was aware that it was on his work phone so he didn't add too many personal details, but kept it all business.

Finally he was ready and logged into StringCan so he sent his first message.

Hi, this is Rob Haines. How can I help?

He waited and looked at his phone but nothing happened. He went back to the help file and flicked through a few pages. Finally he found what he was looking for and peered at his phone. According to the icons, his message had been sent but no one had picked it up at the other end. He felt a bit weird as he'd put himself out there and tried to help and then been rebuffed. He found himself missing the old days when people had land-line telephones and you'd just call someone and talk to them. At least with a phone call, you'd get an instant response, not have to wait for the other person to read it and type a reply.

He had just decided to put his phone away and look at it again later when he got a notification.

OMG that's so awesome. You got the app. Thank you!

How did you find my number?

I saw your website and your a policeman and a detective. And your photo makes you look like a proper dad.

I am a dad. And a private investigator and I used to be in the police. So, can I help you?

Rob looked at the phone and shook his head. While he'd been going through the help file and setting up his account, he'd also switched on message logging. He still felt very nervous about the whole process. But now he was imagining that someone in an office was reading them and he realised how pompous he sounded talking to a child. On the other hand, he imagined the same situation; someone in a suit reading out his words if he'd tried to be all "What's up?" and "cool". It would be worse somehow.

Can you arrest my dad and put him prison?

Rob looked at his phone and shook his head. He had a rose-tinted view of parenting and bringing up his own children. He'd forgotten the, well, there wasn't a better way to say it, childish behaviour. Which was understandable, but he'd always found hard to cope with. It didn't matter what age it happened at, whether it was putting up with an obsession with kid's cartoons or teenage celebrity crushes, it was just part and parcel of bring up children. And, he admitted to himself, as annoying as he found those childish things, he had navigated them and his daughters were now out in the world, living independent lives. Perhaps a little too independent.

He took a breath and looked at his phone again. How to handle this? This didn't seem to be the place to explain the interlinked worlds of the police and the Crown Prosecution Service and how they worked together to move someone down the route from suspect to prisoner. Even if he was still a serving officer, it wouldn't be possible to just arrest someone and send them to prison.

He sighed. He felt confined. He would rather be having a face-to-face conversation than trying to type on his phone's tiny keyboard to communicate. He felt like he was missing out on a huge amount of the information he usually relied on when talking to someone. It was impossible for him explain nuances and ascertain meanings when all he had were the words on his phone screen. But he did need to answer the message somehow.

He took a deep breath and unlocked his phone, still unsure of what he was going to say. He typed without thinking.

Seriously, how old are you? It's not like a kids TV program where the bad guy gets arrested and the next thing you see, they're in prison.

Rob looked at his phone and shook his head. All his great ideas collapsed. He thought he might be a hero who rode in over the internet and saved the day. Now it looked like he was going to be the agony uncle to a bored teenage girl. He weighed his phone in his hand. He was free from the police now, he could be as sarcastic and dismissive as he wanted. And teenage girls weren't really his target market for the private investigation business.

He shook himself mentally. He'd done some research on how to run a business and the one thing he absorbed from it was that you didn't turn down an opportunity. If there was a chance to be kind, then you should take it. You'd never know where it might lead.

I am fifteen you know. I'm sorry you think I'm immature I'm really not. I know how the world works and that the bad guys don't always get caught.

Rob looked at the words on the screen. He was transported back to when his own daughters were teenagers. The teenager really was an inexplicable creature. On the one hand, they were still a child and wanted to be supported and parented. But on the other, they were also desperate for any independence and would take any chance to prove how grown up and independent they were.

Rob set aside all the amateur psychology because it was easy to see where the problem was.

Do you want to tell me about your father?

Ugh. He's like the worst. Won't let me go into town or see my friends. I'm not supposed to have a phone or go on the internet. I literally have no life because of him.

When Rob had been working for the police, he had been painfully aware of all the dangers that lurked around every corner for his daughters. He'd done his best to let them enjoy life while also trying to keep them safe. Was this how he had appeared? As a controlling, watching figure who stopped any hint of fun? He knew he had to tread carefully.

Are you sure that he's not just trying to keep you safe?

You sound just like him. I think he just enjoys it when I'm unhappy.

I don't want to make you unhappy.

Rob looked at the words he'd just typed. Somehow they'd got into strange territory even though they'd only just started messaging each other. He was deciding how to respond when the next message came in.

Later! I can see the school gates so dad alert time.

Rob stared at his phone. Maybe he wasn't used to this strange and disjointed way of carrying on a conversation. When she came back online, would they continue the same subject, or would it be a new start?

He couldn't properly work out where it was going or how he should proceed. He would wait for something concrete to come back from his mysterious contact.

Uneasy with the way the conversation had gone, Rob he decided to put his phone back in the desk drawer and continue with some real work. He had a ten o'clock with a new client.

THERE WAS a rap on his door and he glanced at the clock. His ten o'clock appointment had arrived. 'Come in.'

Following a head injury, Rob Haines had been left face-blind. While he could perceive individual features he could never combine them in his head and then recognise the person. Usually, he had a trick of scribbling quick notes on his pad when he met a new client. It made him look efficient and meant he could then update their file with enough detail to help him recognise them at a subsequent meeting.

The trouble with this new client was that he was hard to categorise. He was average height and build, and had short sandy hair. He was white and probably late thirties or early forties and clean shaven. He didn't wear glasses. Rob looked at the page of notes and knew that he'd have trouble recognising him again.

'So, Mr Church, how can we help you?' He scribbled "Sean Church" on his pad and circled it. He really hoped that any future interaction would be by appointment.

'I've never really done this before, so I'll come straight to the point. I'd like you to follow my wife.'

Rob stopped making notes and looked up briefly. 'Why do you want me to do that?' He liked having everything up front at the beginning.

Sean ran his hands through his hair. 'I don't know really, it's just a feeling. Like, you know, if I call her up when she's meant to be at work then she doesn't always answer straight away.' He paused to gather his thoughts. 'I mean, she usually calls back in like ten or fifteen minutes, but that's long enough isn't it?' Rob frowned at him. 'You know, to get your breath back and put your clothes on and sound like you're at work.'

'Right, yes,' Rob said, still writing. 'And what does she do for a living.'

'She works at an estate agent.' He paused again.

'Listen, I can see you thinking and editing and deciding what to say. This isn't going to work if you hold stuff back. If you think you know who your wife is seeing, then it works best if you tell me. It means we can come at it from both sides, follow both parties.'

'If I knew who she was seeing, then what would I need you for? I could deal with it myself. Don't you see, the problem is that she's at an estate agents full time. She has access to keys to loads of properties all over the place, and she'll know which ones are empty and which ones aren't. She can go out of the office any time her lover is free and claim it's a viewing. Perfect opportunity, keys to an empty house, and out of the office for around an hour or so.' He stopped and shook his head. 'I guess I just want to be sure, one way or another.'

'Yeah, no, I can understand that,' Rob said. 'And that's what we offer here at RHI, certainty. I'll put one of my best men on it, and he can follow her and take photos. If she does a viewing, we'll know who she's in the house with and how long for. You can leave it to us.'

'Us? We? You mean you won't handle it yourself personally. I'm not sure I want lots of people all discussing my business.'

'It'll be me and my associate, Mr Mitchell. We're both former police officers, so we're used to confidentiality and keeping it close. It's what we do. Trust me, I wouldn't have stayed in business five minutes if I wasn't any good at keeping secrets.'

The other man nodded thoughtfully. 'Yeah, all right then. You've got the job.'

Rob then completed the forms for a new job, with Mr Church supplying the details. He also emailed over some photos and other details of his wife straight from his phone. When he was gone, Rob called in Ed Mitchell, the DC he had worked with back in CID.

'New case for you Ed, looks like quite an easy one.'

'What have you got for me then? More late-night lurking in hedges?'

'Should be no late-night work at all. We've got to keep tabs on Nancy Church, and she's an estate agent. The husband has his suspicions, but we're only to follow her at work.'

'Nice, so it's just office hours then?'

'Pretty much. I think he's worried that she's using house

viewings as cover for an affair. So, every time she leaves the office, follow her and see where she goes and who she meets.'

'And I suppose, being an estate agent, she has access to lots of keys and empty properties. Seems quite an easy job. Have we got photos, car details, all of that?' He picked up his phone and frowned as he stabbed at the screen with his finger. 'Oh, yeah. There it is.' He swiped through all the photos and details for a moment. 'I mean, I know you can't judge a book by its cover, but she doesn't look the type, does she?'

Rob looked at his own copy of the pictures. She was certainly a bit dowdy, but more than that, she looked cowed in all the photos. There was no spark or sense of devilment in her eyes. 'I see what you mean. But you know, people always surprise you. There's a reason why there's a stereotype of a frumpy librarian who has a wild private life. Anyway, whatever the truth is, he's already paid his deposit, so we need to get on this.'

'Right you are, boss, leave it with me. I'll get on it for a few days, then we'll meet up and I can tell you what she's up to.'

When Ed had left, Rob got out his phone and turned it over in his hands. As well as the photos of Mrs Church, he had another problem on his phone.

CHAPTER TEN

It was Tuesday evening and Emma was in Lukas' caravan. She was exhausted after her first two days back at work, but she was keen to catch up with her oldest and best friend.

As Lukas shut the door behind her, the weather picked up to squally rain. She settled on the sofa and rain rattled off the windows and the tin roof. Lukas leaned forward and turned the heater up a bit.

'God! This weather,' Emma said as she settled down on the sofa.

'Yeah, this place isn't too bad. At least I can keep it warm. I have to be a bit careful that I don't run the heater all the time, it's on a bottle outside and I can't afford to replace them all the time.'

'Well, I do appreciate it,' Emma said. 'That's the problem with this time of year, I'm going to work in the dark and getting home in the dark.'

'Should have a job like mine,' Lukas said cheerfully. 'I'm out in the fresh air most of the day. Plenty of daylight.'

'Oh, I see daylight,' Emma replied with amusement, 'it's just that it usually has dead bodies and crime scenes in it.'

They both laughed.

'Where have you been? It feels like weeks since I've seen you,' Emma said when the laughter died down. This was about as far as Emma felt she could push Lukas. She knew he was flaky and was prepared to accept this as part and parcel of their relationship. She was also aware that while she'd been sat at home, on suspension and bored, she hadn't seen a huge amount of her best friend. But that was just what he was like. She could accept it because she knew he'd never change.

'Ah, yes, well, sorry about that. You know, the usual story.' Lukas had the good grace to look sheepish.

'New girlfriend?' Lukas nodded so she continued. 'What's her name?'

'Violet. She's brilliant. We met through mutual friends so she's on the same wavelength as me.'

Emma didn't like what she was hearing. 'She's not going to get you back into drugs is she?'

'What do you mean, back into? You know I was never going to go all twelve steps and completely give it up.' He saw the look on her face and held up a hand. 'I know you hooked me up with the caravan park job and the charity and all of this.' He waved his hand around the living room in the caravan that he was now living in. He'd made some progress on decorating it and making it his own place. 'And I'm not going to stuff that up. But plenty of perfectly respectable people end the week with a couple of beers and a smoke. You must know that – not all the drug dealers you arrest are young people in hoodies hanging around dark corners.'

'Well no, yes, that is true. Actually not even most of them are like that.' She paused, wondering how to proceed. 'So, tell me the details. How old is she? What's she like?'

'We haven't really done the whole personal details thing

yet. I guess she's like a bit older than me, you know maybe early thirties. I'm not really sure how to describe her.'

'It's just me, you can tell me. You don't have to be tactful.'

'Well, she's a bit taller than you.' He squinted as if he'd never really seen her before. 'And, I guess, a bit more, erm, solidly built than you?'

'Solidly built? Like she works out?'

'No, she doesn't exercise much, more of a party animal.' Lukas shook his head. 'I never know what to say these days! I mean, she's got a great pair of ... you know, really big.' He trailed off again, looking embarrassed. 'Well and she's, you know, in proportion too. Not like top-heavy or anything.' There was an awkward silence for a bit. 'She's got long dark hair. Not, you know, black, but brown. And her face, the moment she smiles or laughs, she just lights up. She is lovely, you know. I'm sure you'll like her.'

'So, you like someone who's a bit older and a bit larger than usual. You need to relax, Lukas, not worry that everyone's going to be judging you. If she makes you happy, then that's all that matters.'

'I know. I guess that it's just that I think she could be the one, you know.' He looked around at the interior of the caravan. 'I've had a bit of a life already. But all the parties and everything, waking up on someone's sofa and finding a half-smoked joint and can of beer for breakfast. I mean, I've had a blast, it's been a great life. I dunno, maybe I'm getting a bit old for all this.'

'Old? You're in your twenties, not your forties! And even so, my parents are still on the festival scene. Still at the after parties, and hanging around backstage. I don't think they'll ever change.'

'I know that I could do that as well. I'm just not sure I want to. This job is pretty good, I feel like I'm helping, making a difference. And it's nice to have somewhere to go back to. Not a room in a shared house, or a protest camp or squat, but somewhere to call my own. I've had snatches of that moving in with girlfriends but I always knew it was temporary. And I know you say I'm not that old, but maybe I'm at a crossroads. I mean, if I keep drifting around like this, it won't be too long before I'm heading into my thirties. And then, how would I ever get settled down? Without experience I'd end up on zero-hours contracts and insecure housing. Maybe I want more.'

'You're preaching to the choir here,' Emma said. 'I mean, I have the same sort of upbringing as you and I've gone for literally the most stable life I could. I've got the kind of job that people keep for decades and one that defines not just what you do but who you are. For the rest of my life, I'm either going to be characterised as a police officer or as an ex-police officer. So, I think it's great that you want to break away. Don't fall into thinking that it's a black and white situation though.'

Lukas frowned. 'What do you mean?'

'Well, look at Chloe who I helped to find the father of her baby a few months ago. She's chosen a place to live near a good school so her daughter can have a good start. But she still has that free spirit, that lifestyle. I wouldn't be surprised if Coral is going to festivals with her mum. It's a good balance.'

Lukas nodded. 'Yeah, I see what you mean. I think at first I need to go hard in the other direction, in order to make sure I break out of the kind of free-living lifestyle. But you're right. It's a spectrum, I could go anywhere from being a musician playing festivals to a chartered surveyor with a mortgage and kids.' He nodded to himself. 'I just have to choose where on that line to plant my flag.'

'Listen, I could sit here and talk philosophy with you all night but...'

'Here it comes,' Lukas said with a grin. 'What do you want?'

'We've got a new murder. Does the name Bill Hawsley mean anything to you?'

Lukas pursed his lips and closed his eyes. 'Not particularly. Any reason why I might have come across him?'

'He was a drug dealer. Stabbed outside his car, but none of his money and drugs were taken.'

'Ah, ok then. The whole drug scene in Bradwick is much more chaotic since your lot took down King Kabs. It was a big thing, you know. Casual users pretty soon realised that you could just call up a taxi with benefits. It made it a lot easier without dealing with unsavoury characters. I think that people like that, selling out of a car, hanging around on street corners, will die out as Bitcoin gets a hold.'

'I don't think Bitcoin has made much of an impact yet.'

'If you know where to go on the Dark Web, you can order drugs online as easy as buying something from Amazon..' He paused. 'Hawsley? Sounds British.' He held up his hand. 'I'm not going all UKIP on you, but most of the drug trade now is foreigners, coming in and either importing, running county lines or setting up cannabis farms.'

Emma nodded. 'But you didn't have any dealing with this Bill Hawsley?'

Lukas shook his head. 'No, and I haven't heard the name around the site. But then I don't hear much. I'm an organiser, I work for the charity, so in the eyes of the clients, I'm part of the system. I mean, they trust me and I'm on their side, but I'm also not like them, if you see what I mean.'

Emma nodded again. That was exactly how she felt most of the time.

CHAPTER ELEVEN

The office was quiet, but only because everyone was working hard. They'd all got in early and were concentrating on processing all the data that came in the days following a murder. Everything from forensics to door-to-door enquiries was bearing fruit, and all of it needed to be entered into the computer, cross-referenced and sifted for any useful clues.

Michelle Jones came into the office and called the attention of the assembled team.

'OK, I'm going to just put it out there, no preamble. Do any of you think that this could have any link back to King Kabs? I know some of you are new to the team, but others of you were here in those days.'

All eyes in the room turned to Emma Angel and Suse Berman.

'King Kabs?' Emma asked. 'They were wound up after the big drug bust, the one that we went on, instigated by Slater.'

Unbidden memories came back to Emma. Kevin Slater had ordered her to assist in the operation and ultimately arrest Marnie King, the surviving owner of King Kabs.

'Yes, once we arrested most of the key drivers, plus the

radio operator and general manager, there was hardly a company left.' Suse had come to Emma's rescue. 'It was pretty much on its knees before we moved in. I think it would've folded years ago without the dealing and petty crime keeping them in the black.'

Marnie King herself, however, had dodged the proverbial bullet. She had her lawyer ready to go the moment she was arrested and a carefully constructed story to distance herself from the day-to-day running of the firm. With no evidence, she had spent a night in the cells and then walked free.

'Some of you know Marnie King better than me,' Michelle admitted. 'Is there any chance that she orchestrated the whole thing? She could've deliberately sunk her husband's company and got herself arrested to prove that she wasn't involved in the drug business. And then, with King Kabs no longer on the scene, and her both covered by a lawyer and proven innocent, she could have taken over the drug trade quietly in the background.'

Emma chewed her lip. Marnie had more or less admitted to her that she knew about the drug business and had been willing to trade information in return for looking the other way. But now? Emma's gut instinct was that she wasn't involved. She was aware that everyone was still watching her. 'I did get to know Marnie,' she said. 'Back in the day, she was friends with Rob Haines. About twice a year, Rob's aunt threw a party, a big barbecue in the Summer and a Christmas party in December. Obviously, Rob went, but he also made sure that the whole of CID was invited too. The one that I went to had Billy King present and he seemed to be completely at ease. He was with a group of his business associates along with the wives and girlfriends. From the look of him, he was comfortable there, so I'd say he was a regular at the parties too. I didn't see anything overtly corrupt, but you can imagine, food and alcohol, off-duty CID and the local criminals, all relaxing together. It doesn't paint a pretty picture.'

She paused, needing to gather her thoughts. She was on a tightrope now. On one side was loyalty to Rob, her close friend and former boss. But on the other, she had to be honest with her new boss. Or at the very least, she had to own up to whatever her boss had already discovered. And if she had information that could help solve the case, then she mustn't keep it to herself.

'I think, and it's little more than a guess, that Marnie was aware of her husband's business and the quid pro quo that had been established with police,' Emma continued, still picking her words with care. 'But there's no way of telling how involved she was. It could've been a feeling that the business was doing better than it should and that there were some dodgy characters hanging around. Or, she could've been doing the books and actively involved in the business of supply, distribution and laundering the profits. Or anything in between.' She paused, still gathering her thoughts. 'But this doesn't feel like her. My opinion is that she probably had a hand in the operation to bust King Kabs. She doesn't seem to have been financially hurt by the collapse of the business.'

'So, you think that Marnie worked it all out in advance? She tipped us off to raid the office as part of an exit strategy?'

'Looks like it. And I don't think she'd go back to drugs. That was Billy's game.'

'Ultimately, you don't think that she's trying to control the drug trade?'

'No. I think she wanted to have a clean break from King Kabs and the drug business. She's faced the accusations and been proved innocent. That left her free to set up the new taxi company. A new outfit that's respectable and can bid for council contracts and accounts with big corporations. And even if she was going back to the drugs, I think she'd be far more subtle. Think about it. If we're right in what we're supposing about Marnie and her past actions, then she's cunning. She might have arranged to be arrested and then released to make herself immune to further prosecution. That doesn't sound to me like someone who would try to re-enter the trade by crudely stabbing a fairly low-level dealer and then not taking his product and cash. And leaving a body behind with a host of evidence.'

'You might think that,' Suse said, with the voice of experience. 'But I've seen plenty of intelligent criminals make really dumb moves or make bad mistakes. Or it could be that she's building a new organisation and one of the henchmen did this killing? If it's a new enterprise, then she might not have complete control over everyone at the lower levels.'

Now all eyes turned to Michelle as it was clear that a decision needed to be made.

'Emma, out of everyone who's still in CID, you're now the one who was closest to the Kings. So I trust your opinion and your take on the situation sounds right to me. But, all that being said, Marnie King is still a very much a person of interest in this case. I don't think we've got anything strong enough to call her in or make her a formal suspect. But I also think we'd be remiss if we didn't consider her at all. Any evidence that we pull in, let's look at it to see if it leads back to Marnie King. We can re-evaluate if we get anything stronger.' She paused to look around the room. 'Also, just because we took out a major player in King Kabs doesn't mean that we've wrapped up the whole drug trade in Bradwick. In fact, it's more often the case that once a big player is taken out then the smaller fish all move in and start fighting for the remains. I very much suspect that's what we've got here – the beginnings of a turf war.'

'What about the fact that the money and drugs were left on the body?'

'That is something that we'll need to clear up with our investigation. Don't get me wrong, it's a good thing. We've got product off the streets and money out of their pockets. But it is a detail we need to explain. Maybe, it's their first kill, they're stepping up, but they panicked when they'd done the deed and legged it.'

Emma shook her head. 'That's not exactly what happened, is it though? They still had time to put the coin in deep enough that no one at the scene spotted it though. And they took the murder weapon away, made sure they didn't leave any useable prints anywhere.'

'Look, I agree with you.' Michelle said. 'There is enough about this case that simply doesn't add up. So we need to cover all the angles. Was someone personally targeting Mr Hawsley? Did he steal someone's girlfriend or not cover his debts? Or is someone unbalanced enough that they're picking people at random to stab to death and then place a coin inside the body? Have we seen anything else like this around the country?' She paused for a moment to gather her thoughts. 'It's very early days, but we could have some sort of ritual killer. With only one body, we can't say that we've got a serial killer, but there are some elements that are concerning.'

'You think maybe there's some ritual significance to them?' Suse asked.

'I think they have to have some meaning. The problem is in trying to discern the meaning behind actions carried out by someone who'd gut someone and leave them to bleed out in the gutter. We might never figure it out until we catch the killer.'

John had his head down, tapping furiously on his phone. When the room fell silent, he looked up and saw everyone looking at him. 'Just on google,' he said. 'Apparently it's really common to leave coins for the dead. To, you know, pay the ferryman. Charon, it says here. But you'd leave them on the eyes or in the mouth.'

'And also leave a coin that had some value, I'd presume?' Suse asked.

John frowned at his phone. 'Yes, it's either a form or payment or to spend in the afterlife. Or, but I don't think this is relevant, in America they leave coins on graves and they all have a meaning, depending on the denomination.'

'Okay, so we're not in America and the coin wasn't American and not left on a grave, so let's discard that one,' Michelle said.

Suse nodded. 'It is very disrespectful, leaving a coin without any value, and placing it in the wound.'

'So, maybe he hates his victim? We got that from the fact that he killed them?' Michelle said. 'Let's park this for the moment, and maybe come back to it later, if we need to. John, what have you found out from Hawsley's online presence?'

John Fletcher said, 'Yep, give me a minute boss.' Then he fiddled with his laptop, went over to the television in the corner, then back to his desk. 'Here we go. I've just hooked everything up. These are photos I've taken off his accounts. This is a few weeks before he was killed.' A photo of Bill Hawsley standing in front of his white SUV with one foot on the sill came up on the screen. 'This is the day he got his new car. He posted this photo up and tagged pretty much everyone he knew on his feed. Well, more correctly, everyone who's female. Not only is he posing on his new car, look at those trainers.'

There were blank looks around the room. John Fletcher

didn't quite sigh and roll his eyes, but it was close. 'Those only came out a couple of months ago. I had a quick check and I think he had to have ordered them online from America.' He clicked on his mouse and more pictures came up. They all followed a theme of Bill flaunting his wealth. 'These pictures are a selection from a lot that all look similar. He takes these pictures and then tags in any girls he likes at that moment. Some of them like him back, but it's pretty much one way traffic.'

'OK, so that's one dimension of his interest.' Michelle said. 'Is there anything that's more useful out there? Contacts? Known dealers, people we've heard of?'

'Nah. I mean, he was one of those paranoid types. He made a few connections here and there to known dealers. But as soon as they get in touch, it goes all quiet. He's certainly too careful to make obvious deals over the internet. The tech boys went through his phone but there were lots of calls just from numbers. He didn't really go in for storing names in his phone. I mean, they're going to start linking them up to other known names, but it'll be a long job.'

Michelle nodded. 'OK then. We'll let the tech guys go work their magic. I've seen jobs like this before. They'll get the network nailed down. Likewise, the messages on his phone were all in some fairly crude code, but it'll be hard to pin anything down as obviously illegal. Stuff like, "have you got any gear?" replied with "usual place and time". Very hard to prove.'

Emma was hardly listening. She looked at the photo of Bill. He obviously thought he was attractive but his hair was close cropped leaving a curly mop on top. Unfortunately the style made his ears stick out. His teeth were uneven and this was emphasised by his one gold tooth. To Emma he looked like a kid playing at being a gangster.

CHAPTER TWELVE

IT WAS mid-morning and Rob was in his office, catching up on overdue admin. As he looked at the screen, he wondered what he'd signed up for when he'd first replied to Amy.

Sure, what's up?

You know that murder over on Sundown Drive?

I read about it.

He was aware that he'd lied. But she was a stranger and she didn't need to know that he had a possibly illegal source of information from inside the investigation. Rob didn't have to wait long before his phone buzzed.

I thought you were police?

I was. But now I'm not, I'm a private citizen.

But you must have contacts tho?

Maybe. Why are you interested?

The guy who was killed was in the same school year as Sophie. It's properly upset the whole family dynamic.

Who's Sophie?

My sister. She escaped, no contact for nearly a month.

Escaped, Rob thought. That's an interesting choice of word. But he decided not to pursue it at that time. He felt that a soft and gentle approach might be the way forward.

Did you know the victim? How are you coping?

No, he was a lot older. Not my crowd.

What's happened to your family?

My Dad's been totally random. He's not been overly protective, which I would've expected, but he seems more chill some of the time. But my sister vanished before all this kicked off and that's what he's stressed about.

Rob read the message. It was the most she'd ever typed in one go. He was trying to figure out how to respond when his phone buzzed again.

When you were in the police, did you learn about abuse?

I didn't specialise in it, but I did come across it.

So, if I can hear my dad and my mum, you know, doing it? Is that abuse?

Rob looked at the phone and weighed his options. It wasn't an area that he knew well, and he was out of the game. And he had to be aware of his red lines that he'd established in his head when he started the conversation. But, although this was about sex, he thought he could proceed cautiously.

It's not clear. If it was intentional he might be guilty of involving a minor in a sexual act.

But, he thought, it'd be the devil's own job trying to prove it. Maybe he should suggest social services? But then, they were overworked with far worse cases than this.

Well he was bellowing like a wounded cow and the bed was banging against the wall. He must have known that everyone in the house could hear.

I've got a friend who specialised in cases like this. She did all the training. Can I talk about it with her?

He looked at his phone, waiting for a response. He was in a weird situation. In one sense he felt like he knew Amy. But he'd never even seen a photograph of her. She might be fifteen, or she might not. Leaving that all aside, he had the feeling that he was dealing with a scared and vulnerable teenager. He only hoped he'd be able to help.

If you like. Whatever.

There was another pause in the conversation. Rob thought that BaggyAmy had gone quiet when his phone buzzed again.

I've got to go – break is over.

Anyway, he couldn't do anything about it right now, as he had a meeting with Ed. He very deliberately put his phone on silent and into his desk drawer as Ed walked in.

CHAPTER THIRTEEN

'So, I keep meaning to ask, what do I call you now?' Pete asked. There were on the sofa at Emma's house. He'd come back from his training course and straight over to Emma's house. All the housemates were out so they had the place to themselves.

'What do you mean?' Emma answered Pete's question with one of her own.

'Well, do I call you Emma or Angel?' A couple of months ago, it had emerged that not only were Emma's parents old hippies, but they had named her Angel Rainbow Stardust.

She shrugged. 'Either works for me.' Emma considered the question. What was her real name? She'd been called Angel all through her childhood and it had grated more and more until she broke away from her parents and changed it to Emma.

'Were you ever going to tell me? What your real name is?'

'Yeah. It might sound odd, but I don't think about it that much.'

Pete turned to her and frowned.

'I mean, my childhood, and the fact that I changed my

name. I am Emma Angel, that's who I am now.' She snuggled in closer, aware that it might sound like she was pushing him away. 'Listen, I'm sure we would have had one of those "what was your childhood like" conversations eventually. You know, if I hadn't been attacked and all that.'

Pete gave her shoulder a squeeze. 'Just to let you know there are no secrets in my past.' They sat together in companionable silence on the sofa.

'Emma,' she said after a few moments.

'Huh?'

'Call me Emma. Anything else would be weird.' She thought of how Lukas called her Angel, but he'd known her since childhood. And Rob when he was being like an old school boss. And it still was her surname.

'Yeah, I can get with that. You'll always be Emma to me.'

'I do have just one condition though.'

'What's that?'

'I honestly don't mind if you call me Angel or Emma. But never, ever, use the Rainbow and Stardust parts of my name, OK? Those have been firmly left in the past.'

They both laughed. 'So, how do you feel about your parents then? Are they embarrassing, or was there a big feud, or do you still get on with them?'

Emma blew out a big breath. 'It's very complicated. I mean, around work I can't really be seen as having family who are...' she paused, searching for the right words. 'Well, family who don't always follow the law. I mean, I know it's wrong, but I also understand them. They simply believe that drugs, especially those that grow naturally, should be legal. On the other hand, I'm not in a position where I can agree with those views.

'But as parents they didn't do anything terrible as I was growing up. I'm not going to cut them out completely.'

Pete nodded. 'I mean, you tried that, didn't you?'

'I don't think it was ever as formal as me cutting my family out. I never deleted their numbers or blocked them or refused to tell them where I was living.' Emma paused, remembering the past. She'd never had to explain it to anyone. It wasn't planned at all, just happened day by day until they piled up into years. 'It was more that we had an argument and were both too stubborn to back down. Well, me and Dad anyway. You know how much he hates the police, so you can imagine how well it went down when I chose this as a career.' She was appalled that they had spent nearly a decade without talking. 'It's just been easier that we don't talk. But I do think it hurt my mum, having to choose between the pair of us.' She brightened up with a smile. 'Still, there's nothing like having a near-death experience to heal old family wounds is there?'

For a moment, they just enjoyed the silence.

'Do you ever think about where we're going?' Pete asked, slightly hesitantly. 'I mean, I wouldn't even have known your birth name if you hadn't got injured like that.'

'In what sense?' The minute the conversation about her name had started, Emma had known this was the direction it was heading. Not marriage, that was not something she could ever see herself doing. But more stability, moving in, maybe talking about children. It wasn't that she was averse to the idea, it was more that she hadn't considered it. She had so much to do to be taken seriously in her work and to set herself up that she couldn't imagine making a big change in her life.

'Well, I'm in my tiny housing association flat, and you've got this house. I just wondered if you'd thought about the future?'

'I rented out the rooms to my tenants on the basis that I'd only rent rooms out to other women on shift work. I've tried to create a kind of safe environment for everyone here.' She shook her head. 'I mean, I don't want to be nasty to you, and I know you're not that kind of man, but you really can't move in here. It'd change everything.'

'Yeah, I know. And you can't move in with me either. I mean, my flat's hardly big enough for me, never mind anyone else.'

'And I've got Florence the cat. And my tenants. I'd have to look at the mortgage anyway, but I'm sure one of the terms is that I'm meant to be living in the house. I think being an absent landlord would change things.'

'So, here we are,' Pete said.

'Hey, listen, I'm happy, you're happy. We don't have to make any big changes, do we? I mean we can just muddle along.' In her mind, Emma wanted another five years. Get properly settled in at work, take her sergeant's exams, and then look for another posting, move on a bit. She loved Pete, she knew he was one of the good ones, but did he expect children? Would he respect her wish to have a career? She trusted Pete, and hoped that he'd be reasonable. There was a lot to discuss, but she didn't feel that now was the right time.

'No, but, you know, eventually we do have to settle down. Everyone does. You can't live like a student in a shared house forever.' He paused. 'Or in a tiny little flat that's not much bigger than student accommodation.'

Emma was struck by the similarity to the conversation she'd had with Lukas the previous night. Even he thought he'd found the right person and was looking to put down roots. He was doing great work with the charity and had a place to live, but it wasn't long term. It looked like he'd get some experience and move out to a proper house.

'Yeah, I suppose you're right,' Emma said, aware of a swirl of conflicting emotions. She'd gone into the police as a reaction against the freewheeling lifestyle she'd grown up with.

She thought that owning a house with a mortgage would make her feel more secure, more grown up. But was Pete right? She was now living in a shared house, with rotas for the housework and communal areas. Had she tried to move away from her upbringing only to circle back round to it again? She also knew, in the same way that Pete did, that it wouldn't last forever. 'Tell you what, if one of the girls wants to move out then I won't re-advertise straight away. I'll talk to whoever's still here and to you and we'll see where we are.'

'I could move in?'

'Let's not jump the gun. Just see where we are when we get there. What was your big life plan? How long were you going to stay in that tiny flat anyway?'

'It seemed simple when I started. I was going to put up with crappy rental properties, try not to splash too much cash on holidays and cars, and save up for a deposit on a house.'

'How's that working out?'

Pete made a face. 'Not so great. It's miserable and I've got a smidge over eight and a half grand in savings. Even on a five percent deposit, it's still crap. How did you manage it?'

Emma smiled. 'It's my aunt. She put up the deposit. It's part of her life savings. But it's all properly tied up legally. She owns a percentage of the house. And I can meet my end of the mortgage payments between my salary and the amount that I get in rent from Helen and Lucy. The way prices are going, she'll make a lot more than if she just left it in the bank earning interest. Everyone wins.'

Pete nodded. 'So, you've got things pretty well set here.'

'Yes, I suppose I have.' Emma snuggled further into him. 'And we have. I think all of this works well for us. I don't want to be one of those couples where all we have is each other and all our friends drop away. Or, even worse, everything is about our jobs. Listen, you've got your own space and your family.

I've got my friends here and my job. Between us we're both happy. You're always welcome here, no one has a problem with you. Let's not change anything for a bit. We'll meet up when we're free. If we're nearer your flat, we'll stay there, if we need more space, we'll come here.' She paused for a minute. 'If it's not broken, then it doesn't need fixing.'

CHAPTER FOURTEEN

Emma parked up in the carvery car park and turned to face Pete in the passenger seat. 'What are we doing here? Are you sure this is a good thing?'

'Babe, it's a Sunday lunch with your parents,' Pete said. 'Isn't that what you wanted? We can be like a normal couple doing normal couple things.'

Emma couldn't help but feel that "meeting the parents" marked a definite step forward in the relationship. She wasn't sure what it meant, but it felt loaded with meaning. Of course, it wasn't a traditional first meeting with her parents, as they'd met when they'd all gathered around her hospital bed. But this was a proper chance to talk without any pressure. A normal meeting.

'Oh God,' Emma said. 'I know I booked this up weeks ago, but I've just had my first week back at work and gone straight into a major investigation. I'm not kidding, I've worked six straight days and managed to arrange a few hours off today because I'd already booked it.' She paused, weighing up what she could say. 'I don't think it was much of a problem actually. The case feels like it's dead in the water, if I'm honest.'

'What's wrong with it? I thought you said it was a fairly straightforward drug related killing?'

Emma shook her head. 'Not that simple, I don't think. Our best bet is either something personal, or a vigilante. It wasn't either robbery or drug related because we found lots of money and drugs at the scene. All we're doing at the moment is taking the victim's life apart and trying to find his enemies. But he was a careful drug dealer, so it's like pulling teeth. It's slow and tedious.'

'You do sound tired,' Pete said. 'But it could be good to have some time off with your parents, recharge your batteries a bit.'

'Yeah, but now I feel like I've messed it up,' she said. 'I've invited Lukas along. Was that the right thing to do? What do you think?'

'Actually, I think that's a really good idea,' Pete said. 'The whole meet the boyfriend thing could put a big spotlight on me. You know what parents can be like. Whatever your differences in the past, no matter how much you grow up, you'll always be their little girl. This could've turned into a job interview for me. So, spreading the attention around a bit will help both me and you, if nothing else. Besides, they knew Lukas ages ago, they'll probably be grateful of the chance to catch up.'

Emma nodded. 'But it's Lukas. I know he's got a lot better recently, but we can't tell when he'll arrive, or what state he'll be in.'

'It is Lukas, and everyone at the table already knows what he's like. And these are your parents, they can cope with a bit of chaos. In fact, it's what they're used to.'

They both turned to look at the carvery. It was raining gently and without the engine on, the view across the car park was slowly disappearing behind rain spots and the screen fogging.

They both thought the same thing. They were meeting Emma's parents, who lived an alternative life and this was possibly the most normal, mainstream chain restaurant possible. The contrast couldn't have been more stark.

'Come on you!' Pete took Emma's hand. 'It won't get any better just sat in the car, staring at the door.'

As always, they started with the whole process of confirming their booking, being seated and given menus. Unsurprisingly they were the first there. They nervously looked around as they waited for the rest of their party to arrive.

The place was busy, most of the tables were occupied by families. Emma wondered if The Question would rear its head; did she want kids with Pete? Would he want to get married first? Marriage and children. It would certainly be hard to ignore with all the children around and her parents at the table with them.

Lukas was the next to arrive, with a woman in tow. She looked older than him and they were holding hands.

'Angel, babe! How are you? And Pete.' He got a curt nod of the head in return. 'This is Violet. I know it's kind of a last-minute thing, and I really shouldn't be asking but we overslept. And then I remembered that I had to come here and I just couldn't kick her out and tell her to go and get her own lunch while I came here. So, I know it's unplanned, but could she join us? We'll pay our way, of course, but well, we've only been going out a few weeks and I didn't want to stand you up, but then I didn't want to abandon her so here we are...'

Pete and Emma exchanged a quick glance. It was a done deal. Neither of them were prepared to start a scene and watch Violet walk away when Lukas had brought her down here. Beside which it would change everything. Either Lukas would stay and bring the mood down, or he'd leave with a very big and obvious hole in the group.

'Of course,' Emma said, finding herself the spokesperson for the group. 'Sit yourselves down and when my parents show up, we'll ask the waitress to set another place.' A cynical part of her wondered if this was calculated, and whether it came from Lukas or Violet. Once she was here, no one could reasonably say no without coming across as the bad guy.

As they sat down, she quickly assessed Violet. After her chat with Lukas, she'd known what to expect. Violet reminded Emma of Dawn French in the Vicar of Dibley. Not exactly the same, longer hair that was more brown than black. And where Dawn French had a sense of merriment, there was some wariness about Violet.

The waitress came over and took their drinks orders. 'Oh, and we've got an extra one in our party,' Emma said. 'Could you bring over another chair and everything for when the last two get here please?'

For a fraction of a second, the waitress's eyes widened a little. Then she regained her composure. Emma was used to picking up these signals but she was sure the others had missed it. 'Of course, I'll get those drinks, then I'll lay up another place.'

As she turned around, Badger and Jenny arrived. There was a bit of shuffling as the waitress stepped around them, and Emma stood up to give her mum a hug.

'You know Lukas, of course,' Emma said, 'and this is Violet.' She waved slightly awkwardly, as if just starting to be aware of the trouble she'd caused.

'Oh, right,' Badger said tightly. 'Didn't know you'd be joining us as well.'

'Last minute thing, Dad,' Emma said. She hoped calling

him Dad would console him a bit. 'The waitress is just sorting another place setting.'

Badger held out a chair to let his wife sit down as Emma returned to her seat. This left him standing at the side of the table, glowering with a look that clearly told Violet that she'd taken his rightful place, but he was too much of a gentleman to make a scene.

The waitress brought their drinks, then bustled off to get a chair. There was a lot of standing up and shuffling left and right, finally Badger was sitting at the table. He looked expectantly for the waitress, but she'd gone again.

'Bloody drink would be nice!'

'Badge, remember, it's not her fault. She just works here, and look at the place, the poor lass will be run off her feet. And she won't be getting paid enough for her trouble either.' Jenny fixed her husband with a look. 'Let's just settle down and enjoy being here. I'm sure everything will be sorted soon.'

Emma watched the harassed waitresses walking to and fro, always managing to avoid catching her father's eye. In the end Emma noted the table number and went to get the drinks from the bar herself.

Finally, the waitress came back and everyone opted for the carvery option except Violet who tutted and sighed over the menu before ordering the vegetarian cheese parcels wrapped in filo pastry.

Once they were in the queue, Badger muttered to Jenny and Emma, 'Who the hell brings a vegetarian to a carvery? I mean the main thing here is roast meat.'

'Dad, shhh!' Emma raised her eyebrows at Lukas who was ahead of them in the queue with Pete.

He nodded, then said, 'Why the hell are we queuing for our food anyway? I mean, they've got waitresses and tables. Don't see why we couldn't just bring the food to us.'

'It's just the way it is,' Jenny said with a consoling hand on his arm. 'Listen, we're here with our daughter and her friends. Isn't this what we always wanted, what we've been waiting for?'

'Yeah, I suppose so.' His face brightened a bit. 'So, what does this Pete do then? Same thing as you?' He couldn't quite bring himself to admit what his daughter did for a living.

'Similar, but different,' Emma answered. The queue shuffled forward a bit and Emma grabbed some plates and handed them out to her parents. 'He's not actually like me,' she continued.. 'He's a civilian who works for us. He does all sorts of complicated technical analysis. To be honest, the way the world is now, he's probably more important to making sure that criminals end up behind bars than I am.'

Badger frowned for a moment. He was about to ask something when they reached the front of the queue. The conversation was on hold as they all chose their roast meat and shuffled forward to get vegetables and gravy. Finally they walked back to the table, walking in a long single file through the tables.

When they were eating, Badger spoke to Pete. 'So, Angel tells me that you aren't in the police, but you actually work in the technical side of things? She even said you're more use at catching criminals than her.'

'Dad, you're stirring things up. What I meant was that nowadays, nearly everyone has a mobile phone, most criminals have laptops, and everything's on the internet and cloud servers. If you can't get to that information, you can't get a conviction. That's where you come in, isn't it?'

'Yeah, pretty much. I mean, I can't arrest people like Emma can, but I do get to process and handle evidence. You know, keeping the chain of custody intact. And, occasionally, I need to go to court, to explain what we've found.' He shrugged half-apologetically. 'I do enjoy it. It's nice to work with computers and I feel like I'm doing some good.'

'Hold on a minute, Lukas said you were police but I didn't believe him.' Violet was wide eyed with surprise as she turned to Emma. 'But Pete just said you can arrest people. Is that true?'

'Yes,' she said with a sinking feeling. 'I am a detective constable.'

'But Lukas said that you've been friends with him since you were kids. How exactly does that work? I mean, what happens if, you know, you see some of his stash, or come round when he's smoking a joint?'

'It's never happened,' Emma said firmly. 'Because he's a good friend and he knows not to put me in an awkward position.'

Violet's eyes sparkled. 'What if I told where his gear was? Or that I'd seen him smoking a joint? I mean, then you'd have to act on that information, wouldn't you? Or at least choose between arresting your best friend or breaking the law?'

Emma sighed. This was not the conversation that she wanted to have right now. 'We do have some discretion, you know. We don't actually have to arrest every single person we see breaking the law. Or follow up every piece of information that we receive.'

Violet's forehead crinkled. 'So, I could light a joint in front of you, right now? And you wouldn't be able to do anything?'

Emma gave her a hard stare. 'Apart from the fact that you can't smoke anything inside any building, this is a public place. Of course I'd have to do something.' When the silence grew longer she continued. 'Listen, if I get a call that some man is beating the crap out of his wife, I leap in my car and head over there. What do you expect me to do if I drive past a group of teenagers obviously passing a spliff around? Or if I get that call about domestic violence in the middle of nicking someone for speeding? I make the decision. It's like that, but on a bigger scale. We have operational priorities and we don't allow ourselves to become distracted by more minor crimes along the way.'

She took a breath after her big speech. As soon as she'd heard that Lukas had a new girlfriend, she'd braced herself for the jealousy. She was the friend from way back who was also female.

She saw Lukas reach across to Violet's forearm and give a little squeeze. In return Violet's eyes narrowed as she glanced sideways at him. Emma wondered what Lukas had got himself into.

The awkward silence only lasted for a moment before Jenny said, 'So Pete. Tell us about your work. You must be awfully clever to do all of those things with computers.'

'It's not that difficult really,' Pete said. 'I mean, I always liked computers from when I was at school. Everyone's good at different things. I'm not brave like the police who actually confront criminals and arrest people. But I'm glad that I'm able to help. I could've had any other job in IT, but this one actually feels like I'm helping in some way, you know?'

Jenny nodded. 'I mean, I know that we seem all anti-establishment and everything, but,' she gestured around at the restaurant. 'All of this is only possible because people like you keep the peace.'

'Aye, that's not the part of it that I have a problem with,' Badger said. 'But you see, it's your bosses. It doesn't take long before they forget that they're the servants of the public. That's always been the problem with humans. Put a group of them together and give them a uniform and a bit of power and that's where your troubles start.'

Jenny looked at him sideways, but Emma spoke before she

could rein him in. 'It's all right, Mum. I've been away for a while and I've kind of missed this. And Pete and I won't be offended. We didn't join up thinking everything would be rosy. We know what some people think of the police and we'll be the first to admit that there are problems.'

'And, you'll get to the top, won't you lass? And then you can make some changes.'

Emma couldn't believe her ears. Was her father actually proud of her? At least, he did clearly believe in her.

Pete thought for a second and then said, 'So, Badger, you're in favour of small government?'

'Ah, yes, kind of.' He held up a finger. 'I know where you're going with that. Small government can be a cover for right wing views. Low regulation and leave everyone to sink or swim on their own. But I think that you could have left wing small government. Not go poking into everyone's lives, but have a safety net there if anyone needs it.'

Pete nodded. 'But what you said about the police, tending towards becoming authoritarian, I think a similar thing happens with government. You get bosses and managers who are secure in their jobs and then they start to want to expand. They'll increase their remit, and try to get more staff. Give it twenty years and you're back to big bloated government.'

'Yeah, that's true. And trying to make government departments go capitalist obviously isn't working-'

'Oh my God!' Violet broke into the conversation. 'I can't believe you're actually discussing forms of government. I thought you'd all be anarchy and let people do what they want. This is more like a sociology seminar than anything else. Shouldn't we just let people do what they want, govern themselves?'

Badger pursed his lips. 'You'd think, but then the strongest would come to the top of the tree. Look at the drug trade.

Because it's illegal, you just get the strongest and the most ruthless running everything, with no morals. It's unfortunate but humans need organising. They need someone in charge to tell them to be kind.'

'Well, this human needs some dessert. Lukas, are you going to come with me and pick something from the desert trolley?' Without waiting for an answer, she got up and Lukas trailed after her looking slightly lost.

'Who the hell is that?' Badger asked.

'Lukas has a new girlfriend. He sprung it on us when they showed up. I invited him on his own, because, you know, he's part of the old crowd.'

'Yeah, Lukas is sound. But his choice in girlfriends...'

Emma nodded. 'You never know what you're going to get with Lukas. I mean, I love him, as a friend. I don't know where I'd be without him.'

'You see,' Jenny said. 'That right there. You've known him forever and you just said that you love him as a friend. You're going to need to dial that right down around Violet. She's just playing up to mark her territory and claim her man.'

Emma shook her head. 'I'll keep my head down till they're over the honeymoon phase. Maybe once they've settled down a bit we can get on better. Shall we go and look at these desserts then?'

For the rest of the meal, Emma did her best not to engage with Lukas too much and make sure that she leaned in towards Pete slightly. She felt foolish playing games, but it seemed to work. More importantly, it was clear that her parents had warmed to Pete and that was what she really wanted to achieve.

CHAPTER FIFTEEN

Emma cradled her petrol station coffee in both hands in an attempt to keep warm. The sky above her was studded with stars which meant that there was no cloud cover, making the night literally freezing. It was now past one in the morning, and she'd been summoned out to inspect a body.

The person who found it had been on his way home from the pub when he'd been caught short. After a bit of cajoling from the first attending officer he did point out the tree deeper into the park where he had eventually relieved himself.

She was joined by John Fletcher who was yawning and scratching his head. 'Where'd you get that?' He pointed at her coffee.

'Petrol station on the way in. There's another one in the car.'

When he had retrieved the coffee, they went over to inspect the body. The crime scene officers were already set up and had the area ringed with bright white lights. They were arranged around a tree that grew from a flower bed by a wall. 'It's fairly easy to see what happened,' Fletcher said. 'Our victim, Dr

Nicola Donnelly, walks from her surgery on her way home, right past this gate.' He indicated an opening in the red brick wall that led to the main road. 'It's dark but there are streetlights on the main road. The murderer pops out once she's gone past and grabs her from behind. Drags her back here into the shadows and then he stabs her. Or, maybe he stabs her as he grabs her. Either way, she's pulled back here and laid under this tree.'

'There's a lot of blood,' Emma said, peering at the earth where the blood had pooled and soaked in. 'Likely that the stab wound caught one of the internal arteries or organs. They can bleed a lot.' She was shaken but John Fletcher didn't notice. 'There's only one stab wound,' Emma said when she'd recovered. 'I think that we have to consider whether there could be a link with our previous victim.'

'I don't see it,' John said. 'This is a woman, and she's in a nice place.' Emma looked at him. 'I mean, the other one was in a seedy location and he was a seedy character. Just take a look at the crime scene. Hawsley, our first victim, was dumped where he fell, in the gutter of car park, with the litter. Here, she's not only been dragged off the street, but she's been laid out below a tree, in a park.'

'I didn't know you did the whole criminal profiler thing.'

'I know I don't come across as serious, but that's just banter with the team. I do know what I'm on about. And I just don't see why you would link a teenage drug dealer with a GP, literally a pillar of the community.'

'It's the weapon,' Emma said. 'I don't like the thought that there are two people running around Bradwick with a big knife, stabbing people. And I know this is a nicer place than the car park, but they were both left where they were killed. And both attacked in the dark.'

John nodded. 'That only applies if you've got a killer

picking random victims though. Most killers stick to a gender or race or have something that links them.'

They looked at each other, the same thought dawning on them both.

'You mean the football coin?' Emma asked.

'I know one was left in the first body,' John said. 'But to be honest, I'm not even sure what a football coin is.'

'They were an old promotional item from petrol stations. You know, buy so much petrol, get a free coin. Then you keep going back to collect the set. You could even buy a folder to keep them in if you wanted. I think it all happened back from the seventies through to the nineties. Once our victim is opened up, then we'll know.'

'Or, we could find out now. Here's Dani, let's ask her.'

'Ask me what?' Dani had just arrived, and like the other people there was dressed in a white forensic suit.

'Whether she's the next in a series, together with our dead drug dealer, Bill Hawsley.' Emma said, gesturing at the body. 'I think there are similarities, one stab wound, body dumped pretty much where it fell, no witnesses.'

'But,' John countered, 'the two victims share nothing in common. A male, teenage drug dealer and an older, female GP. It's hard to see the same person being responsible for both attacks.'

'Well,' Dani replied, 'there's no way to tell until I get her back to the mortuary and start the autopsy.'

'Couldn't you just look in situ and give us a quick yes or no?' John asked.

'I can't compromise a crime scene just to settle a bet between two detectives.'

'It's not just between the two of us,' Emma said. 'We've got two bodies now and the first had a coin left in the wound tract. This one has some similarities to the previous ones and some big differences.' She nodded to John to acknowledge that he did have a point. 'The presence or absence of that coin would be the defining factor. It would greatly help the investigation if we knew whether we were adding this one into the existing major investigation, which could indicate a series of murders. Or it could mean that we need to get a whole new SIO and a second major investigation team established. Really, this is key information as to how we go forward. Has the killer we're after changed his MO and branched out, or do we have a whole new case?'

Dani thought for a moment. 'I can take a quick look in the wound. If I see something, I'll leave it there until I can safely remove it in sterile conditions. And of course if I don't see anything, that's not to say that nothing's there. I might find it later anyway. That's the best I can do.'

With care she knelt down by the body and opened up her kit. She held a probe in one hand and a torch in the other. Completely absorbed in her task, she leant in close, moving the probe and torch around. Finally she packed away her kit, stood up and looked at the two officers.

'Well. There is something in the wound. It looks to be shiny and metallic. Probably a few millimetres thick and maybe ten or more millimetres across. I can't really tell any more detail at this stage. Obviously I'll know more back at the lab.'

'Did it look to be the size of a large coin?' Emma asked.

Dani nodded. 'If I was looking at it edge on, then yes it could be.' She held up a finger as a warning. 'But don't quote me on any of it. There's no way I can make an official report while kneeling in a park in the small hours of the morning.' She paused and softened her tone. 'It's entirely reasonable that it could be another coin in the wound tract. And that injury does bear some of the same characteristics of the previous body. The weapon could easily be the same one. But that's as far as I'm going. As I said, I'm not going to remove it here. I'll do it properly when the body has been processed back at the morgue. And then, once you've got it, you can work out what it is and where it fits in.'

Emma smiled and touched Dani's elbow. 'Thank you! I'll keep your name out of it. I know it's your professional reputation at stake. But that does mean that we can roll this into the existing investigation. I'd better take some notes and head back to the station.' She turned to John. 'Looks like I won this round. To be honest, I thought you made good points. And you're right about one thing – nothing about this makes sense.'

'Yeah, you got that right.'

'And it means we've now got twice the evidence in our major investigation, whereas we could have been faced with two separate cases.'

'Well, I suppose we ought to head into the office, start phoning everyone and get the new information added onto the system.' John Fletcher still seemed a bit down, but it could have just been the hour of the morning and the fact that they were at the scene of another brutal killing.

CHAPTER SIXTEEN

Rob looked up from the notes he'd been preparing as Ed knocked on the door before entering and sitting in front of the desk.

'Ed, what have you got for me?'

'Two thirds of nothing, boss.' Ed looked downcast. 'I followed the brief. It's not really a difficult job, there's a coffee shop over the road that has clear line of sight on the estate agents. I just sit there all day till she comes out. I usually park in the same car park, so it's easy enough to naturally walk back to my car if she leaves the office and follow her.'

'And? What happened?'

'Honestly? She showed houses to folks.' Rob's face fell. 'Listen, she met with all sorts of people. But if there was ever a single man, I kept a close eye on things. And guess what? They never closed the curtains. I had a walk by every time. I left it for five to ten minutes before checking in on them. I figured that if she was playing away, then that would be the perfect amount of time for them to get their clothes off and get caught at it. And every time I could see people, upright, fully clothed, and walking around. And when they came out, they never looked dishevelled.'

Rob nodded slowly and shook his head. 'Ten minutes. I mean, even if they're really keen, get in there rip each other's clothes off...'

'... even if they're really quick, they're going to have finished and be smoking cigarettes by then. Certainly they won't be dressed. Yeah, I really don't think she's playing away. I mean, I saw them, ten minutes after entering the house, through the window. All fully clothed and to be blunt, like they were buying a house.'

Rob rubbed his chin. 'Absolutely nothing I can report back? We don't usually get people willing to pay if there's nothing going on at all. By the time they're ready to pay us they already have some pretty strong suspicions.'

'There was one house, she went in to view with a bloke about her age. I thought we could be on. I waited ten minutes, had a walk by, couldn't see them through the window, so I knocked.'

'And?'

'And nothing. I gave them some flannel about my missing cat, and they checked the garage and shed. But they were very professional with each other. No knowing glances, neither too close nor too distant. Neither of them looked particularly red in the face or breathless or with their hair messed up. Not a button out of place.'

'So, in total, we've got nothing.' He shook his head. 'This is the trickiest part – telling someone they've just paid money and got nothing back.'

'Surely he'll be happy. His wife isn't playing away. Won't that be what he wants to hear?'

Rob thought back to his first meeting with Sean Church,

his client. He didn't seem like the sort of person who'd take the news well.

'Listen, boss, I've taken some photos.' He slid an envelope across the table. Even in this digital age, he knew that Rob would be happier with real photos printed on paper. 'They're all time stamped so you can see her going in, meeting people and leaving again. They might convince him.'

'Thanks.'

'What do you want me to do now?'

'Leave off for a bit. Don't let the wife get too used to seeing you. I'll call a meeting and we'll see what the client wants to do.'

CHAPTER SEVENTEEN

EMMA ANGEL and John Fletcher were already in the office when the rest of the team started filtering in from seven thirty onwards. The pair of them had spent the rest of the night drinking coffee and carrying out as much research as they could while most of the world was asleep. They were also rapidly approaching the stage where coffee would stop working to keep them awake. When the whole team were assembled, DI Michelle Jones called the meeting to order.

'As I'm sure you all know by now, we have a second victim.' She tapped a photo on the board. 'Once again, it wasn't a robbery, so we have all her bank cards, plus her photo driving licence. It looks as if this person is, or was, Dr Nicola Donnelly. Obviously, we have contacted the next-of-kin and as soon as the morgue is ready, we'll arrange formal identification.'

'How do we know this is the same killer?' Suse Berman asked. 'Why aren't we spinning up a new major investigation?'

'Dani Price carried out an initial examination at the scene and made an initial assessment that there could be a coin in the wound tract. Obviously, we're once again waiting on the pathologist to properly confirm. But for the moment we're working on the assumption that this is Nicola Donnelly and she's the second victim of the same killer. And it's looking like a strong assumption.'

'But it's still an assumption though, isn't it?' asked John, picking up the thread.

Michelle nodded. 'That's true. But it's a good assumption. What's your problem with it?'

'Well, if this is the same killer, then we have to ask ourselves how he's picking his victims. The first was a low-level drug dealer who was operating out of a carpark on the edge of the Seaview. Why has he switched over to a respectable, middle-aged, female doctor? Almost every characteristic of the second victim is the opposite of the first one.'

Michelle nodded. 'You're right, the whole victimology is problematic. But I have one further problem that I think trumps your concerns.' The whole team went quiet as they watched the exchange between the two of them. 'If you're right and this becomes a new case with another killer, then we have two people in Bradwick who have each, independently, decided to start stabbing people with nearly identical long knives. And inserting coins into the wound as well. I don't like co-incidences, and this seems far beyond the realms of what's possible. Which leaves us with the other option – this is the work of the same person. I have no doubt of that and we must also bear in mind that the murders and choice of victims make sense in his head. If we can't catch him by working out what links the victims, then we're going to have to work the evidence. Two bodies mean like we've got a lot more to work with.'

'Emma and John, you were on the scene in the middle of the night, so I'm ordering you two to work till lunchtime, then go home and get some rest. I know that this development doubles the amount of evidence that we have, and will provide a lot of work. But I need everyone sharp so we're not going to work more than twelve-hour shifts.

'This is a much more promising crime scene as well. Dr Donnelly was walking home from work at seven in the evening. That gives us a whole host of opportunities. We can start with car dash-cams and check any shops along the route that have CCTV. Hopefully her phone will give us enough tracking data to narrow down a timeframe.' Michelle Jones then started allocating tasks out and bringing in more uniformed officers to help with the sweep. Before she left, she looked at Emma and said, 'DC Angel. My office, please.'

Confused, Emma followed her across the open plan working area. She quickly reviewed all her actions since she had been called out to the body early that morning. She couldn't find anything that she'd done wrong or that she had missed. So it was with a clear conscience that she sat opposite her boss in her office.

'So, Emma, you've been working with John Fletcher since early this morning.'

'Yes, ma'am. We were both on the on-call rotation and it seemed like a major incident so we both attended. Is everything OK?'

'Oh, yes, everything is fine. Textbook, the way you dealt with it and set up the incident room before everyone else got here.' She paused and pinched the bridge of her nose. 'Listen I've got to compile a report on Fletcher, since he's a trainee detective constable. Make a recommendation. So I'm carrying out an informal three sixty review. Getting input not just from those above him, but those who work alongside him. Aside from that first day when he turned up late, he hasn't put a foot wrong. But he has, for want of a better word, a bit of an attitude. I guess, you've been in this team longer than most, you'll know what makes it work. You'll know who'll be good for the team or and who won't.'

'You want me to recommend whether or not John should stay in CID?' Her head was spinning. After a long night she couldn't believe that she now had to make a decision that would affect another officer's entire career.

'Oh God, no! I would never do that to you. No, the decision will be mine and mine alone. And I'll stand by it. I just want a well-rounded view and you work with him day to day, whereas I'm his boss. So, it's just your opinion of what he's like to work with. And it won't just be your opinion, I'll be asking around the whole team. So don't worry about what you say. It'll just be part of the bigger picture.'

'Right, yes.' Emma breathed out and gathered her thoughts. 'Well, I know he comes across as a bit abrasive, but I honestly think that's just how he is. He's... ' She stopped speaking. She'd been about to say a different generation, but that wasn't completely true. They were roughly the same age. But she'd been brought up by her hippy parents and sometimes that felt like a different generation. There was no way that now was the right time to start discussing her upbringing with her boss. 'He's one of those people who grew up on the internet. His idea of normal is YouTube and now TikTok and all the social media. Banter is like a second language to him, don't read too much into it.' She paused and Michelle nodded slowly. Emma was aware that she hadn't answered the question. 'All that aside he is a good officer. I mean, he showed up at gone one in the morning, near freezing temperatures, and didn't bitch about it at all. Just did the job. And when we were back to the office he carried on without complaint. Didn't try to shirk or give me the difficult jobs. We divided it up fairly and, yes, he was fine.'

'So, no problems then?'

'Not really.'

'He did push back on the linking of the two murders though.'

'Yes, but I think that's a good thing.' Michelle frowned at Emma so she continued. 'I mean, the last case I was on, I had to stick to my guns.'

Michelle nodded. 'And it got you suspended.'

'But I was right. I think you need different voices. And you need detective constables and sergeants who aren't afraid of you and will speak up.'

'Yes, you are right.' She had been making notes but now she clicked her pen shut and closed her notebook. 'Thank you. Very useful. And I meant what I said about going home. Lunchtime at the latest.'

Emma returned to her desk and tried to keep her eyes open as she waded through the vast numbers of reports coming into CID at the moment. When the preliminary report came through from Dani Price the pathologist, she saw immediately that the argument was over. A football coin had been removed from the wound tract. It was the Charlton Athletic coin from the same set from 1972.

Michelle had obviously seen the same report as she came over to Emma's desk. 'Emma, have you found anything about those coins yet? Now we've got two, I think we need to be on top of it.'

Emma had noticed that the coins were left out of the general briefing. 'I did have a quick search around when the first showed up. The bad news is that there are plenty available on eBay, or any of the other online sales sites. The only thing I can tell you for definite is that anyone with internet access and about thirty pounds spare could get a set.'

'Is it worth getting a warrant and a list of recent purchases in the area?'

Emma pursed her lips and then shook her head. 'No, I don't think it'd get us very far. I mean, not only are there lots out there, but there are also bricks and mortar auction houses and boot fairs. Not to mention those lower end shops that are halfway between junk and antique shops.'

Michelle nodded. 'I can see your point. But this person needs to be caught. I know that it's a bind, but can I put you onto this? I'll get the legal guys to try to get a list of users from the internet who've bought one recently. In the meantime, can you go around all the bricks and mortar places in the area? See if there are any specialists or anything like that. Have you got any other ideas?'

'Well, from a bigger perspective, I did some poking around on the internet. As John said, it's actually from Greek myth, the idea of leaving coins with the dead. It's payment for Charon to ferry the body across the River Styx.'

'I know what you mean.'

'And the coins are usually placed in the mouth or over the eyes. But there wasn't too much more info that seemed relevant.

'Yeah, it is weird, especially the coins not being in the right place. And, from what you've said, the coins are nearly worthless. It's not much in the way of payment, is it?'

'But, it does add up, doesn't it?' Emma was getting excited now. 'I mean, we think this guy is a vigilante, so he doesn't think his victims are worth anything.'

'Well, we'll keep it close to our chests for now. Just within CID. This will sort out the attention seekers from the genuine tips and if we do, God forbid, get a copycat or anything, we'll know.'

Emma nodded and returned to her work. After another

hour, she realised that she'd read the same screen three times without taking it in, and remembered her boss's words. A glance at her screen revealed that it was nearly three pm. She looked out of the window and saw that since the frost of the morning, rain had moved in, darkening the day.

When she got back into her car, she kept on turning over the conversation she'd had with DI Jones. Did she really want to work with John Fletcher long term? She accepted that he could be a bit brash and hard to rub along with. But she couldn't decide if he'd be an asset or not.

She shook her head. This wasn't what she wanted out of the police. She didn't want to decide who stayed and who was sent back to uniform. She thought she was working towards a place where people rose on merit and corruption was a thing of the past. In which case she supposed that she'd have to recommend John Fletcher. She'd seen nothing that would suggest he was corrupt. And he did seem to be a good investigator.

She decided the best thing to do would be to drive home carefully, and get some rest before the next round of the case.

CHAPTER EIGHTEEN

AMELIA GOT out of the car with her gym bag and went up the stairs to the dance studio. There was the usual bustle of parents and girls, all fussing over hair and clothes, tracksuits coming off, leotards being straightened. She always left her mum in the car, so she could have these few moments of peace. She could almost feel like a grown up. She could almost feel free.

When she got to the door however, the teacher pulled her to one side.

'Amelia, could I have a word?' Shona, the teacher, had her concerned face on. Amelia nodded. 'Is your mother or father here?'

'Mum's waiting in the car, shall I fetch her?'

'Yes please. The fees haven't been paid. And they weren't paid last month either. I know it's awkward, but we do have policies. And we don't want to be unfair to the other girls.' She looked around as if the other girls were worried that Amelia was getting a free ride but they seemed oblivious.

Amelia couldn't speak around the lump in her throat. She

nodded quickly and blinked to try to avoid the tears. She stumbled down the stairs and back to the car.

'Amelia? What's wrong?'

'Nothing, it's fine. Just didn't feel like it today.'

'Really? Are you sure? I thought you liked dance class? Have you gone off it?'

'No, just, you know, didn't want to.'

'Are you not feeling well?'

Amelia reached for the lifeline that was offered her. 'Yes, that's it. Stomach cramps, you know, time of the month.'

Her mother turned around to look full at her daughter. 'You know, I can always tell when you're lying. What's really going on?'

Amelia took a moment to clear her head. She knew when her mum got into a mood that she wouldn't let up. But she didn't want to tell the truth either. She was afraid of where that conversation might go.

She shook her head and her shoulders shook with the effort of keeping it all in. After a few moments of sobbing she took several deep, shuddering breaths to calm herself down. 'The fees haven't been paid.' She paused again and shut her eyes. 'Apparently the payment for last month never went through either.' She opened her eyes and blinked the tears away. 'Shona wants you to go up.'

'There's nothing I can say. You know your father won't even allow me to look at the bank account.' Her mother paused, unsure what to reveal. 'He did say something a while back about reducing outgoings. You know what he's like. He goes off on these rants about how his money doesn't stretch and we have to live within our means. And then in two months' time, he'll have forgotten and we can go back to normal. You just have to weather the storms.' She paused and glanced at her daughter. Her words hadn't been enough. 'I'm sorry, honey, I didn't know he'd cancelled your dance class.'

Amelia snuffled and rubbed her nose on the back of her hand. In a small voice, she asked, 'Why do you stay with him, Mum?'

'What do you mean? He's my husband and I love him. I made promises, legal ones and ones in front of God. Things you just can't go back on. And neither of us want you to grow up in a broken home either. Do you have any idea what the statistics look like for children of divorced parents?' She stopped and saw again that she had lost Amelia. 'Listen, sweetie, I know you're butting heads with him at the moment, but that's just the age that you're at. He's a good man underneath it all. Everything that you don't like, that's just him trying to protect you. That's what you don't understand. He's doing what's best for you, for this family. Sometimes he has to do things that you don't like, but in the end they work out for the best. And do try to remember that he works hard, he's the one who earns all the money. That means you owe him respect.'

Amelia tried hard to work out how cancelling her dance class was protecting her, but didn't dare to ask. She knew that her mother was on the same side as her father. What had she been thinking, asking a question like that? She should keep her mouth shut and her head down.

'You want me to go up? See what I can sort out?'

Amelia shook her head. 'Is there any way we could just go and never come back?'

In response, her mother nodded and started the engine.

THEY GOT HOME in a sombre mood. Neither of them had spoken in the car. Amelia had crossed an unspoken line by asking about her mother's marriage. And now she had to decide whether or not to confront her father over what had happened at the dance class.

Neither of them said anything, but they both knew that their response would depend on the mood of the man of the house when they returned. Sitting on the drive, Amelia silently pulled down the sun visor and flicked open the mirror. She peered at her face. Wordlessly, her mother handed her a wet wipe from her purse. The teenager acted quickly, trying to hide any sense that she'd been crying. She did what she could, but there wasn't much she could do to hide the splotches on her face.

They went in through the front door, alert to the atmosphere inside. But the house was empty, with all the lights on. Amelia went straight to the kitchen and looked out of the window above the sink. She could see down the length of the garden to the shed at the end. Well, shed wasn't quite the right word. There was a brick-built workshop there when they moved in and Thomas had expanded it with a couple of large sheds. Every summer, he bought a new machine for it. When he needed to unwind, that was where he went. His hobby was making wooden toys. Everything from intricate match-the-shape games for toddlers, up to rocking horses. Everything was sold for charity, he didn't even take the costs of his wood, paint and varnish.

The lights were burning bright down there, throwing rectangles onto the lawn. Amelia nodded to her mother. 'He's in the workshop.'

Both of them breathed out. They looked around the house as if it were a new building, assessing how long he'd been there, how long they had.

Tom being down at the workshop meant that he could not be disturbed. Once he'd passed that door at the end of the path, it was as if he ceased to exist. None of the women in the house ever went into the workshop. Neither of them had even seen enough through the door to be able to describe the interior.

'I'll put the oven on, make a start on dinner. Check the fridge has enough beer in it, would you?' Sharon asked.

'There's only two bottles left, will that be enough?' The two looked at each other, a silent calculation being carried out. Tom being annoyed at not enough beer – was that better or worse than if he got drunk?

There was no time to rectify the situation though. The lights in the workshop switched off and they could see Tom making his way up the path, wiping his hands on a towel.

'You're back early,' Tom said, as he came into the kitchen. 'Everything all right?' It was impossible to tell from the tone of his voice what mood he was in.

'Yeah,' Amelia said carefully. 'Just not really in the mood for it today. I've been thinking I might quit, actually. You're always saying how it costs money and it's not fair to expect you to earn it all while we spend it.'

There was a pause, as he digested this news, nodding slowly to himself. 'Well, why don't you think on it?' Then he broke into a broad smile. 'Hey, Sharon, have you started cooking yet?'

'Yes,' she said nervously. 'The oven's on and I was just looking through the cupboards and seeing what to make. Is there anything you'd like?'

Instead of answering, he got his wallet out and held up a couple of notes. 'Tell you what, why don't you take the night off? You're always cooking and cleaning and ferrying Amelia around. Pop down the chippy, get dinner for us three.' He crossed to the fridge and peered inside. 'And pickup another four pack of beers from the corner shop. I feel good today, and I think that we should all have a good evening. I'll put the kettle on so you can have a cup of tea when you get back.'

That evening, Amelia lay in bed. She was full, having eaten battered fish and chips and should've felt, warm and contented. Her father had even let her have some of his beer. She didn't like the bitter taste, but she didn't want to break the good mood of the evening. Now her head felt pleasantly swimming and her eyes were heavy. But she found she couldn't sleep and relax.

Why was her dad in a good mood? How long would it last? If it did come crashing to an end, would she be to blame? She lay there, staring at the ceiling as the thoughts circled in her head.

CHAPTER NINETEEN

DI Michelle Jones turned to the white board and gestured at it. 'OK people we now have a second column on the board. Not what I wanted to see, I'll be honest, but let's try to make it the last one. I know we're all in early, and the last one has left us all tired, but let's crack on with it.'

'What do we know, boss? Are we still looking for a vigilante?' John Fletcher said.

'No.' She shook her head. 'Unless our second victim, the good lady Doctor Donnelly had some secrets that are so well hidden that we haven't been able to find them.' She looked hopefully at DS Suse Berman who'd been leading the initial investigation into the second victim.

'Seriously, Boss, we've not found a thing. Initial search throws up nothing on any of the police databases. Not even a parking ticket. As far as we can tell she hasn't been even a witness to a crime. She's on DVLA, she passed her test at nineteen and her car is a five-year-old Mini.'

'Anything else, hobbies, social media profile, anything?'

'Not much of anything,' Suse said. 'Although to be honest, we all know how many hours GPs work, and from what we've seen, she was committed. I don't think she had time for any extracurricular activities. She was dedicated to her job. She went on extra training courses so she could help more people. The few complaints about her were that she was taking too much time with her patients.' She shook her head. 'We had a preliminary interview with her husband, took a deep dive into her private life. She worked all hours as a GP and looked after her family. There wasn't really much time left for anything else.'

Emma had a thought. 'Do we know if she was local to Bradwick? I mean, I know she worked here, but was she a local? Born here?'

Suse frowned, and looked at her notes. 'We've made a broad strokes outline of her career. Went to university, did her medical degree and then went to Bradwick General for her foundation year. She obviously liked the sea air because she stayed for her specialist training, then went into one of the local surgeries. Been here ever since.'

Emma nodded. 'And where was she from originally?'

'Err,' Suse leafed through her notes. 'Bexley, in the London suburbs, medical school in London, then out here for the postgrad.'

'Right, thanks.'

Michelle fixed her with a stare. 'Emma, what are you thinking?'

'Well, I'm thinking we've got to find some similarities between the victims. They're obviously not both criminals, so they've got to have something in common. Hawsley was a Bradwick lad, and I just wondered if Dr Donnelly had also gone to Bradwick High or not.'

Michelle frowned. 'I see what you mean. And there might be a link somewhere. It's not like either of them have just arrived in town.' She nodded decisively. 'OK then, people.

Let's see what else links the two victims. What else do they have in common?' She looked at Emma again. 'Emma, we've got a slot booked with the practice manager in an hour. Can you take that? Take John with you.'

Emma nodded. She still wasn't certain that she knew what to make of John Fletcher. He seemed keen to make the right impression, but at the same time he seemed to be doing all the wrong things.

EMMA AND JOHN shared an awkward car journey into the outskirts of Bradwick to talk to the practice manager. After a few comments from John about why she was in the police, which bordered on sexist, she decided to turn the tables.

'So, John, what about you? What made you want to be a police officer?'

John looked nervous and made a show of concentrating as they turned right off a main road. When it was clear that he couldn't dodge the question, he said, 'Well, it seemed like a real job, you know?'

'A real job?'

'Yeah, you know. So many people when I left school just kind of fell into gig work, deliveries, zero hours at coffee shops, bit of this, bit of that. And I thought that, you know, when I got older, and people asked what I did, what would I say? A bit of this and a bit of that? Or if I said I was a police officer, well, you know, it sounds a bit more real.' He paused uncertainly. 'Sounds stupid, now that I say it out loud.'

'Doesn't sound stupid,' Emma reassured him. 'But why police? There's lots of other real jobs.'

'I dunno. I've always been fit and good at sport, so there's that. And I like talking to people, you know, sorting out problems. And it's interesting, you know, always something new and different.' He seemed to run out of steam. 'I applied for a few things, but got in the police, managed to get through the training.' He indicated and pulled into a car park. The surgery was situated in the middle of a housing estate and was a modern, low, brick-built building, surrounded on two sides by a car park.

They navigated the reception and were shown into the practice manager's office. They sat with the two officers on one side of the desk and the manager on the other.

'I'm Margaret Fisher, practice manager, how can I help?'

'I'm DC Emma Angel and this is DC John Fletcher. We're here about Dr Donnelly. We are sorry for your loss, it must be such a shocking time.'

Margaret's face fell, but she held back tears. 'Well yes. I mean, you always think of such things happening in big cities at night. But for it to happen to Nicola on her way home from work. In Bradwick, our own sleepy seaside town.' She stopped, unable to continue.

'Well, you might think that–' John started saying, but stopped when Emma kicked his shin. He looked at her and her eyes told him to shut up, without using any words. Luckily Margaret Fisher was looking for a tissue and hadn't noticed the hurried, silent exchange. 'I mean,' John recovered, 'we were shocked as well. Someone who dedicates their life to helping others, well, it's not right, is it?'

Margaret blew her nose and Emma tried to change the direction of the conversation. 'Are you all right to answer a few questions about Dr Nicola Donnelly?'

'About her, yes,' the manager said carefully. 'As I'm sure you're aware, we can't really comment in any way about her patients. As upsetting as this situation is, we really can't compromise confidentiality.'

'We are aware of that,' Emma said. 'But we also need to find who killed her, and I'm sure you want that too.' The other woman nodded. 'So, what was she like as a doctor? Was she a good colleague? Easy to work with?'

'She was good at her job. Knowledgeable and very able at diagnosing patients. I'm not sure what else you need to know.'

'Well, I'm sure all GPs are good at their jobs and well trained. But they're also people. Was she known for taking a long time over appointments, or was she brusque? How well did she treat the receptionists? Did patients request her specially or did they try to avoid her? Was she popular?'

The manager looked thoughtful.

'We won't record your thoughts with your name against them,' Emma said, 'if you'd be happier. There's no need for this to come out in court. It's just building up a background.'

'No, it's not that. I was just gathering my thoughts and mentally checking everything against ethics and privacy concerns. No, Nicola was lovely. She was one of those genuinely warm people. In fact it was more a case of telling patients that they'd have to wait to see her or they could see one of the other GPs more quickly. She was always taking more time with her patients than the allocated ten minutes. I mean, she didn't mind staying late to catch up at the end of the day, but the appointments did get progressively later throughout the day. I did have to remind her on more than one occasion that she could schedule follow up appointments or to get her patients to book double appointments. But it wasn't really a problem, more a sign of how dedicated she was as a doctor.' She paused for a second. 'In fact, she was training to become a family counsellor. She could've done that in addition to her GP hours. That's what she was really interested in, helping people holistically, not just prescribing them some pills to alleviate the symptoms of whatever was bothering them at that moment. And not that fluffy complementary medicine, but solid science based therapy. If you make patients feel better in their minds, if their lives are happier, then that can have an effect on their bodies. Once their minds and emotions are sorted out, often their bodies follow.'

Emma nodded, and noticed that John was taking notes, keeping his head down and not saying anything further. 'What about hobbies, interests out of work?'

Margaret gave a sad little chuckle. 'Obviously you don't know what the life of a GP is like. Some of the older doctors move to locum work and have a bit of spare time. But Nicola was one of our partners. When she finished seeing patients, it was after six most evenings. Then, she'd have to help run the surgery. I mean, I know I'm the manager, but all I can do is prepare reports, sort out personnel matters, and then allow the partners to make their own decisions. For a committed doctor like Nicola, there weren't enough hours in the day to do everything. So I can say she didn't have a social life or any hobbies. It's sad, but it's the reality for GPs.'

Emma nodded. She knew that being in the police was equally likely to consume as much free time as it could. There was only one more question she needed to ask and she thought she already knew the answer. 'Can you tell me, without details, if there were ever any formal complaints against Dr Donnelly? Or any patients that you had to move off her list to someone else?'

Margaret thought for a moment. 'I don't have to look it up, there were no complaints. Neither from the patients nor from Nicola. She didn't have a problem with any of them. And as I said, the only blot on her record was that she took too much time. I always thought that she'd have to slow down sooner or later, or she'd burn herself out.'

This time, John chose to keep quiet. But they were both

thinking that the doctor would never get the chance to slow down. Emma nodded to herself, then they thanked Margaret Fisher for her time and they made their way back to the station.

The journey back was quiet. Neither of them referred to Emma kicking her junior, nor the fact that once again he had been tactless.

CHAPTER TWENTY

While the Major Investigation Team were assembling several hours after the second body find, Rob was in the office early to try and get all his paperwork in order. He also wanted to catch up with his contact on StringCan. He'd got used to Amy's routine. She wasn't allowed to have a phone at home, so she tended to send messages either late at night, when presumably her parents weren't around to watch her, or sometimes while walking to school. She had said that her father was a teacher at her school, so it was hard for her to message while there, but she occasionally messaged during break time.

When Rob's phone beeped with a StringCan notification, he instinctively checked the time to see why Amy was able to message him. Then he realised it was pointless, because even when his daughters were in secondary school, he had no idea what their school day looked like. Obviously he knew that they left after breakfast and came back between three thirty and four, but aside from that he had no idea when the break times were. He shook his head at his foolishness and unlocked the phone. Of necessity their conversation was slow and stilted, but Rob was slowly getting used to it.

Do you think I should go on anti-depressants?

Rob stared at his phone. It must be a short break time by the way she dived straight into the subject. But this was such a loaded question to come from someone he was just getting to know. He guessed, as he had no real way to evaluate her mental state, that what she really wanted was a general opinion on them. But he was also aware that he could be treading on thin ice if he interfered in BaggyAmy's family dynamics or offered up medical advice.

I think they can help in some cases. What do your parents think?

My dad says only weak people who can't cope with life take them. Same with shrinks. Doesn't think you need anyone poking around in your head.

If I'm honest, I used to think the same way. But I changed my mind.

Rob wondered how far he'd go, what he'd say to her about his past.

What changed?

I had a head injury a while back. Had to deal with all sorts of shrinks and head doctors. Actually found it did me some good. What does your mum think?

She has no opinion unless dad says it first.

Are you thinking about it?

The doctor said that it might help. I feel anxious and have trouble sleeping. She's also worried that I'm losing weight.

And what do you think?

I think no one has a clue. I'm glad I'm losing weight and everyone I know is anxious. It's impossible being a teenage girl and being happy today.

Rob pursed his lips as he looked back over the conversation. While this hadn't crossed over his red lines, he did feel that he was straying into dangerous territory. Although, why was he in this conversation, unless it was to help her through difficult times? In the end he decided to reply.

If the doctor thinks it's a good idea, maybe you should consider it?

Maybe. She's one of those busybodies who wants to fix everyone. But now she's ghosting me. Probably moved onto the next project.

Rob looked at that and couldn't think of an answer. It felt like a test. A point in their relationship where they would either fall out or move closer. In the end, Rob decided that she'd come to him because of who he was. So if he stopped being himself now, then there was no point.

But you do have problems. Otherwise why have

you contacted a stranger off the internet? That's not something happy, well adjusted people do.

LOL. Your right I guess.

So, you could find a new doctor and discuss this with them?

Might do. Gotta go, break time over.

Rob looked at his phone as if expecting something more, but he knew that it was futile. Once she said that it was time up, then she wouldn't reply. It could be hours or even days before he would hear back. He wandered over to the window and looked out. The weather was still grey and miserable, and the garden was still immaculately groomed and soulless. Rob gave himself a shake and sat down tidy up his files.

CHAPTER TWENTY-ONE

'I TAKE it that you've heard about the second killing?' Emma asked Rob as she reached for another slice of pizza. She was round at Rob's house and as Jem was out, he'd gone for the quick and easy option of ordering takeaway.

'The doctor? I might have heard a few things here and there.'

Emma chuckled. 'I didn't think it'd get past you. What do you think? Because, to be honest, we have absolutely no idea now how the two victims are linked.'

Rob frowned. 'And you're absolutely certain that they are linked?'

'Yeah, no doubt about it. What we've got is a genuine signature killer. We just have no idea what he's doing or why he's doing it.' Again, she mentally reviewed what she knew and whether there was any value in telling Rob about the coins left in the bodies. And, once again, she decided there was nothing but downsides in telling him that one detail.

'So,' Rob said, 'don't focus on what you don't know, but look at what you do know.'

'Well, both victims lived in Bradwick.'

'OK, but in what sense?' Emma looked confused, so Rob continued. 'I mean, did they just move here or were they part of the town? Had they been here for ever? Were their parents from around here?'

Emma nodded. 'I see what you mean. Well, Hawsley, our first victim, was in Bradwick High for what time he did spend in school. And he died just after his twentieth birthday so we know he spent at least the last ten years here. We can always go back and check his records, and try to build up a fuller picture.' Rob waved a hand to indicate she should move on. 'Our GP, Dr Donnelly, has worked at the surgery for over ten years. I think, without checking the file, that she was a GP in the area before that.'

Rob pursed his lips. 'So, both Bradwick locals. Another few years and they might not be considered incomers. I wonder if that means anything?'

Emma frowned and let the silence stretch out. 'You know, I think it does help. All this time we've been focused on the fact that we have two very different victims. We couldn't see how or why our killer was choosing them.'

'But now that we've established that they're both local, then maybe our killer is too?'

Emma nodded. 'That make sense. And it does narrow it down to a few tens of thousands of people who live in and around Bradwick.' She held up two fingers. 'We've got some kid who's just out of school and a GP. It might be that one of those two is where our killer crossed paths with them.'

'It might be, but I'm not sure how it helps,' Rob said. 'I mean, it doesn't narrow down the field of people. If you're already looking at people in Bradwick then most of them would have gone through Bradwick High. Or they'd be friends with people from there. It's where friend groups usually form, especially among twenty-year-olds. And likewise, everyone needs a GP.'

Emma sighed. 'So, it doesn't really help. I don't know how many GPs there are in Bradwick but we'll have a devil of a job getting the data out of a practice. I mean, it's medical privacy. They're not going to hand over the details of all the patients on a list just on the off chance one of them could be a killer.'

Rob shook his head. 'That'd definitely be a fishing expedition. And, we'd have to go deep into the records and find a list of all her appointments. There's no way they'd allow that.'

There was a pause, longer and more awkward than usual between them. Finally, Emma said, 'What's up with you?'

'What do you mean?' Rob looked evasive.

'Come on, we've been friends for a while now. And I know when something's bothering you. You've seemed a bit distracted since I got here. Like you want to say something but don't know if you should. And before you speak, you're going over everything and checking whether you should say something or not, all while trying to hold a conversation with me.'

'Damn! You always were a good judge of character.' The silence stretched out again. Finally, he asked, 'Have you heard of an app called StringCan?'

'Yeah, wasn't there some big fuss about a year ago? People using it for either grooming or bullying? I haven't heard anything else about it since then though. I mean, there's all of these apps popping up and going out of fashion. But the big ones like Snapchat, WhatsApp and the others remain.' She paused and looked at Rob. 'Why, what have you done?'

He paused again, but then said, 'I've been contacted by someone over StringCan. Someone who needs help.'

'Why am I guessing that it's not some middle-aged businessman who needs a private investigator to either vet his employees or follow his wife, and is willing to pay handsomely?'

'Hey! Don't judge me! It was you who said I should do things that are good for my soul. No, it's a troubled teenager who needs a mentor.'

'Oh my God, why would you do that?' Emma put down her slice of pizza and put a hand over her eyes. 'Even if you're completely above board, all it would take is for them to make one false accusation and everything would come crashing down. It doesn't even have to be true. You've put your life, well, your social standing, your marriage, your business, well, pretty much everything, in her hands.'

There was a strained silence between them. Finally Rob said quietly, 'Remember when you first joined the police? Those first few years in uniform?'

'Of course I do.'

'Do you remember arresting the same teenagers over and over for shoplifting and anti-social behaviour? And how completely hopeless it felt, knowing that they'd started on a path the meant they'd carry on being arrested for the rest of their lives? You know you'll be scooping them up at kicking out time until you end up arresting their kids. The whole family will probably end up going in and out of prison.'

'Well, not all of them. Plenty of people go a bit wild in their teenage years, then calm down as they get older.'

Rob gave her a sideways look, wondering what she was hinting at. 'Yeah, but some of them don't calm down. Anyway, haven't you ever thought that they were just one good influence away from being saved? One positive role model in their lives might just turn them around?'

'And that's what you're doing? That's who you are? A positive role model?'

Rob nodded slowly. 'Don't look so surprised. I know I've

made some bad decisions in my life. Maybe this is time to, you know, start to make amends.'

'Do you even know if this teenager is in trouble? Likely to go off the rails?'

'No, but you never do, do you? I mean, if you could tell, it'd all be a bit Minority Report. All you can do is do what you can.'

'Well, it's very noble, but I can still see so many ways that could go wrong.'

'Yeah. I've got a friend who worked in child protection, she's agreed to help me have a look over things. Kind of acting as a second pair of eyes, and a check.'

'Well, that's something at least.'

There was a break in the conversation, so each of them grabbed another slice of pizza. After a couple of mouthfuls, Emma picked up the thread again. 'So, how's it going? Are you returning this troubled teen back to the straight and narrow?'

Rob took his time answering. 'I don't know. I've been looking back at my own daughters with rose-tinted glasses. I mean, Amy, that's her name, can be really annoying. She's very young and immature at times. But at others... ' He paused. 'I don't know. I think there's more ways you can have a messed-up childhood than the obvious.'

'Like what?'

'Well, she's fifteen but she has no independence. Like, she's not even meant to have a phone or access the internet. She has this old phone that a friend gave her and she has to keep hidden. It's weird, we have these odd, disjointed conversations because she has to keep switching it off and hiding it. Also, she seems to think that her father is very controlling. He's a teacher in her school, so he's around all the time.'

'And how much of that is real, and how much is just teenage girl complaining?'

'I don't know. Do you have any idea how many teenagers have smartphones?'

'Pretty much all of them,' Emma said. 'But I think it's a bit of a reach from there to full on child abuse.'

'Yeah, I'll hang in there and see how it shakes out.'

Emma glanced at the clock. 'I'd better be off. You know how these kinds of cases go.'

'Yeah, go home, get sleep while you can.'

CHAPTER TWENTY-TWO

Rob felt strangely nervous as he approached the chain coffee shop. He'd arranged to meet his friend Liz Baker there. She was the local expert in all things child protection. She had retired from the police but become a freelancer who advised, wrote reports and delivered training in the rapidly changing field. Rob had worked with her years ago and counted her as one of his closer acquaintances, if not an actual friend.

Soon he was sitting down with a black coffee that was too big and too hot for him. He'd decided not to have a muffin or any of the other tempting cakes.

He was still navigating the world of being unable to recognise faces following a brain injury. He hadn't seen Liz for a couple of years so he didn't trust himself to recognise her. Instead, he arrived early and deliberately sat where he'd be clearly seen if Liz walked in and went straight to the counter.

He had three or four worrying minutes to wait. What if she had already arrived and was right now sitting at the back waiting for him? There was nothing he could do though, except to wait and check every person who entered, looking for a thin woman of about his age.

But, before his coffee had cooled down enough to drink, his friend had arrived, waved to him and went to buy a coffee. Soon she was setting down her coffee and putting her coat and handbag on the back of her chair.

'So, Rob Haines has come to me for help? It must be serious.' Liz sounded harsh but was teasing her old friend.

'Not so much serious as outside my experience. I must be getting older, because I'm finding it easier to ask for help. Either that or it's easier now that I've left the force.'

She laughed. She was about the same age as Rob, and had the same disregard for fashion as him. Her grey hair was cropped short and managed not to look elfin while her clothes were also no nonsense. 'So, what it is you want to know?'

'Well, I've been contacted by someone over StringCan and I wanted you to review the conversation. Maybe give me some pointers?'

'It's on StringCan and you've come to me? Are you doing some off the books work? Have you come across a cat-fishing vigilante who's trying to drag paedophiles out into the light? That can be fraught with danger.'

'No, nothing like that. I've been contacted by someone who's got the underage marker on her account. I've been careful and set the app to keep logs of everything.' He opened the app and slid his phone across the table.

Liz pursed her lips and blew out as she picked up the phone. She frowned and started scrolling through the messages. 'It's a ballsy move. Middle-aged man chatting to a young girl. Even if you're bright enough to avoid any traps, you know people will jump to conclusions if they find out. Let's have a look at the evidence, shall we?' There was a tense silence as she swiped through the messages on his phone. She nodded occasionally and at other times pursed her lips.

Finally she put the phone down and stared out of the window for a moment.

Rob had felt like a schoolboy presenting his work to a teacher and he wasn't in the mood for playing waiting games. 'Well? Have I completely screwed it up? Am I finished?'

'No,' she said, drawing the word out as she thought. 'No. I mean, there's no law yet that says that two people can't have a conversation, even if one of them is a middle-aged man and the other a teenage girl.' She did frown though. 'Unfortunately, in this day and age, it could be considered at the very least unwise. The world is full of talk of grooming and gaslighting. Even something that appears innocent now can be made incriminating if it was viewed as the beginning of a grooming experience. If this was ever taken out of context and read out in evidence it could be sticky.'

'Evidence? Court? I hardly think it'll go that far. She's just an unhappy teenage girl. She hates her dad and wants to talk to someone as a father figure. No more or less than that, that I can see.'

'You be very careful then. Make sure you stay in that role and nothing else.'

'I do have two happy grown-up daughters, you know. I do know what to do.' He paused, then said, sounding weak, 'I just thought I could help a bit. What do you think is going on with Amy?'

'Based on this?' She tapped the phone. 'There's not a whole lot to go on. Have you ever heard of coercive control?'

'It was being talked about before I left work. I think I was meant to go on a training course, months down the line.' He looked wistful. 'Never going to happen now.'

'Well, it's far too big a subject for me to explain while we're sitting in a coffee shop. It's basically where an abuser, usually a man, carries out a series of incredibly small actions that, taken individually, are not illegal. Some may actually be beneficial, like love-bombing, to keep the victim off balance. But when looked at as a whole, you realise the victim has no control over their life. Everything has been surrendered to the abuser. Look for things like women who don't have keys to their house, who have to check in with husband every five minutes, who can't access their own bank accounts.'

'Oh, I have heard of stuff like that.' Rob clicked his fingers. 'What was the name of that woman who bashed her husband's head in with a hammer? She admitted she did it, went to prison and then was released on appeal.'

'Yes, Sally Challen. It was a landmark case in how the courts view mental health.'

'I still don't get it,' Rob said. 'I mean, she killed her husband, she admitted to it, the evidence backed it up. She should be in prison.'

Liz patted his arm. 'Oh, Rob. Perhaps it's a good job that you did retire. If someone is pushed into a place where they have no alternative, then is it fair that the system should punish them? Besides the fact that usually it's the other way around. When the woman tries to leave, then more often than not, the man kills her.' There was a short pause, but Rob couldn't see any value in continuing the argument. 'Anyway, I'm sure you didn't get me out here to discuss the ins and outs of historic cases and the future of the criminal justice system.' Liz picked up his phone again and scrolled lazily up and down, not really reading the words. 'I mean, hopefully, this won't go so far. But, she is a child, even if she's a teenager. But there are certain features here that could lead to concern.' She held up a hand. 'Sorry, badly phrased. I don't mean I'm concerned by your behaviour, but that of her father.'

'Her father?' Rob considered the question. He wanted to say that not having access to the internet couldn't be child abuse, but he'd already been stung by the earlier conversation. He felt like a dinosaur and didn't want another challenge on his world view.

'Yes. From what she's said, he does sound very controlling. Like I was talking about earlier.'

'The fact that she doesn't have a phone? I thought that was just a teenage girl complaining?'

'It is a warning sign, a red flag.' There was a pause as she considered her next words. 'Rob, when you were at school, how did you go home? And what did you do on weekends and holidays?'

Rob frowned, but answered the question anyway. 'Well, by secondary school I was walking to and fro with a group of mates. And at weekends and holidays, we went into town, or just hung around the waste ground.' He shrugged. 'Looking back, we didn't do much really.'

'Knowing you, you were probably looking for someone who'd sell you cigarettes and trading pages out of porn mags.'

'It's like you were there.' Rob smiled. 'Where are you going with this?'

'Well, it's part of growing up. You need somewhere to go where the adults aren't observing you. It's where things come up, from Beatlemania through to Tik Toks and Fortnite dances.'

'And that's a good thing?'

'Very. There's a lot of psychology that I won't bore you with, but basically it's part of leaving the nest, of forming your own identity.'

Rob nodded, relived as he started to pick up where the conversation was heading. 'And you think this Amy hasn't got that safe space? That her father's always there?'

'In a nutshell, yes. It's particularly concerning that he's

also a teacher at her school. And here she says that he watches her at break time.'

'But surely he's being a good father in keeping her away from the internet? I mean, we started out this conversation talking about grooming. You're not suggesting that he expose her to all of that?'

Liz held her hand out flat and waved it up and down. 'I'm afraid it's not as simple as that. Obviously a parent has a responsibility to keep their children safe. But simply cutting them off from their friends, from everything that can be gained from the internet? That can't be good. A responsible parent should have an arms-length approach. Make sure that they're being safe online but also that they have their own space to develop.'

'So, you're saying that Fortnite and Tik Tok are essential in child development?'

Liz laughed. 'No, not exactly. But kind of.' She picked up the phone that had now locked itself. 'This Amy girl, she has no space to grow. She's watched at home, watched at school, doesn't seem to go out anywhere. It is certainly a concern.'

'So, broadly speaking, I'm on the right track? She does need help.'

'I still think you're a bloody fool. But an idealistic one who wants to do the right thing. And you're not hide bound by all the regulations like you would be if you were still on the job, so that's easier.' She paused, sizing Rob up. 'Would you be open to meeting me once a week? Show me the latest messages. Just to make sure you stay on the right track.'

'I think that'd be a good idea.'

'And there is a concern. If a woman tries to leave a controlling man, then that's most often when murders happen.'

'You can't think he'd kill his own daughter?' Even as Rob said it, he realised that he'd seen enough of it in his career.

'Again, there's not enough evidence here. If he discovers that she's broken the rules and got a phone, then who knows what might happen. We have to bear in mind that in our respective careers, we see the very extreme, the worst that could happen. It might be that he grounds her for a week, or doesn't allow her any chocolate or even just locks her in her room. We mustn't leap to conclusions.'

Rob nodded.

'I do think you have a vital role here. But be careful to act like a sounding board. She'll be very impressionable, try not to tell her what to think, just give her a safe space.'

'I think I can do that.'

'And obviously, avoid anything that could be seen as even remotely dodgy.' She held up a hand. 'I shouldn't need to say that, but it'd be wrong if I didn't mention it.'

'Well, I'm trying to stay firmly in the role of father figure, so I should be okay.'

'Unless she's been sexually abused and sees her only value as a sexual being,' Liz said darkly. 'But there's no evidence for that, so you should be okay.'

The two looked at each other. 'Thank you for your time, Liz. I think you've put my mind at rest.'

'Well, I think you're on the right track. But do keep in touch. I'm quite concerned about Amy. I'd like to know that she's all right.'

'Same time, same place, next week?'

'Definitely.'

Rob hoped that it wouldn't have all gone wrong by then.

CHAPTER TWENTY-THREE

THE MEETING with Liz had taken longer than Rob had expected, and he only just made it back to the office before a scheduled meeting with Mr Church. As expected, his client was perfectly punctual.

'Ah, Mr Church, thank you for coming in.' Mr Church just nodded and took a seat. 'Or shall I call you Sean?'

'Mr Church is fine,' he said, completely deadpan. 'What have you found?'

Rob slid an envelope across the desk. He had set up secure servers with access for each client so he could download the photos and reports at their leisure. He would follow up the meeting with an email that gave his client the links. But he still preferred the old-school approach of having real, glossy photos. It was more theatrical, and it was easier to point out details to someone with a bit of paper on the desk.

'Hmmph,' Mr Church said. He flicked through the photos. 'Are these available online as well?'

'Of course, I'll send the email at the end of this meeting.'

The other man nodded and waved the photos at Rob. He

frowned. 'I'm not seeing anything incriminating here. No smoking gun.'

'We did what you said. We staked out her work and followed her to the viewings. As per your instructions we focused especially if she met any men on her own.'

'But you didn't bring me proof of her affair or the identity of the man she's cheating with!'

The two men stared at each other for a moment. 'We haven't left anything out,' Rob said. 'How certain are you? It might be that there's nothing there to find.'

'I'm not wrong,' Mr Church said. 'I know something's wrong. You're just not looking hard enough.' He lowered his head and leafed through the photographs again. He stopped, pulled one out and slid it over the desk. 'Him. What's his story? Who is he?'

Rob looked down at the photo. It showed a man in his thirties, wearing a dark suit, red tie, striding away from his car towards a house on a new build estate. 'A customer. He was shown round the house. Obviously, as per your instructions, we took an interest in him. We looked through windows and my colleague even rang the doorbell with a made-up excuse. As far as we could tell, there was nothing going on apart from someone viewing a house.'

Mr Church nodded to himself slowly. 'So, they were maybe casing the place out? Seeing if it's OK to come back to it later?' He tapped the photo. 'Can we find out who this man is?'

Rob sucked air over his teeth. 'I suppose it could be done if we got lucky. But all we've got is this one photo. I mean, we know he had an appointment with an agent, but it'd be tricky to get into their systems and find out who he is.'

'But you've got a clear shot of his number plate right here,' Mr Church said, tapping the photo again. 'You used to be in the police, surely you can make one phone call and see who owns the car? That'd be a good place to start.' He paused. 'Obviously, I'd pay extra.'

Rob shook his head. 'That's just not possible. Maybe when I started in the police, you might have got away with it, but I doubt it. Now, they've got everything tied up and secured, data protection and all that. And you have no idea what computers are like. Every single search on the DVLA database is logged with a user and a date and a time. If that can't be allocated across to an active case file, then you'll be in trouble. Even if you hide it inside a case file and it gets audited, well more trouble. I can't think of anyone I'd trust to do it for me.' He paused a moment. 'Or anyone who I'd want to get in that much trouble.'

Once again an awkward silence fell across the pair. 'What I'm hearing is that you don't want to do it. Let me make my own enquiries, we need to know who he is and what he's doing with my wife.'

'Obviously that's your prerogative, if you want to carry out your own enquiries. Do you want us to carry out any further work?' For reasons he couldn't put into words, Rob found himself hoping that this matter was closed. He was about to be disappointed.

'Yes, keep on with what you were doing. Maybe keep an eye on her when she goes out shopping. I can text you if she leaves the house and tell you where she claims to be going.' He picked up the photo again. 'And find out everything you can about him. Obviously, everything legal, I wouldn't want you to get into trouble.' His words were clearly sarcastic.

Rob was tempted to tell him that it was his business and he wouldn't have it shut down just to satisfy this person's whim. Instead he said, 'We can do that. You do realise, of course, that there'll be further charges, especially if you want on call availability and some out of hours work?'

Mr Church waved his hand. 'Yes, yes, whatever. I've already paid your last invoice by direct bank payment. Do you need anything up front, or can we continue on that basis?'

'No, no, that'll be fine,' Rob said. He felt that it would be anything but fine.

CHAPTER TWENTY-FOUR

'Right so, where are we now?' Michelle Jones asked. 'Emma, did you get anywhere with the surgery? Was it a minefield of rights and permissions?'

'Yeah, I got on all right,' Emma said. She proceeded to recap what she'd learnt, which wasn't a huge amount of anything.

'And no links between the two victims?'

'Not that we can see. I mean, she could've been Hawsley's GP, but you know, data protection and all that.'

John Fletcher spoke up. 'You can get the area served by the surgery off the website and cross reference that with Hawsley's address. Might give us something.'

Michelle nodded. 'Okay, you do that. Let me know what you find.'

The meeting was called to a close but before Emma could look at her list of actions, her personal mobile rang. She saw Lukas' name and went out to the corridor as she hit the button.

'Lukas, what's up?' She was instantly concerned. Lukas was far more likely to text or message rather than make a call.

'Err, well, I'm kinda at your work. Downstairs.'

'Downstairs? You mean you've been arrested? What for?'

'Well, I was hanging around with Violet when a couple of her friends called by in their flash new car.'

Emma had a sinking feeling. 'Let me guess, you went for a ride. And also, let me guess, they didn't exactly own the car?'

'I can see why they made you a detective, Angel. Can you do anything?'

Emma took a deep breath. 'I'm not sure. I mean, it doesn't sound like you've been actively involved in the theft, but it wouldn't be much of a stretch to charge you as accessory to the crime.'

'And what about the drugs?'

'Drugs?'

'Just like personal use, a few bags of gear, nothing heavy.'

Nothing heavy, Emma thought. But cannabis had been reclassified to class B and more than one bag could be stretched to possession with intent to supply. Lukas could be charged as a dealer.

'But, it was all on the floor of the car, so we're not connected to it at all. It won't come back to me.'

'OK, Lukas, give me a minute.' She tugged on her earlobe and ran a finger over her knuckles. 'First off, co-operate. Play nicely. The uniformed officers are holding all the cards. They have a range of options all the way from charging you for theft and dealing, right up to turfing you out of the door. But you've got to give them a reason to let them go.'

Now it was Lukas' turn to be quiet. 'Violet might not go for that. She's very up on her rights. I don't think she's even given them her full name.'

'Then, you've got to change her mind. This is me you're talking to, so I totally get fighting the system. But right now, she's got a choice between three to five years inside or being free. She can do a lot more good if she's not behind bars.'

'Yeah, I know that. She's got a thing about being a grass though.'

'She doesn't have to give them all the details. Just play it dumb, couple of friends called round, didn't think it through, don't know anything about the drugs. That kind of thing.'

'I guess. I'd feel better if you could help, you know, have a word or something?'

'Oh, Lukas, you know I can't do that.' She didn't elaborate that it'd cause irreparable damage to her career and that uniform wouldn't appreciate CID elbowing in to one of their cases without being asked.

'Yeah, I know.' He sounded downcast.

'Listen, stick to the story, sound a bit stupid, don't embellish and you'll be out in no time.'

'Yeah, yeah, I know what to do.'

Emma disconnected the call and turned the phone over in her hands. She knew she was in a precarious position as Lukas' best friend if she ran up against the new girlfriend. But that didn't alter the fact that she had a bad feeling about Violet. She knew the kind of person she was, the type that always attracted trouble. And if she had a chip on her shoulder about the police, then she'd either have to change her ideas or get used to a lifetime of being arrested. The trouble was that she didn't seem to be the sort of person who'd change her mind.

THE REST of the day was frustrating. More physical evidence was trickling through, from the crime scene techs and CCTV. And the research on both victims was continuing. But there was a fundamental problem. No matter how much work they did, the same conclusion was reached. The two victims were definitely killed by the same person, but there was no tangible link between their lives. A twenty-year-old drug dealer and a thirty-seven-year-old GP just didn't intersect.

By the end of the day, she was tired and frustrated. As she started driving home, she saw the familiar lanky form of Lukas slouching away from the station. He'd obviously been released, and Emma was pleased to see that he was alone. She could do with a word without Violet around.

'Hey, Lukas, want a lift home?'

'Angel, how you doing? Yeah, that'd be great. I've been stuck in there too long.'

'Where's Violet?' Emma asked. 'Does she need a lift too?'

'No.' Lukas shook his head. 'Looks like they're taking a bit longer to process her. She was arrested just before lunch so she might be in till tomorrow morning. I'll go home now and get the place all set and ready for her.'

Emma knew what was going on. It was likely that Violet had been aggressive and hard to deal with. She had no idea if her advice had been taken or not, but she was sure that Violet would have started out on the attack. And she knew that the attitude of the police was to leave her to calm down.

'So, how are things between you and Violet?'

'Fine. I actually think that this is my chance to settle down. She feels like the one.'

For the first time in ages there was a long, awkward pause.

'So, you know, what was the deal with that meal that we had,' Emma asked.

'Oh, you mean the way she behaved?. I know she can be a bit much, but she was completely overwhelmed, you know what with meeting you and your parents and Pete and everything. Quite a big deal. And she gets a bit loud if she's put on the spot.'

Emma thought fast. It really wouldn't do any good to point out that Violet hadn't been invited to the meal at all. Maybe that was why she felt overwhelmed and under pressure. But Emma had a strong suspicion that Violet was one of those people who breezed through life assuming that she was welcome anywhere she chose to be and not understanding the conflict she caused.

'Listen, Angel, babe. Can you give her a chance? You can be quite intimidating, what with your job and everything. You're kind of like the one who was like us, but got out. There are so many people in our world who just party and do drugs and, well, they just live like they're never going to get old.' He paused for a moment, looking thoughtful. 'I don't know. Maybe you were right. I mean you've got a life. You actually do something worthwhile with your life.' He paused again, for longer this time.

'Well, you're doing the same thing as well,' said Emma eventually. 'You've got the caravan park, your work with a charity that helps people. And that's important, because, you know, you're like the people you're helping. You are a living example that it's possible to break out of that pattern. You don't have to live the party lifestyle all the time. You can still to do some good.'

Lukas nodded, absorbing this. 'I guess you're right.'

'So, you think the fact that we're making something of our lives means that Violet feels insecure and that's why she's acting up?'

'And you've known me forever, so you know it might seem that we're shutting her out. That we have our own history, one that she isn't part of.' He paused, scraping the hair out of his face. 'Violet's important to me. I can't always be just mooching around, parties, drinking, all that. I got to settle down at some point. And having a decent relationship is part of that.'

'And you think that Violet is the sort of person that will change with you? Are you sure she won't just tempt you back into the same old ways?'

'No,' Lukas said thoughtfully. 'I think that it'll settle out to something a bit better than today.'

But why with that woman? Emma thought. 'Yeah, I know. I'm not going to be checking up on you and your relationships.'

The silence stretched out and Emma concentrated on driving for a moment. She turned left at a T junction and started driving along the sea road. It was dark, but she could still sense the sea off to the right.

'Angel, could you pull in at this petrol station?'

She indicated and looked across at Lukas. 'Are you sure? It's still half a mile to caravan park.'

'Yes, I've got nothing in at the moment. I usually walk down here to get some shopping and you've just saved me walking both ways.'

She pulled into the parking spaces and the harsh fluorescent lights illuminated the inside of the car. Lukas suddenly seemed older, the light picking out the flaws in his face, making him seem thinner than usual.

'Why don't we get together one evening this week? A double date, just you and Pete, me and Violet.'

'Yeah, we could do,' Emma said without much enthusiasm. 'But you've got to tell her to wind her neck in.' Lukas looked sheepish. 'I mean it. In my job, I can't have people taking the piss. If she gets some illegal drugs out in my presence, I can't afford to look the other way. All it'd take is for another off-duty officer to be in the place and notice and I'd be toast. I've had enough run ins with Professional Standards to last my whole career.'

'Yeah, I'll have a word with her.' He opened the door and let a blast of wintry sea air in. It gusted and rustled the packets in the footwell. Lukas got out, then leaned back in and gave Emma his best smile. 'Trust me. It'll be brilliant.'

CHAPTER TWENTY-FIVE

Rob was trying to prepare for a client meeting when the StringCan message pinged onto his phone. He could see that it needed a quick response so he put his folder to one side and concentrated on his phone.

What's up?

Have you seen that doctor on the news last night? The one who was murdered?

He'd seen the news reports when he woke up, but they held a lot less detail than Emma had given him. A local GP had been found dead, foul play suspected but no more details at this stage. His instincts, honed over years in the police were tingling. How was Amelia connected to the murder of the GP? He couldn't see it at the moment. But one thing was certain – now she had his full attention.

What about her?

I knew her. She was like the only person who understood me. And now she's gone.

I'm so sorry. I don't know what to say.

I've got to get up now. Can I voice call you on my way to school?

Rob breathed a sigh of relief. This was a tricky situation and he found it so difficult to carry on a conversation over text. Nothing made him feel his age more than squinting at a tiny screen and trying to hit the right buttons with his thumbs. He nodded at the phone and then realised he had to reply.

OK.

Rob tried to compartmentalise. Somewhere in Bradwick, a teenage girl was getting up and going through her morning routine. He glanced at the clock, glad now that he'd come in early to prepare for the meeting. The meeting was a weekly catch-up with Ed to review all the active cases. He'd already texted Ed and moved the meeting to half-nine. Now he had enough time to prepare for the meeting and talk to Amelia.

His phoned buzzed on his desk, breaking him out of his reverie. He looked at his phone, aware that he was about to cross a line in his relationship with Amelia. His phone looked odd, the graphic for an incoming call from StringCan looked different from the usual phone call, although it still had familiar green and red buttons. He pressed the button and raised the phone to his ear.

'Hi, this is Rob Haines.'

'Hi.'

There was a silence on the line as both parties tried to feel their way through.

Rob decided to break the deadlock. 'So, tell me about this doctor.'

'She was really nice to me. I felt like someone understood how I felt, you know? How trapped I was living at home. And now she's gone and I'm alone. It's like I had a route out, a way to escape.'

'I'm here, I can listen.'

'Oh, I know that. But she was different. She was a GP and she made me feel like I wasn't mad or making it all up.'

'I don't think you're making it up either.' He paused. 'How is your father today?'

'Oh, he was awful this morning. Last couple of days, he's been all chipper and happy, whistling under his breath.' She paused. 'I mean, it's kind of better than him being the bastard he usually is. But then you're just waiting for the next storm to come so you can't really enjoy it. And it's worse today when I feel like my life is over and I've just lost my escape route. And he's all like "cheer up, smile!" when I just want to crawl under the duvet and not come out again.'

Some connections were being made in Rob's head, but he needed confirmation. He knew he'd have to tread carefully. 'Amelia, do you feel safe at home?'

'Safe?' She rolled the word around her mouth, getting the feeling of it. 'Safe? You know, I think I do. But I think that's actually the problem. I'm so safe that I can't breathe. I mean, I can't go out with my friends, can't do anything other than go to and from school and go places with my parents. How can anything happen to me if I'm not out anywhere on my own? I actually think I'm too safe.'

'Hmmm. So you're not afraid of your father? Of what he might do?' Rob couldn't help thinking about his meeting with

Liz, what she said about children needing a private space to grow up.

'I dunno. He can be a moody bastard. I never really know what he's going to do next. But he's not abusive. He's never hit me or my mum. He says he does what he does for the family, to protect us from the world. And he's got a good job. Mum doesn't work so he provides everything for us.' Her voice dropped a bit quieter. 'But, behind that, I actually think he's just a bastard. He likes making our lives a misery and all that crap about protecting the family, that's just his justification. He just wants to be in control over us.'

'That's a bit harsh,' Rob said automatically.

'Meh. You don't live my life. Listen, I've got to go. Nearly at school, don't want the bastard seeing me. Later!'

'Bye, Amelia.'

And the connection dropped, leaving Rob holding his phone and wondering what the conversation meant. He wasn't quite sure what his intuition was telling him, but something was definitely up. He shoved it to the back of his mind and left it in the background while he prepared for his meeting.

'WHAT'S UP ED?' Rob asked as his former colleague came in and settled in the chair with a hangdog expression. In many ways it took him straight back to when he was a detective chief inspector and Ed worked for him.

'I'll have to come off the Mrs Church case. I've been spotted. Bound to happen sooner or later with only one of me. I stayed on it longer than I should have.'

'And that was my fault. I didn't want to farm it out or bring someone else in from outside. We've already done the groundwork so it made sense to carry on. To be honest, I should've knocked it on the head ages ago.'

'Why didn't you?' Ed asked.

'Because it pays the bills. And you haven't met the lovely Mr Sean Church. He won't take no for an answer. He's a bit volatile. That's another reason I wish I'd never taken this case. What do you make of his wife? You've been following her for a while now.'

'Honestly? I think she looks broken down. You know, you look at some people when you do this job and you can tell they're having an affair. They have a bit of a spring in their step or a sparkle in their eye. Especially when they're heading off for a rendezvous. But Nancy Church? She's kind of going through the motions of life. She goes to work, comes home, goes out shopping. Gets herself a low-calorie lunch from Boots three doors down from the office. Always head down, always looking drab. It's a bit sad really.'

'Yeah, you see, that's what I'm worried about. Sean Church has a short temper, especially when dealing with me. One minute he's fine, then he blows up, then it's all over. But he won't let this go. I can't shake the feeling that we're on the wrong side of this one.'

'That makes sense of what happened this morning. I was sat there in the coffee shop, newspaper out and just keeping an eye on the estate agents. Anyway, she comes out the front door, so I get up and get ready to leave. Usually she goes to the car park round the back and I can get there thirty seconds behind her. But this time, she changes her mind in the car park and turns round. I was caught out and she damn near walked into me. And when she saw me, she looked straight at me and said "You can tell that no good husband of mine that I won't be intimidated. You can follow me around all you want but it won't work. Tell him from me that I've had enough of his mind games and bullshit. I'm leaving!".

'What did you say?'

'What could I say? I blustered a bit, told her she had the wrong person, that I had no idea at all who she was. But she just looked at me, kind of pitying me almost. I could see it in her eyes. I'm certain that she knows. Then she nodded as if it proved she was right, and said "When you've finished, crawl back to Sean and give him my message". There didn't seem to be any point in carrying on from there really. I mean, she knows who I am and who sent me. She's not going to do anything if I'm following her.' He stopped and sighed loudly, blowing his cheeks out. 'Anyway, she's not playing away. I'm certain of that. I don't know what's going on, but I'm sorry boss, you're going to have to put someone else on it.'

'Yeah, no. You did the right thing coming straight back here. This is a bloody farce and it's gone on far too long. I'm not going to put anyone else onto it. I should've pulled the job weeks ago. I'll give him a ring now and see if he can come back in today. But this time, I won't take any more bullshit from him. This job is over. At this point I don't even care if he pays his final invoice or not. Do you mind staying on for a bit, in case he's got any final questions?'

'Yeah. I'm kind of intrigued now, to be honest. I've met one half of the couple, I'd like to see the other side.'

HALF AN HOUR after a terse phone call, Sean Church came back into Rob Haines' office. Usually at this stage in a case, Rob would be on friendly terms with the client, but somehow Sean managed to bring a stiff formality in with him.

Rob settled in behind his desk, and introduced Ed who was sitting in the corner.

'So. You said on the phone that you had an update for me. I trust that you have some good news.'

'Well, unfortunately, it's bad news. We haven't found anything.'

'What do you mean, you can't find anything!' Sean Church banged Rob's desk with the flat of his hand.

'OK,' Rob said in a dangerously neutral voice. He had been on the training courses and he knew how to de-escalate a situation. He should speak in a calm voice and say nothing to provoke the other party. On the other hand, he wasn't in the police anymore and he wasn't about to let a customer come into his office and try to intimidate him. He shot a quick glance at Ed and saw that he was on the edge of the seat, ready to intervene if needed. 'And please keep your voice down. I'm right here and I can hear you just fine.'

To Rob's surprise, Mr Church collapsed backwards into his chair. 'Sorry.' He waved a hand vaguely. 'It's just that I love Nancy so much. And the sanctity of marriage is important too. You've got to find it. The proof. I know it's true.' He paused, considering how much to reveal. 'You know, I couldn't be seen to be the one cheated on. The cuckold. That would be intolerable. I mean, you're a man, you know what it's like. What people would say, how it would look. Women can't be trusted. She's up to something, I'm sure of it. I won't be made to look the fool.'

Rob sat back in his chair and steepled his fingers. 'I'm not sure that we should continue working together. We've carried out an in-depth investigation into your wife and there seems to be no indication that she's anything other than loyal. I really don't see what else we can do.'

He wanted to keep Ed's news up his sleeve for the

moment. Hopefully he would be able to bring the relationship to an end without revealing it.

'You can keep doing what you've been paid to do. I don't care how long it takes, sooner or later she's going to slip up and when she does, I want you to catch her.'

'If you want my advice, you'll stop now. I honestly don't think there's anything there for us to find.'

'But I'm willing to keep paying and I'm telling you to keep looking.'

Rob shook his head, then admitted. 'The truth is that we stayed on this case too long and your wife, Nancy, became aware that she was being followed. I'm afraid that that's the end of the line.'

'End of the line? What do you mean? I'll pay for more people.'

Rob stayed firm. 'I was already thinking that if we've gone this far then there's nothing to find. This last event just confirms that we've run out of road.'

'But you could have a rotation of people watching her so she doesn't get wise to it.' Rob said nothing and Mr Church changed tack. 'Your man must've been sloppy to get caught, she's a dozy cow. I can't imagine her spotting you. He must've been waiting right outside her office or something.'

Eddie bristled in the corner. 'I can assure you Mr Church, that I was nothing but professional,' he said crisply. 'It used to be my job in the police and I've been on surveillance courses. Ultimately if you have a small team following a single target, it's just a matter of time before your target becomes aware. And in this case, we have run out of time.'

Mr Church pursed his lips and stared out of the window. The silence stretched until it became uncomfortable. Rob was used to using silence to draw confessions out of suspects, but this was different. Sean Church radiated a barely supressed energy. Finally he said in clipped tones, 'You're trying to tell me that you've failed. I keep coming back here, writing ever larger cheques and after all of that you've got absolutely nothing to show for it?' He looked around the office for a target and settled on Ed in the corner. 'You. Were you the primary operative following Nancy?' Ed nodded. 'What makes you think she figured out she was being followed?'

'She turned back and nearly walked into me. It was clearly a deliberate move. She'd figured it out and she wanted to confront me.'

'So, there's no way you could be mistaken?'

'No. She looked me in the eye and said -' Ed stopped, realising he'd gone too far. They'd had no real intention of passing Nancy's message on.

'Said what?' Sean Church pounced. 'Come on. Don't lie to me now.'

Rob caught Ed's eye and nodded imperceptibly. Ed's shoulders slumped. 'She said that she knew you'd sent me. Told me to tell you to stop all the bullshit. That she was leaving.' As soon as he said this final word, the atmosphere became even more hostile.

'Leaving? You've really fucked this up, haven't you? Not only can you find no evidence that she's playing away–'

'I've told you before, Mr Church,' Rob interrupted, 'sometimes we don't find anything because there's nothing to find.' His voice got louder until he was nearly shouting.

'I know what you said! Do you think I'm stupid? That I can't remember your lies and excuses from one day to the next? I know Nancy, and I know what she's like. Or do you think I'm lying about that as well? She'd never leave me. And if she does, then I'll know that it's your fault. Putting stupid ideas in her head.' He saw the looks on Rob and Ed's faces and continued. 'You think I don't know my own fucking wife?'

'You could be mistaken–'

'No! Enough of this fucking charade!' He stood up, his chair skittering and falling behind him. Ed and Rob shifted in their seats, very slightly, ready to spring up if Mr Church got violent. 'I'm done! I'll try to find a competent firm who know what they're doing. You're just a bunch of con artists! You think because you can get a bit of skirt to sit behind a desk and rent a fancy office with carpet on the floor and nice desks that somehow it makes you respectable but it doesn't. You can polish a turd all you like, but it'll still stink of shit!'

Born of years of experience, Rob and Ed stood up and moved cautiously so that they were one either side of the desk. They looked relaxed, shoulders loose and hands open by their sides, but they were ready for any violence that might happen.

'Oh, you don't have to escort me off the premises, I'm done with you.' He turned to leave, but stopped in the doorway. 'You have no fucking idea, do you? Who you're dealing with? I know the mayor, same class as me at school.' He looked smug. 'Yeah! And the Chamber of Commerce. Not so fucking sure now, are you? I'll bury you! You won't be able to rent a table at a fucking Starbucks when I'm through with you!' The door rattled in its frame as he slammed it shut and stormed down the corridor.

Rob caught Ed's eye and they burst out laughing, releasing all the tension that had built up over the meeting.

CHAPTER TWENTY-SIX

DC EMMA ANGEL had a map spread out on her desk and some coloured felt tip pens. DS Suse Berman wandered over. 'What you doing? Some down time to do some colouring?'

'No,' Emma said defensively. 'I'm just working on something. We've got two victims, one fresh out of the high school and the other working as a GP in one of the bigger surgeries in Bradwick.' She paused and then realised that mentioning Rob Haines' name wouldn't win her friends. With some misgivings she continued. 'I realised that both places have catchment areas. So I thought that if I drew them out on the map, I could see if they overlapped. Maybe plot any other points from the case as well.'

'And?' Suse bent over the map and peered at it.

'And it's a bust. Bradwick High is the only secondary for miles, so its catchment area is all of Bradwick and over half the small villages that surround it. And the GP surgery is just over half a mile away from the school. So,' she indicated the map as she spoke, 'the catchment for the surgery fits inside the area for the school.' The map clearly showed how the one was inside the other. 'And here are the two crime scenes, plus the home addresses of the victims.'

'They all fit inside the Bradwick High area,' Suse said thoughtfully. 'And everything is all centred around the northern end of Bradwick.'

'Yes, I was wondering about victimology. We've all been so caught up in how different our two victims are, but I've found a few things that they did have in common. They've both been in Bradwick for over ten years. Hawsley was born here, went to school here, died here.' She sighed and tapped the map. 'This was a long shot, but much easier than my other plan. I thought I might start a family tree of Bill Hawsley. He might well have aunts or uncles who would be closer in age and maybe even social status to the GP. We could see if they intersected somehow.'

Suse nodded. 'Sounds like a good plan. Carry on.'

Emma turned back to her desk although she had a sinking feeling that looking into the Hawsley family would be a futile exercise. Her desk phone rang and she picked it up. 'DC Angel? It's Martin in the custody suite. We've got a prisoner down here. Been arrested on a drug charge. Only now she's asking for you. Said about how you were CID and could help?'

'Fine,' she said. 'Who is it?' She mentally ran through the contacts she'd been trying to cultivate. She couldn't for the moment think of any women who she'd tried to recruit.

'It's some woman called Anna Blackton?'

Emma frowned. She rolled the name around in her mind. It did ring a faint bell. 'Does she have a middle name?' She wasn't sure why she asked, but she trusted her instincts.

'Let me check her form.' There was a pause. 'Anna Violet Blackton. Is she one of yours?'

'Short, long dark hair, heavy built IC1?'

'That's the one.'

'Yeah, I know her as Violet. I wouldn't exactly say one of mine. She's not connected to CID, she's a friend of a friend. Wasn't she picked up yesterday though?'

'Yeah, we're nearly up to our twenty-four hours. We'd normally turf her out and move on but it's taken us this long to get her name out of her. She's been in and out on minor drug and disorder offences for quite a few years. Usually cautioned or just a friendly warning. But she's being defensive and this is a bigger case, stolen car, drugs and weapons found. We were trying to link her to it, but then she dropped your name into the conversation.'

'I'll pop down and have a word.'

SOON, Emma was in the doorway of the cell. It wasn't strictly speaking an interview and she'd be in trouble if she got any information she could act on. Also, she'd be in worse trouble if Lukas found out she'd taken something that Violet had said and used it against her.

Violet was sat on the bunk, slumped against the wall. She had her lower lip stuck out. 'There you are! God, I've been so bored just sat here! I cannot believe that they kept me overnight. When can I go home?'

'It's not quite that easy,' Emma said.

'But you're in the police. That's what you said. Can't you just use your discretion? There must me some loophole or something that only police officers can do.'

Emma sighed. 'This isn't a hospital. You've been arrested. I don't have a lot that I can do because it's not my arrest. I mean, if you were my confidential informant, then maybe I'd have a bit of leeway.'

'Oh God, no! I'm not a snitch. Never have been, never will be.' She shut her mouth and shook her head violently.

The two women looked at each other for a moment, at an impasse.

Finally, Violet thought of a play. 'What about Lukas? I know you don't like me, but if you get me out, then it'll be a favour for him. I can put in a good word for you. If not, well, I'll tell him you've been mean to me.'

Oh my God, Emma thought, it's like being back in the school playground. She took a breath and calmed herself down. 'It's not that simple though. You were found in a stolen car with drugs and weapons. You need to give them a reason not to charge you as being involved. Otherwise you could be facing serious charges.'

Violet's face fell as she started to realise what kind of trouble she was in. Then she regained her usual composure. 'Whatever! Can you help me out, or do I have to tell Lukas that you don't like me? Make him choose?'

Emma took a deep breath. She knew from bitter experience that someone like Violet would never listen to explanations about personal responsibility. So she decided to save her breath. She also knew that the hole was a lot deeper than Violet realised. She had been formally arrested, so there would be a report from the arresting officer, another one from the custody sergeant. There was a mountain of paperwork already generated and more to come. 'I know you don't want to be a snitch. I get that. But you need to talk to the police. This whole clamming up and refusing to even give your name isn't doing you any favours. It just makes them think that you're involved and have something to hide.'

'What would I have to do?' Violet was a sulky child backed into a corner.

Emma lowered her voice slightly. 'Listen, the guy driving and his passenger, is this the first time they've stolen a car?'

Violet laughed. 'What? Paul and his mate Aiden? No, they're always involved in something.'

'Right, so. In that case they're known to the police. The chances are that they know what they're up to. They'll be more than willing to pin this on them and get them locked up for it.' Emma frowned. 'It doesn't really count as snitching if you're just confirming to the police what they already know.' Emma mentally crossed her fingers. She knew that confirmation was really useful to the police, but she was willing to bend the truth.

'So, I can just confirm who they are and what they do?'

'Don't go that far. Play it down. Like you're just know them vaguely, see them around. You had absolutely no idea that the car was stolen and no knowledge at all about what was under the seats.'

'Well, I'd only been in the car like ten minutes when we got pulled.'

'Perfect. That'll do. Keep it simple.'

The was an odd silence as the two women considered each other.

'I've got to go–'

'Thank you–'

They spoke over each other. There was a pause then Violet said, 'Thank you, Emma. I know we don't see eye to eye. But we both know Lukas would want us to get on.'

'Well, yes. Hope it goes well and you're out soon.'

Emma shut the door and went back up to the office. As she climbed the stairs, she considered what she'd said. She wondered if she had done the right thing. She knew Violet was one of those people who attracted trouble. But Emma genuinely believed that in this case Violet was simply in the wrong place at the wrong time. Of course, the way she lived her life meant that she was far more likely to get into these situations than anyone else. She just hoped that her advice was general enough and wouldn't come back to bite her later.

CHAPTER TWENTY-SEVEN

THE TEXT MESSAGE from Rob was, on the surface, completely innocent. "Do you want to pop round for a bite to eat tonight?" And to be fair, Emma loved going round to Rob and Jem's. She knew they were missing their grown-up daughters and the chance to eat at a table in good company was never to be passed up. Without them, she'd survive on ready meals eaten in front of the TV on the sofa. And this deep into a major investigation, she'd be lucky to get that. It was more likely to be takeaway and petrol station sandwiches.

She texted back, but she wasn't fooled. Rob needed something. For the brief time that he'd been her boss, they had had worked well together. She'd provided a good sounding board for him and was able to provide her own ideas, to pull together the threads. She also hoped that he'd be able to help with her current investigation, which was grinding to a halt.

She slogged her way through the rest of the work day, typing up reports and making sure everything was on the computer. Usually at this stage in an investigation they'd be working hard, looking for suspects and throwing theories around. But the truth was that they had no idea. It was still early days, but Emma thought this case might be one that became a cold case. It was the eternal problem that faced the police with a persistent murderer. If they stopped of their own accord, then there would be no fresh evidence and it would get kicked into the long grass, to be reviewed every year. But Emma wasn't able to wish for the other option, that he'd keep killing and generate enough evidence to catch him.

In the end, she rubbed her eyes, switched off her computer and left the office at seven thirty. Suse and Nick were still in, but they were head down at their computers. The whole mood was low, so when she called out good night, she just got a couple of waves in return.

When she got to Rob and Jem's she found out it was Indian takeaway time.

'I got you lamb biryani. Is that OK?'

'Great thanks.' They'd been doing this for a while and Rob knew what to order. Soon they were eating from plates sat around the table. Jem had excused herself to eat in front of the TV, tactfully leaving the pair of them to talk shop.

'I've got this client,' Rob started. Then he held up his hand. 'Of course, it's all confidential.' Emma nodded her agreement. 'Anyway, this client, he's actually an ex-client. We finished the job today and it didn't go well. Not at all, in fact he stormed out of the office shouting threats and slamming doors.'

'That sounds like fun. What was the problem?'

'Well, he wanted us to follow his wife. He thought that she was playing away.'

'So far, so standard,' Emma said.

'Yeah, the problem is that we didn't find anything.'

'What, nothing at all?'

'Not a thing.' Rob paused, then continued. 'Not that she

didn't have any opportunity. She works as an estate agent, so access to the keys for a lot of empty properties.'

Emma nodded. 'Yes, I mean, if you wanted to have an affair, then that's the perfect job for it really. Unless you work in a hotel, that is! But didn't you say that most people who are willing to spend the money on a private investigator already know that something's up? That they wouldn't start down that route unless they were already quite certain? I thought that this kind of job was your bread and butter?'

'It is usually,' Rob admitted. 'And you know Ed from when he worked in CID. He's a good sort. He's reliable if you put him on a stake out. And this was quite an easy job. I mean, she went out and about a bit, but it's easy enough to follow her and mostly in office hours.'

'So? Turn in the photos, send an invoice and move on. At least there'll be one happy couple out there in Bradwick.'

'That's the problem. The husband doesn't want to stop. He's absolutely convinced that he is right and the reason we haven't found anything is because we're not looking hard enough. He's going to go somewhere else.'

Emma pursed her lips. 'Sounds like a narrow escape. But surely you can't be worried about losing business? Not if he was so hard to deal with.'

'It's not about the money!' Rob said. 'It's... I can't quite put it into words. Something about him makes me uneasy. I'm wondering now if I've ended up on the wrong side of things. If he's the bad guy and I'm just enabling him.'

'What, you mean like stalking his own wife? That's a bit weird, isn't it?' She added a bit more sauce to the pile of rice on her plate.

'It's not that weird if you think about it. If the husband is paranoid, he can't exactly follow his wife around. She'd recognise him, she'd know what car he drives and besides, he works, so he can't spend all his time on it.'

'But, if he hires you,' Emma picked up the thread, 'then you can do it all for him. And give him photos and details of where she's been when.'

Rob nodded around the mouthful of curry he was eating. When he'd swallowed, he said, 'That's what I was worried about. What if I've been doing the dirty work for him? It doesn't help that I recently had that chat with Liz Baker.'

'Is that the ex child protection officer you were going to talk to about that teenager you've been -' Emma stopped, unsure of how to proceed. 'You know, the one you're talking to.'

'Yes, mentoring is the word you're looking for. But the point is that Liz was telling me about the different types of abuse, things like gas-lighting and coercive control.'

'Right, and you think that's what this husband is up to? It certainly does feel like it. Are there any other red flags?'

Rob nodded. 'His mood is one of them. Even when he's dealing with me, in a perfectly normal meeting, he can't keep a check on his emotions. He goes from normal, to angry and then despairing, all in a matter of minutes.'

'That is bad. If he has no idea of how to regulate his own emotions, then that makes him dangerous. What do you want me to do?'

'Well, the first thing is that I wanted to bounce it off you and see if you agree with my assessment. I can tell you're as worried as I am. Which leads on the next problem.'

'Confidentiality.' Emma thought for a moment. 'If you seriously believe someone is at risk, then that's out of the window.'

Rob nodded his agreement. 'In that case, I need you to run

a name through the system. Pass it across the desk of the guys in domestic violence. See if there's anything on the system.'

Emma nodded and said, 'It'll also put her on their radar. Might make the response better should the worst happen.' A silence stretched out between them. 'Rob, I'm gonna need the name. It'll make things easier.'

'Right, sorry.' Rob pinched his nose and looked pained, but he did comply. 'Sean Church and his wife Nancy. I can ping you over the address.'

'Thanks. Any kids?'

'Don't think so. Never mentioned them and Ed saw no sign of them.'

'OK, I'll pass it on and let you know. What is the latest with your teenager then?'

'Amy? I'm not sure. The reason I was talking to Liz is that something is off in that family. She thinks the father maybe controlling the family. She shouldn't even have the phone she's using.'

'How old is she?'

'Fifteen.'

'Well, that is a bit weird. I mean, unless they're like, you know, the Amish or some other ultra-orthodox religious group that doesn't live in the twenty first century.'

Rob shook his head. 'No, I looked it up. It's more than a bit weird. Over ninety percent of children her age have their own phone. Hell, even primary school kids have smart phones. That was on the same survey too – over half of them have a smart phone. No idea what they do with them, but hey.' He shook his head. 'When you consider that as well as no phone, she also doesn't have a computer or anything at home that connects to the internet, she's in a group that's in the low single figures in percentage terms. And that makes her very isolated, at the mercy of her parents.'

'OK, so you're right, that is a bit concerning. But not everyone can afford a phone. Or they don't have the technical knowledge, the level of education to think that it's a good idea.'

'No, I wondered that, but the dad's a teacher. And there is internet in the house. Apparently if she has homework to do, then he'll demand to see the worksheet, and then will sit there looking over her shoulder all the time she's there. It just sounds very...'

'... controlling?' Emma nodded. 'I'm starting to see what you mean. It must be stifling to live like that with someone always there.'

'It's worse because he teaches in her school. So his work colleagues are her teachers; even in break times, he'll be watching.' He paused, poking the food around on his plate, and considering his next words. 'I've been back over the messages. The language seems to me to be reminiscent of those interviews I used to do with domestic violence victims.'

'In what way?'

'You'll have seen it too. The victim, or in this case Amelia, is always referencing their abuser or the person who's controlling them. Everything she says is about the father and how he's feeling, what mood he's in. It seems that she's putting all of her energy into understanding him and appeasing him.'

There was a long pause, as Rob considered his options. Emma knew that he was thinking and let him carry on, knowing he'd reach his destination. 'I might have a long shot for you in your murder case.'

'Go on. We're not quite at the stage of listening to the local psychics and weirdos, but there again, we're not far off it. We have nothing at the moment.'

'This girl I'm talking to, Amy, she has suspicions about her father.'

'Yes, I think we've covered that.'

'No, I mean, well I think, suspicions that he might be the murderer.' Emma let the pause hang in the air and Rob continued. 'I've checked this on the news sites, and the messages on the phone, but the morning after both murders he seemed to be in a good mood.'

Emma pursed her lips and rolled the idea around in her head. She stroked her earlobe and ran a thumb over her knuckles as she thought. 'I can see good sides and bad sides to that as a theory.'

'Go on, then what are the upsides first?'

'Well, victim number one, Bill Hawsley, was a pupil at Bradwick High, dropped out about four to five years ago. But it does sound like there might be an overlap with the father who teaches there. He'd certainly be aware of him. And we could run down an address and see if the family falls in the GP catchment area.'

'Shouldn't be too hard. There can't be many teachers at Bradwick High who also have children there.'

'But, on the downside, this isn't exactly proof. It's not even close enough to warrant an arrest or to launch a formal investigation. For all we know, he's just an evil bastard who takes joy in the fact that someone has been killed. It'll be impossible to prove the difference between him seeing the murders in a news the morning after and him being involved. Both of those could put him in a good mood and only one is criminal. There's another big problem.'

'Go on, then. I can tell you've stopped because you don't want to say it out loud. I'm big enough and ugly enough to take it.'

'Well, if it did become part of a formal investigation, we'd have to look into where the information came from. Which means a team would probe you and your connection to Amy.'

Rob spread his hands open. 'I've got nothing to hide. I've done this properly, all above board.'

'I know that. But it could leak. Rumour and innuendo could spread. You have to think about the effect on your business and your family. You know that something doesn't need to be proven true to cause damage.'

Rob stood up and gathered the plates, walking into the kitchen and stacking them in the sink. It was a delaying tactic, something to do while he thought. Emma collected what was left and followed him into the kitchen. He turned and leant on the worktop, facing Emma. 'You're right. It pains me to say so, and I still maintain I've got nothing to hide, but I think it might be best. You running a tip line yet?' Emma nodded. 'If I drop an anonymous message on there, can you be sure to pick it up? Say, around ten tomorrow?'

'That will be enough to at least allow us an initial look.' Emma knew that the tip line was often derided by officers, but the DCs were still on a rota to check each one out. Hopefully no one would question why she chose that particular tip to follow up.

CHAPTER TWENTY-EIGHT

Amelia woke up early and lay in bed, listening to the sounds of the house. She thought that she could hear someone in the kitchen. She heard the distinct sound of her mother going downstairs, so she deduced that her father was already up. Now that neither of her parents were on the same floor, she crept across the floor and got her phone out. With one eye on the door, she powered it up and had a quick check of her overnight messages. She knew she should be more careful, but she couldn't wait for the walk to school to check her phone.

There was a flurry of activity as her friends organised a trip to the shops at the weekend. They'd tell their parents that they were Christmas shopping but mainly it would be a chance to gossip and try on party clothes in the shops. She quickly typed a reply hoping that she hoped to join them, before hiding her phone again and going downstairs.

Her father was sitting at the table, eating toast with one hand. He was flicking through his phone with the other and barely looked up when she came into the room. Amelia quietly seethed with anger. She was hiding upstairs, guiltily using her phone while always being afraid of discovery. She couldn't look at the home computer without him hovering over her shoulder. And with all of this fear and anxiety, she came downstairs to find her father using his phone at the dining table without a care in the world.

But she knew better than to say anything to him about it. She kept her thoughts well buttoned up because she realised that there wasn't a mood that he could be in that would make it acceptable for her to criticise him.

She silently slid around the kitchen and flicked the kettle on. A voice came from behind her. 'Damn! Do you have any idea how many registered sex offenders there are in the UK?' Without waiting for an answer, he continued. 'Over eight hundred thousand, that's like, nearly a million!'

'A million what, dear?' Sharon looked up from where she was watching television and drinking her tea.

'Perverts! In the UK alone. How many towns and cities do you think there are in the whole country?'

Amelia looked at her mother who gave a half shrug with raised eyebrows. An answer seemed to be needed.

'I don't know? Must be thousands?' Amelia said. She didn't add that she could look it up on the internet if she had a phone.

'Sounds about right,' her mother said hopefully.

Tom's forehead furrowed in thought. 'So, there must be hundreds, maybe even thousands in Bradwick alone. It's a frightening thought. Amelia, I think you should stay in for a bit, at home, where it's safe.'

'What about school?' Amelia asked. 'I can't just miss a day.' She couldn't miss a day using her phone and meeting her friends.

'Don't worry about that,' her father said airily. 'I'll tell them in the office that you're off sick. Won't be a problem.'

For once in her life, Amelia couldn't keep quiet. 'But that's not fair! It's not like I go out and attract perverts to me.'

'Oh really?' Tom turned to his daughter with an icy cold demeanour. 'I don't know about you, Sharon, but when I was growing up we didn't have jewellery shops that actually target pre-teen girls. I mean, there's a whole industry now based on providing princess type experiences to young girls. Like I said, it didn't happen when I was young. Why would a ten-year-old girl need earrings and make up? It's just to entice and entrap all the perverts.

'And have you seen those pageants in America? Young girls all dolled up like they're going to a ball and they've barely learnt to read and write. No. My mind's made up.' He got up and put his phone on the table. He strode from the room and within a few seconds the two women heard the sound of the back door locking. Tom came back into the room, tossing and catching a bunch of keys. 'Back door is locked. I've got the spare keys. I've got to go to work. You two will be safe in here.'

Without waiting for an answer, he picked up his phone and left, locking the front door behind him and taking the keys. Mother and daughter looked at each other, speechless. Once they were sure that Tom had gone, Amelia said, 'What the hell? I mean, he can't just do that, can he?'

'He just did,' her mother said simply.

'But it's nuts.' She paused and thought for a moment. 'And, we could just go out of a window. The ones at the front, the sills are low, it's easy to get in and out and Dad would never know.'

Sharon thought for a moment. 'No. Don't do it now. Where could you go? You can't go to school, because he'd find you. And if you wander around town, then you could get caught for truancy. You know how he is when he gets into a mood like this. We'll just keep our heads down and wait for it to blow over.'

Amelia's mood instantly deflated. She thought round and round in circles. There had to be a way around her father. But if there was, she couldn't find it. She wanted to go upstairs and look at her phone. But the thought of sitting there, in secret, watching her friends chatting and talking about school was too painful.

She drifted into the living room where her mother was watching daytime television. 'Mum? You must know that this isn't right. Even you can't defend him this time.'

'Amelia, you're a child, you have no understanding of how adult relationships work. Surely you can see that he's doing this because he loves us, he wants to keep us safe.'

'Safe? We are now literally prisoners in our own home!' She flung herself into an armchair. 'Ugh! Why don't we just leave him? Just you and me? We could make a go of it.'

'Oh, Amelia, you just don't understand, do you. What would we say? To the people around us? To our friends? He doesn't take drugs, he doesn't hit us, he's a good man with a steady job who provides for us. I've never had to work. Don't you think it would be selfish for us to just up and leave after he's done all that for us?'

'Yes, but -'

'No buts. This is what I mean about you not being old enough to understand. We can't just go. If we left, we'd have to go to a whole new town. He works here and lives here and we'd never be free unless we really left, went miles away. And I don't have a job, and I haven't had a job for ages so it's not like I've got skills. You need to know how a computer works these days or no one would even look at you. So we'd end up claiming benefits, living in some God-forsaken bed and breakfast hoping we don't get put on sanctions. And we'd be doing all this miles away from here, away from all your friends and my friends and our family. We'd be miserable and without any support. And it'd be hard to make friends, because everyone hates benefit claimants. Your father isn't the only one who reads the papers. Believe me, we couldn't survive out there on our own.'

CHAPTER TWENTY-NINE

'Are you Robert Haines?'

Rob frowned and looked at the two people on his doorstep. It was Friday morning and with no meetings in the diary, he had chosen to work from home. Although he liked his office, once in a while he preferred not to go in. Now he was glad that he had made that decision as he was able to face these two instead of leaving Jem to answer the door.

He inspected the two visitors and immediately knew who they were. One was a woman in police uniform, the other was in a man in a cheap suit with his tie loosened, both were white. He was obviously CID with a uniform to accompany him.

'What do you want?' Rob asked.

The man, slightly balding, frowned. 'I want to talk to Robert Haines.'

'That's me.' Rob had already assessed him as a bit of a plodder, concerned with getting each fact confirmed before moving on. 'Now, what do you want to talk to me about?'

'Maybe this would be easier if we came in,' the man said, taking a step forward.

'I don't think so,' Rob said. 'First of all show me your warrant cards. Can't be too careful.'

There was definitely a look between the two officers, but Rob was within his rights, so with an air of resignation they handed them over. Rob peered carefully at the cards. Laurence Astor was the detective constable and Ruby Clovis was the PC. Both were down from Bristol. 'What departments are you from?'

'I'm in a specialist computer crime department and Ruby is in child protection.' He paused and looked up and down the street. 'Are you sure we can't come in? I wouldn't want your neighbours to get ideas, seeing us stood here on the doorstep, talking to you.'

'Do you have any idea who I am? What I did for a job before I retired?' They both looked blankly at each other. 'I was a detective inspector in the local CID. Served over twenty years. None of your tricks will work on me. My neighbours know me so it won't be weird that I'm talking to the police. And, I know my rights, you can't come in without a warrant, and you won't get one without reasonable suspicion. And if you had reasonable suspicion you wouldn't be standing on the doorstep having a chat, would we? You'd have arrested me and I'd be halfway to Bristol by now.' The two officers looked at each other and back at Rob. 'Right, so, we've cleared that up, how about you tell me what the hell this is all about?'

Something passed between the other two officers. They looked increasingly uncomfortable. Finally Astor nodded briefly at Clovis, then answered. 'There's been a long legal battle between the owners of an app called StringCan and the authorities. A settlement has finally been reached, it's something of a compromise. The owners have agreed to provide us details of likely grooming events. In particular, the parameters were set to select all children who are in active contact with men over the age of twenty-one.' He raised his eyebrows at Rob. 'Now, with all your experience, you must be able to see why we'd be concerned about contact between a man in his fifties and a girl of thirteen. Maybe you'd like to clear up the exact nature of your relationship for us? We've also got forms here for you to waive your right to privacy and allow us to view your conversations.'

Rob closed his eyes and pinched the bridge of his nose. Thoughts flowed around his head. Amelia was only thirteen, not fifteen, he thought. As if that made any difference. And he was trying to remember every single conversation he'd had and if they could somehow be incriminating.

'Well?'

Rob opened his eyes and saw DC Astor holding out a form on a clipboard with a pen.

'Here's the form. Just sign at the bottom.'

'No, thank you.' Rob reached a decision.

The three of them looked at each other, at an impasse. PC Clovis said tentatively, 'You really should co-operate, you wouldn't want...'

'... to look guilty,' Rob finished the sentence for her. 'I told you. I was doing this long before you were a probationer. What's next? If you've done nothing wrong, then you've got nothing to hide? I'm not going to be bounced into anything.' The other two officers waited in silence while Rob thought through the situation. 'Give me some time to get a solicitor organised and I'll come in and give you a statement. How about tomorrow morning?'

'You're not in a position to set the timetable. We're in charge of this.'

'And we've already established that you don't have

grounds to make an arrest. I'm co-operating with you and I've agreed to come in and help.'

Again they'd reached an impasse. But Rob was far more experienced at the waiting game. It was one of his favourite tactics in getting suspects to talk.

Finally, DC Astor cracked. He looked uncomfortable, but he did reluctantly nod. 'Come in to the office at ten tomorrow morning. We're in the headquarters out in Portishead.' He handed over a business card. 'Ask for me when you sign in at reception. Don't be late.'

'Listen,' Rob said, 'I am one of the good guys. Honestly. Nothing dodgy at all is going on. But I'm not going to be railroaded. Like I said I've done this for a long time and I know what happens once the decision is made and the evidence is bent to fit it.'

'We don't do things like that anymore,' DC Astor said stiffly. 'We just want to see all the facts and then we'll decide. On that note, don't delete any messages.'

'I'm not stupid. I know that everything is on a server somewhere or waiting to be downloaded no matter what I've done with my phone. Trust me, I'll sort out a solicitor and see you tomorrow at ten.'

With that he went inside and shut his door, leaving them on the doorstep. He paced around the house for a bit before making himself a cup of tea. Then he did what he'd been putting off and phoned a criminal lawyer. He didn't have one as a matter of course, so he picked the name that he'd most hated when he'd been interviewing suspects.

The phone call was about as awkward and awful as Rob had expected. It was clear that Mr Malone, the solicitor, remembered him with as much fondness as Rob had toward him. But they ended with an eye-watering amount agreed as a retainer and an appointment to meet at nine the following morning for a meeting in a coffee shop in Portishead. Rob wondered how much of the charge was for weekend rates and how much was added on because he didn't like the police.

That unpleasant business concluded, he opened a new pack of biscuits and settled down to watch some daytime TV. The knock at the door had disturbed him and he had no urgent work to complete and no desire to do any.

He soon realised he wasn't concentrating on the television so he worked through what he would do if he was on the other side of this situation. He knew that if he'd still been in the police, then this would've looked really dodgy. All the misgivings he'd had when he started messaging Amelia came back in full force.

If he were investigating then the next step would be to talk to Amelia. And that couldn't happen in isolation if she really was thirteen. Far too late he realised where the danger was. Amelia shouldn't have that phone. Over the course of their conversations, he'd been more and more convinced that she was in genuine danger from her father. The same man who'd banned his daughter from owning a mobile phone.

He got the card of the officer and dialled the number. He got put through straight to the detective inspector who was running the investigation.

'Right, so you're Robert Haines, are you?' He tried to picture the woman who spoke to him.

'Yes, I was visited by two of your officers this afternoon.'

'I know. They spoke to me afterwards. Apparently you were less than fully co-operative, as if you had something to hide.'

'Not at all, it's just that I know what my rights are.'

'Ah yes. The former police officer.' She drew her words out. 'Former Detective Chief Inspector Robert Haines.'

'That's me.' Rob's words were tight and clipped. 'I just

wanted to impress on you that I have serious concerns for the welfare of Amelia Bagshaw.'

'The girl who you're in correspondence with? Strangely enough, we also have concerns for her welfare.'

Rob thought fast. 'That's what I was talking about. Amelia's father has banned her from owning a mobile. The one that she's using now, she's not supposed to have. As I said, I think that Amelia's father presents a real danger to her. Especially if he finds out that she's been going behind his back and using a phone.'

'Right. And what do you think we should do about it?'

'Well, not tell her parents what's been going on. I think you'd be exposing her to a credible risk of harm.'

There was a long pause in the conversation. 'Let me tell you something, Rob, if I can call you that. When my officers phoned in about their little doorstep chat, I did some digging. Well, that's not quite the right word, because nothing was particularly buried. It's all there on the surface. Robert Haines, disgraced former cop. Somehow managed to escape some very serious corruption charges. Now runs his own private investigation agency. He finds himself accused of grooming a young girl over the internet. So, he calls up the inspector in charge of the case and does the old buddy routine. We're all cops and on the same side. We're concerned for the young girl's welfare. Only, would we please not contact her parents? Which, of course, means that we can't get her side of it, without getting social services involved, which would tip the parents off anyway.

'So, you're seeking to control the entire narrative and not have us hear the other side. Now, bearing all that in mind, and with your previous experience, what conclusion would you draw?'

This time the silence was strained and awkward. There was nothing more that Rob could say. Except, 'Well, OK then. I'll see you at ten tomorrow morning.'

'Oh, I'll be looking forward to it.'

Rob put his phone down and closed his eyes. It was only now dawning on him how deep in trouble he was. He hoped that Malone was worth the money and that things would look better in twenty-four hours.

He picked up his phone and went to the app before he remembered the words of the solicitor Malone. He really must drop all contact with Amelia until this had been sorted. That had been the gist of the conversation – complete disclosure and a temporary cutting of contact. Once he'd been warned, it'd be ridiculous to carry on chatting as if nothing had changed.

But, on the other hand, he couldn't let Amelia go straight home into what could be a dangerous situation. It was already half past two so if he messaged her now, he could catch her at school or on the way home. He could give her a little bit of warning, then it'd be up to her how to deal with it.

Or, would he be interfering with an active investigation? They'd already pegged him as trouble and found out about his record. He knew that everything he'd done had been done for the right reasons. And he also knew how thin that sounded.

Fuck it, he thought. If he was going to get buried, he might as well go down properly. He would never be able to live with himself if something happened to Amelia. Her father Thomas had been getting increasingly erratic. The latest flurry of messages had detailed how he'd locked Amelia and Sharon in the house, but then come back in a surprisingly good mood. Before he could stop himself, he picked up his phoned and tapped out a quick message.

Just to let you know, the police are investigating my contact with you. They'll want to speak to you and your parents and see your phone.

CHAPTER THIRTY

THE NEXT MORNING, Amelia woke up with a sense of dread. She hadn't forgotten yesterday's insanity from her father. Being locked in the house all day and not going to school had been a weird experience. She'd mostly been bored, lazing around watching rubbish on television with her mum.

She knew from experience that her father's weird moods were often short lived. So when she woke up she decided to go through the morning as if nothing out of the ordinary had happened twenty-four hours earlier. It was a strategy that had risks, but she knew she'd be able to tell soon enough if the madness was continuing for another day.

Walking on eggshells, she negotiated her way through breakfast and packing her bag with nothing out of the ordinary from her father. She could hardly believe her luck when she walked out of the door with her uniform on and her bag over her shoulder.

The day passed completely normally at school. She looked at the teachers around her, the administrative staff and assistants and contemplated telling them. How could she approach anyone at the school and tell them that their beloved teacher was nuts? That the man who did after school clubs and fetes and charity events had locked her in the house yesterday. That she could never tell from one day to the next how dangerous he would be?

No. There was no way she could do that. She mourned the loss of Dr Donnelly, the one person she thought might have listened. She'd been waiting to see if she could be trusted before she said anything and now the chance had gone.

Somehow she made it through the day. Five lessons and two breaks with her thoughts swirling around her head. But finally the bell rang and she was free for the weekend.

Amelia had worked out down to the last second exactly how much she could dawdle on the way home from school. It was her one brief periods of free time. During school breaks, she was never certain whether her father was watching or not, meaning her time on the phone was always anxious. But, after school her father usually stayed late, tidying his rooms and writing up reports. She could be certain that her mother was at home, so for this brief seven minute period, she could walk slowly, chat with her friends and use her phone.

As always, as soon as she left the gates with Sara, they powered up their phones. And on Amelia's there was a message from Rob Haines. This was unusual as she usually started the conversations. When she read the message she was even more alarmed.

He was being investigated by the police for grooming her! She couldn't figure out why he had told her or what she was supposed to do with the information. But she did realise that he probably shouldn't have told her and therefore it must be important.

Her consternation must have shown on her face. Sara stopped walking and asked, 'What's up, Amelia?'

Instead of answering she showed her phone to her friend.

'Shit! That means the police will want to talk to you. And they'll want a parent or responsible adult present.' They'd covered internet safety in PSE classes recently. 'How exactly are you going to explain to your parents that not only you have a phone when you shouldn't, but also strange older men are contacting you on it?'

'One man,' Amelia said sharply. 'And he's not strange. I mean, he's a bit cringe like a parent, but he's okay really.'

'Whatever! Not really the point. You know what your dad is like. Do you want me to take your phone?'

Amelia screwed her face up to think. 'No, that won't work. I'd still have to explain to them what's been going on. If the police know, they'll know I have an account on StringCan and they won't believe me if I don't have the phone that goes with it.' She paused again. 'Shit! We're stuffed. I'm stuffed.'

'What are you going to do?'

'I dunno. Go home and work it out. I mean, how bad can my dad be?'

'OK. See you after the weekend.' Sara paused with perfect comic timing. 'If you survive that is!'

They went their separate ways. Amelia was only two corners away from her house and Sara lived in the other direction. But Amelia soon realised things were moving faster and more seriously than she'd imagined.

She stood at the end of her road and saw her mother on the doorstep, talking to two people. One was in a police uniform. They were here already, before she'd had time to plan anything. She felt the weight of her phone in her blazer pocket, damning her.

Now she understood what Rob's message had meant. It was a warning, a chance for her to plan. She knew what she had to do. She already had it as a vague thought, but hadn't dared acknowledge it until now.

She ducked down and looked at her front door through the windows of a parked car. Her mother was scanning the road, looking for her. She was talking and gesticulating to the two police. Amelia could imagine that she was saying that her daughter would be home any minute now.

Sharon darted back into the house and came back with a phone to her ear. Amelia knew how paranoid her father was, how he was always checking his wife's phone. He was the only person she'd be calling in a situation like this.

Amelia kept below the level of the car window and jogged away from her home. As soon as she turned the corner, she straightened up and started running after Sara. She tried to imagine the route her father would take home and cut through a couple of streets to avoid it. Finally she saw Sara up ahead and raced to catch up with her. 'Police are already there,' she said breathlessly, as Sara turned round in surprise. 'What do I do?'

Sara didn't hesitate. 'Come home with me for now, then we can talk about what to do next'.

Amelia felt giddy. She was going over to a friend's house, like a normal teenager. Sara's mum was, well there was no better word for it, she was normal. Light and breezy, she took the extra teenager in her house completely in her stride.

Amelia was allowed to take food and drink as she wanted, and then she went to Sara's room to plan. The two sets of parents knew each other, although not well, so their time was limited. Eventually Amelia's mother would phone round to see if anyone had seen her. She only had one clear aim – to find her sister Sophie. They hadn't spoken since Sophie had left the family several weeks ago, but Amelia held onto the fact that Sophie had managed to escape. Unfortunately, she only had the vaguest idea of what direction she had to head in to find Sophie, and no idea how to get there.

After some quick discussion, Amelia borrowed a bag and a couple of changes of clothes from Sara, and changed out of the school uniform she was wearing. Then, with the further loan of a ten-pound note, she went downstairs and stood by the front door with Sara. Amelia opened the door and a squall of rain hit her in the face. She looked up and down the street. It was dark and cold and the streetlights had come on. She suddenly felt very small and alone. She couldn't go back home and she didn't want to head out into the unknown. She imagined the homeless people she'd seen around town, sleeping in the bus station or underpass. In her head they all smelt faintly of piss and held cans of cheap lager. She couldn't go out to that as a future either.

Amelia turned and looked at Sara, panic on her face. Sara nodded slowly, but she was thinking fast. She glanced up the stairs, then raised her voice, to make sure that her mother, who was cooking would hear. 'Bye then Amelia, I'll see you on Monday.'

Amelia caught on fast. 'Thank you for having me. Have a good weekend!'

Sara slammed the door shut with both girls still inside the house. Amelia crept up the stairs with Sara walking normally alongside her. When they got into the room, still not speaking, Amelia went and lay down on the floor on the far side of the bed from the door. Sara went to the doorway and confirmed she'd be hidden.

Then she fired up her Bluetooth speaker and they hatched a plan. Amelia would hide in Sara's bedroom until the morning and then she'd sneak out of the house. Sara had a friend whose mother cleaned self-catering houses so they'd try to get access to a place for Amelia to hide while she searched for Sophie.

CHAPTER THIRTY-ONE

EMMA ANGEL COUNTED along the cubicles and then stopped and pushed aside the curtain. She stuck her head in and found she'd got the right place.

'You know, I already see way too much of this place with work, I don't really need to come here when I'm off shift.'

'I see that you've been notified then,' Lukas said lightly. 'Nothing gets past you lot, does it?'

'Well, that's kind of the point really. Modern policing should be intelligence led. Doesn't really work if we don't know what's going on.'

Lukas laughed, then stopped. 'Oh God, don't do that. Makes me hurt.'

'What the hell happened to you?'

'Well, Violet,' he paused for a moment. 'Do you think you could find where she is in this place? Anyway, she knew someone who knew someone who was having a party. So we went there but it wasn't really happening, until one of the guys there got a text about a beach party. So a whole group of us from the party went down there to have a look, and well, you know, one thing led to another.'

Emma frowned as she took in his injuries. 'And you got into an argument? Someone beat you up?' Emma was unsure of this as Lukas was one of those people who made friends with everyone.

'No, nothing like that. Some of the neighbours complained about the noise and they must've called the police, because next thing, your lot showed up. So we all split in different directions. I went to jump over this low wall in a car park, only I kind of misjudged it. Caught my foot and went down like a sack of potatoes. Got all cut up on some broken glass and kind of half fell, half rolled into the subway. You know the one, goes under the main road by the kebab shop?'

'So, what's the damage?'

'So far, just cuts and bruises. Feels like hell if I take a deep breath but apparently there's no broken ribs on the x-ray. Nothing serious, but I'll probably feel like crap for a few days. Now I'm just waiting for the paperwork to get sorted and get some painkillers. But it's a Friday night, so it's busy and nothing's open. They're looking for enough for a couple of days and then they'll give me a prescription.' He looked around the cubicle, obviously concerned. 'Listen, I'll be fine. It's Violet I'm worried about. Could you, you know, ask around a bit, see what's happened to her?'

'Is there any reason something would've happened? I mean, should I be asking the nurses or my colleagues?'

Lukas had the good grace to look sheepish. 'Last I saw her, she was in the back of one of your vans. I mean, I had one plod wait by me till the ambulance could pick me up.'

'And would Violet happen to have anything about her person that could interest my lot?'

'Probably. She usually does. I don't know if she ditched it before she got nicked.'

'Lukas!' Emma was exasperated. 'I thought you were getting yourself sorted? How's this going to help with straightening yourself out?'

'I dunno. I mean, it's not serious. Just a bit of smoke now and again. And like I say, we were going to a party. Be rude not to show up with something that you could share.'

Emma shook her head, but she did stand up from the uncomfortable plastic chair she'd been sitting on. 'I'll ask around, quietly. But I can't make any promises. This isn't like the old days, you know. If she's caught, fair and square, then she'll just have to face up to it and take her punishment.'

Lukas looked downcast. 'Yeah, I guess. Well, you know. Do what you can.'

Emma left him and started hunting around for a nurse or another officer to find out what happened to Violet. But Friday night in A&E was not the right time to find a member of staff or to ask for favours. As she looked for anyone who might help, she mulled the problem over in her head.

If she was the long-term best friend who warned Lukas off from his new partner, then that would not end well. Violet had already shown herself to be the jealous type. If Emma pushed Lukas now, made some suggestions that Violet was bad for him, then there would be pushback. And Emma couldn't guarantee which way Lukas would go. She was one of his oldest friends, but Violet was the new girlfriend. And Emma just knew that Violet would pull all the strings available to win an argument for Lukas' affections. In fact, Emma was certain that Violet would fight for Lukas, even if she saw it as a short-term fling. On top of which, a new relationship was a strong pull and she'd seen enough people ditch their existing friends the moment that their new other half said a word against them.

She finally found a uniformed officer at the coffee

machine in the waiting room. 'Hi, can you tell me if you arrested a Violet Backton? Or if she's in here?'

He frowned. 'I don't know who's here, I didn't arrest her. But your best bet is to check with admissions.' He indicated a desk behind a glass screen with a long queue. 'Do you want me to radio in to the desk sergeant and see who he's processed?'

'Yeah, if you could do that, it'd be a help. I'll go try my luck at the desk.'

She went over to join the queue. When she finally got to talk to the nurse she found there was no trace of Violet at the hospital, so she walked back over to the officer.

'We've got her booked in at the station now. I think they're just going to caution on all of them. It wasn't anything serious, just some kids on the beach with a fire, drinking and taking drugs. Sarge said the important thing was to break it up and get them out of there. As long as it's all quiet, that's the important thing.'

Emma could read between the lines. No one wanted all the paperwork that would go with so many minor possession cases. And he was right, the main objective had been achieved. The disturbance had been brought to an end.

She thanked the constable and then had to decide what to do next. It seemed to be a good outcome for Lukas and Violet, but not one that she could take any credit for. In the end, she decided that the best thing to do would be to just go back home and try to catch up with some sleep. And let Violet and Lukas figure things out in the best way they could.

CHAPTER THIRTY-TWO

EMMA AND SUSE BERMAN stood on the pavement and looked up and down the street before turning to the building that they'd been called to attend. It was split into flats in an estate that had seen better days. It was on the edge of the Seaview, in a particularly unloved corner of the estate. There was a small car park and footpaths leading off to a cluster of two storey buildings.

'Makes you think,' Suse said. 'The architects designed all this, what, fifty or sixty years ago? And they thought they had something beautiful, a new way for people to live. All these low buildings with paths between them shaded by trees. Everything from corner shops to churches to doctor's surgeries all within walking distance. But you leave it to rot with no attention for fifty years,' she indicated the area with a sweep of her hand. 'And then you wait till it's winter like this and the supermarkets are now all out of town and the buses are crap, so you're carrying your shopping in from the car. Usually when it's cold, dark and raining.'

Emma looked at Suse with a frown. She hadn't put the sarge down as one of life's deep thinkers. 'I didn't know that you knew about the history of the town, Suse. I thought you were a bang 'em up and move on type of person?'

Suse tapped her nose conspiratorially. 'You know me better than that, Emma. I'm always looking for the next way to move up. Sooner or later, I'll be going for interviews where they need me to think strategically and not just tactically. That's where the really senior jobs are. So, I had a look around to see if there was anything I wanted to study further.'

'And you chose the history of Bradwick?'

'No! I chose the impact of urban design on crime. Think about it, you put an underpass next to a line of cheap shops, like charity shops, pawn brokers, vape shops etc. and suddenly it's full of teenagers leering at the public and being a nuisance. It takes budget to keep the lights on and paint over the graffiti. But if that same crossing is replaced with traffic lights or a bridge, and you mix in a bank or an upscale coffee shop, then the whole nature of that one tiny area changes. Once you start to look at it like that, the whole subject is fascinating.'

Emma nodded. 'You could be right. Although those teenagers will still need somewhere to go.'

'You see, you do get it. It needs to be a package of facilities, all interlocking.' She stopped as they reached the crime scene. She indicated the flat in front of them. 'And then you get places like this that are, whether the authorities will ever admit it or not, dumping grounds. Places to house those people who the world would rather forget.' They both approached the front door which was slightly open and guarded by a PCSO. Judging by the grim set of her face, what was inside was not pleasant.

'Hi,' Emma greeted the PCSO. 'DC Angel and DS Berman from CID. Are we the first ones here?'

'Yes, SOCO and the pathologist are on their way.'

'OK, we'll have a quick look. Just through the door, we know the score.'

She gently nudged the door open with her foot and the two detectives peered inside. In the hallway, a body lay on his side, the red of his intestines piled up in front of him. He had other marks, long slashes on his forearms and bruising around his face. There was blood everywhere, splattered around and pooled underneath him. There were marks on the walls and even a few drops on the ceiling and the lampshade. The stench was unbearable and flies buzzed around. The body was pale, the pallor now tinged towards green. Emma wrinkled her nose and stepped back for a moment to get some fresher air.

'How did you find the body?' Emma asked the PCSO.

'Benjamin Scott is on probation. Was on probation. He missed his last meeting with his probation officer, and it's on my beat, so I was asked if I'd look in and check to see if he'd done a runner or there was any other reason for skipping out. The door was locked, so I went to look through the letter box and the smell hit me. I only forced entry to confirm it really.'

Emma thanked her and went to sit on the low wall at the front of the property, and got her phone and tablet computer out. She chatted briefly and scrolled through information on her screen before she hung up and turned to Suse.

'Assuming the body in there is what's left of Benjamin Scott, I asked Nick to run a quick check on him, why he was on probation that kind of thing?'

'And? How naughty has he been?'

'Well, it didn't put Nick to any trouble. His name and this address are the same as on his criminal record. And the answer to your question is, very naughty. He was done for possession of obscene images of minors, collected while he was a teacher. He's only been out on licence for six months.

What's more interesting is that Nick also ran a regular internet search. Mr Scott turns up on a lot of the "do you know there's a paedo living in your town" type websites and his face has been splashed all over social media with some fairly heavy hints as to where you might find him.'

Suse nodded. 'It figures. I mean, once you're on the register, there's very few jobs you could get. Especially if people are busy outing you and putting your face all over the internet. He probably didn't dare to go out much either.'

'So this could be the same killer? Going back to the same pattern as when he started with the drug dealer? Cleaning up the town?'

'If it is the same one, then it leaves us with the same problem as before. Why the GP? I suppose we'll have to wait and see what Dani finds.' She raised her voice slightly, nodding at the figure of Dani Price, who was standing on the pavement a short distance away, squirming into a white suit.

'You could at least let me get in there and see the body before you start asking,' she said, a joking tone to her words.

'You know what we're going to ask,' Emma said.

'Yes, yes. I'll have a quick look for the coin. What do you think? Part of the same pattern?'

'Don't know,' Suse answered. 'Could be. He's certainly been attacked with a knife and gutted like the others. But it looks like he fought back, so that's a difference. And he's a paedo out on license, so there'll be no shortage of suspects.'

'I'll do my best.'

Dani went into the building to start her painstaking work.

'He looks like he's been there for days, any idea when the missed probation meeting was and when last contact was before that?' Suse asked.

Emma called the PCSO over and asked her what she'd been told about Benjamin Scott.

She consulted her notebook. 'He had a routine check in appointment at two o'clock yesterday afternoon and didn't show. I think they wanted me to check on him quickly in case he'd done a runner.'

Emma nodded and thanked her. 'So, he was dead yesterday. I'd guess he's been dead for at least a couple of days.' She looked at Suse.

'Yeah, might be even less. The heating was on, and his guts were out. I doubt he looked or smelled that great at any point.'

'Well, Dani will do her thing and give us a timeline.'

Suse nodded. 'And we can always work his contacts. Although I doubt anyone would admit to being friends with a murdered paedophile, let alone tell us when they last saw him.'

'That's probably true,' Emma agreed. They looked up as the full scene of crimes unit arrived.

'They're going to be tied up here for ages,' Suse said. 'Let's see what Dani thinks, then I want you back at the office while we make a start on building up a victim profile.'

'Who's going to cover the scene then?'

'I'll get John Fletcher down here. It'll be a valuable part of his training. You wait here until he can relieve you. While you're waiting, summon up some uniforms and start a door to door.' She looked around the area, scanning high up along houses and peering at streetlights. 'Not a lot of CCTV, and it doesn't look like the kind of area for too many video doorbells. But, on the plus side, it's a Saturday morning, so the door to door should find plenty of people in.'

Dani Price was just emerging from the house, carefully removing her mask so she could speak to the officers. 'I know what you're going to ask. It's another stabbing in Bradwick so I did have a quick check. There is a metallic object lodged inside the body, a few millimetres thick. Obviously this one's a bit more of a mess so it was hard to establish where he'd place the coin. But I think I've found it.' She smiled. 'Obviously full details and evidence will have to wait until I get back to the mortuary. Should have something by the end of the day.' She glanced at the open door where the SOCOs were all busy securing evidence before the body could be moved.

'Thanks, Dani,' Suse said. 'We'll get out of your hair now. This will let us tie it into the existing major investigation.'

She left the scene, and Emma was left alone to be the CID presence. She had plenty to organise while she waited for John to arrive.

CHAPTER THIRTY-THREE

'All right everybody. Some quiet please. Let me give you the potted history of one Benjamin Scott.' Michelle Jones now had the attention of the room. 'He had a very undistinguished childhood, went to university for three years and came out with a 2:2 in Business Studies. After that, he took a few starter jobs, office admin, customer service phone centres, data entry, that sort of thing. Then, at twenty-three, he changed direction and went to convert his degree to a teacher training certificate. However, in his first year as a probationary teacher at our very own Bradwick High, some of the year seven girls at his school reported him for being generally creepy and being too keen to wander unannounced into girls' changing rooms and toilets. Thankfully, the safeguarding team were on the ball, and the head launched an investigation. They found some cameras hidden in the girls changing room and seized his laptop. The cameras were synced to his work laptop, so they called us in. We arrested him and under a PACE search, we found that he's been looking at the kind of pictures that you really don't want a prospective teacher to be interested in.

'So, he goes to prison, spends a good few years in solitary, dodging those hardened criminals who are fathers to young girls. He was released and, against all the advice, chose to come back here for his probation.'

'Isn't that really unusual?' Suse asked.

'Yes, he served his time at a specialist unit in the north-east, to keep him out of the area where his offending took place.'

'But he chose to come back here?'

'Yes. And this,' Michelle indicated the photo of the body on the board, 'was the result. But it gives us a whole lot more leads. We believe these three murders are linked. Now the problem is that Bradwick High has over a thousand students, and hundreds of teachers and ancillary staff. If you factor in close family members of any of the girls affected, then you're probably linking in to pretty much the whole population of the town. But we need to find an overlap with our first victim. Obviously, he dropped out of Bradwick High in year eleven, at which point victim three was in prison.'

One of the technicians looked up from where he'd been scribbling on a piece of paper. 'Do you have the dates of, uh, Scott's time in prison?'

Michelle read them out from her notes. 'Yes, he started at the school in September 2011, was arrested in 2012 and sent down in 2013. Why?'

'Well that means our first victim, Hawsley, would've been year seven at the same time as Scott did his probationary year.'

Michelle furrowed her brow. 'Scott's thing was young girls though. I can't see how he'd be connected to Hawsley. But it is a link.' She looked at Nick Dent and said, 'Can you look into that? See if anyone has records from that time. If Scott ever taught Hawsley, anything like that?'

'Will do boss! And I'll look at female students who started

in year seven in the school year 2011. See if we've got any violent relatives in their families.'

EMMA SAT down at her desk after the meeting. The news about Ben Scott and Bill Hawsley had made her think about Bradwick High again. She couldn't help feeling that maybe Bill Hawsley had also met someone there who'd killed him. The trouble was that a single year seven student was in over ten different classes. If you counted in the form tutor, the people who supervised the library, canteen and all the other shared areas, then there would've been up to twenty staff at the school who knew Hawsley. Plus, of course, he'd have mixed with hundreds of pupils, ultimately building his customer base for his short-lived career as a drug dealer.

And, worse, Scott was an English teacher so he taught across all years and all classes. She rubbed her eyes. There was no way to tell if the two victims knew each other. And as Scott's perversion was young girls, it didn't seem likely. And it didn't link into Dr Donnelly either.

DI Jones called Emma into her office. When she was sat behind the desk, her boss began. 'Now we're up to three bodies, I need to know what progress you've got on the football coins.'

Emma took a deep breath. 'We're getting the reports in from the online sites. There are tens of them available within a fifty mile radius but the companies involved will not release details without a warrant. I've started phoning round the shops immediately in Bradwick, but I think it's a dead end. Not many of them keep good records. And that doesn't even include boot fairs and indoor markets, which might have sold them. In addition, those coins are getting on for fifty years old, so the killer may have inherited them.'

'Do we have anything else on the cards?'

'We have got a long shot. I've picked up a tip from the phone in line and I've fleshed it out a bit.'

'What have you got?'

'Anonymous tip about a girl called Amy who's at Bradwick High. Apparently her father is the one we should be looking at and he's a teacher there as well.'

Michelle nodded. 'It does all seem to be centred around that school.'

'Yes, I made an unofficial enquiry and out of the four teachers with children there, I found one called Amelia Bagshaw, with her father being a Design and Technology teacher, Thomas Bagshaw.' She left out the fact that Rob Haines' contact was called BaggyAmy, further confirming that she had the right person. 'Even more intriguing is that the family lives in the catchment area for Dr Donnelly's surgery. So he does have a potential link to all three victims.'

'Potential, yes,' Michelle Jones said. 'But it's probably something he shares with thousands of local residents.'

'I've been keeping an eye on her,' Emma said, ignoring the questioning look her boss was giving her. 'And today Amelia went round the system as a missing person. I'm not sure, but it feels like something is going on in that family.'

'And you just picked this out of the hundreds of leads on the list?'

'Yes, ma'am.' The two women looked at each other over the desk. Michelle clearly knew that something was up, but she obviously decided to leave it for the time being.

'OK, then. Keep an eye on it for now. And if you need to action anything, run it by me first, OK?'

Emma nodded and left the office. The tension had been obvious when talking to Michelle. Emma knew her story hadn't been believed, but as she was still allowed to run with it, she counted it as a win for now. Given that her boss had not only worked at Professional Standards in the past, but also investigated Rob Haines, she was going to keep his name out of this for as long as possible. She just didn't know how long that would be.

CHAPTER THIRTY-FOUR

By the time Rob had got through a sit-down with his lawyer, then been signed into the police station, he felt guilty. The entire process was designed to make anyone feel like a criminal.

DI Ruth Peterson was as he expected – in her forties, thin, white, with ginger hair that was kept short. She looked tired and pinched, but Rob knew what the job could do to a person. When they were all sitting down, she said, 'This is a meeting with DI Peterson, DC Astor, Robert Haines and his solicitor, Joseph Malone. Although this interview is being recorded, Mr Haines is here of his own free will and hasn't been read his rights.' She stopped and looked expectantly at the two men on the other side of the table.

Malone was the first one to speak. 'I want to start my asserting that my client is completely innocent. He has been mentoring a troubled young girl, who incidentally lied about her age, using his experience as a father to guide her through a difficult time in her life. Obviously, we can see how this would look incriminating, so we've prepared a folder of paperwork.' He tapped a folder that he'd laid on the table. 'We have everything that you want in here. Printouts of all Mr Haines' activity on StringCan, plus authority to check that nothing's been deleted or omitted, and a waiver so you can contact his internet service provider. But, before we hand this over, we do have some conditions.'

'Conditions?' DI Peterson was icy cold. 'I don't think either of you quite understand the severity of this situation. You're not in a situation to make any requests. I suggest you hand over that file right now, and let us do our job.'

'Would you hear us out please?' Rob said, before his solicitor laid a hand on his arm.

'Maybe conditions was the wrong word to use. More of a request.' He inclined his head and smiled to show that this wasn't a confrontation. 'My client has a standing in the community of Bradwick. He's a family man with a small business and a retired police officer.' Malone caught the glances that passed between the two officers on the other side of the table. 'We'll have none of the sly looks either. He retired on medical grounds, after being injured in the course of his duty. Specifically while keeping the public safe. Anything else you may have heard is pure speculation and will play no part here.' He paused and took a breath. 'Sorry, I went a little off track there. It's quite simple. We want this meeting, here today, to be kept private. No leaks to the press, no social media, nothing.'

The other two officers looked at each other. Finally Peterson said, 'What about when he's charged? That'll be a matter of record.'

'*If* my client is charged or arrested then obviously the whole matter is moot. But until that point, discretion is the word of the day. What we don't want is a repeat of that fiasco a few years ago in the Bath area, where that neighbour of the young girl who was killed was arrested. He ended up with his name all over the papers, and it turns out he was innocent after all of that. Ruined his life, it did.'

'Yes, I think you've made your point,' Peterson said.

'I do have one more point. No coded messages either. If anyone in Bradwick reads about a "retired senior police officer who's now a private investigator" being investigated for grooming, well, they won't need to be Sherlock Holmes to identify my client, will they?'

Rob could guess Peterson's thoughts. If he'd been the other side of the table, he wouldn't want to accommodate a suspect's requests, however reasonable they might be. She took a deep breath and laid her hands flat on the table. 'Right. Nothing will come from this station. We'll keep everything quiet here. I have a good team and they'll do what I say. Now, can we please see what's in the damn folder? Let us know what we're looking at.'

There followed an excruciating few minutes while the two officers flicked through the file. 'Well, everything appears to be in order,' Peterson said. 'We'll also need to seize your phone and any computers in your home and business. Can we arrange a time for our technical officers to come round and collect them?'

'No,' Rob Haines said simply. He glanced at Malone who nodded at him to continue. 'My business is as a private investigator. The very nature of that means that my most valuable asset is the trust my clients have in me. I have thousands of photos on there, some that are of a sensitive nature. People come to me to investigate cheating spouses and thieving employers. I'm sure you understand that without a warrant, there's no way that you're seizing any computer equipment.'

'What my client means to say is that while he's willing to co-operate, he has certain business commitments that means he is unable to hand over any material that may compromise that business. You will see in the folder a waiver so that you can check with StringCan's servers to ensure this is a complete and true record of the conversation you're interested in.'

The two officers nodded to each other. 'Well, we'll review this and find enough to get a warrant. We will need to check other devices to see if you switched to a different channel to have a more personal conversation. I think that's about as far as we can go today.' But then Astor pointed at an entry on the page. The two officers leant their heads together and whispered.

Malone raised his voice. 'There's no point in taping proceedings if you're going to whisper.' Pointedly he leaned towards the microphone. 'Officers Astor and Peterson are having a whispered conversation.'

'Fine,' Peterson said sharply. 'We haven't been able to contact Amelia Bagshaw yet. It appears that she's hiding from us.' She tapped the transcript. 'And it also appears that, if you read the last message you sent, it was you who warned her off. Interfering with our investigation.'

Malone leant forward and read through his own copy of transcript. 'I think that if you read it carefully, my client simply informed the other party of events that had, in fact, taken place. I'm reading this and I can't see any instruction to flee, or delete messages, or in any other way interfere with your investigation.'

DI Peterson opened another folder and ran her finger down a list of actions. 'Yes, but the course of events clearly shows that my officers visited Mr Haines, then he phoned to tell me that I shouldn't contact the other party, and when that didn't work, he sent the message. That shows quite clear intent, to me.'

'It's all circumstantial,' Malone countered. 'I think you

need something more solid if you're really going after perverting the course of justice.'

The two officers looked at each other. 'Well, we can put this to one side for now,' DI Peterson said. 'But you'd better hope that Amelia shows up sooner rather than later.' She picked up the file from Rob Haines. 'We'll look through this and be back in touch. Please don't do anything stupid in the meantime, we'll need to know where to find you.'

Rob considered what had just happened. When he'd been on the other side of the table, he wouldn't have rolled over quite so easily. He might have told Amelia something that was true, but it was still sharing details of an ongoing investigation with someone in that investigation. His only conclusion was that they were still treating him softly, letting him out with enough rope so that he could incriminate himself later.

Rob briefly considered telling them that as he hadn't been arrested, then he was free to go where he liked. But he didn't want them to think that he was becoming hostile. More than that, he felt beaten down. He'd been taken through a system that treated him like a criminal. And all he wanted now was to get out of there and start feeling like himself again.

CHAPTER THIRTY-FIVE

'PETE, I wish you could find some weird computer trick to untangle all of this and point to the killer. You've done it before.' Emma and Pete were entangled on the sofa in her house. It had been a long day in the office, with the third body and no further ideas as to who the killer was. They'd eaten and were ignoring the TV which was turned down low in the corner.

'Well, tell me what you've got and we'll see.'

'We've got three murder victims, all undeniably killed by the same person, but aside from that, there isn't really any other link between them.'

'Go on, then, tell me, there must be an overlap somewhere.'

Emma was annoyed by his confidence. He hadn't spent two weeks bashing his head against the brick wall of this case. She laid out the facts as some sort of challenge to him. 'Well, two victims are linked, the first and third. One was a drug dealer who was just a few years out of Bradwick High. And the other was a teacher from the same school who got caught with a hidden camera in the girls' changing room. He was just a few months out of prison. From the looks of it, he was teaching at the school while victim one was in year seven, then he got arrested over the summer holidays.'

'There you go then!' Pete said excitedly. 'You can make up one list of people who were in school when the dodgy teacher was there, and another of people who were there at the same time as your drug dealer. Start with everyone who knew them, even down to cleaners and support staff.'

'But that'd be two lists with hundreds of people on each.'

Pete shrugged. 'Spreadsheets don't care. You can put in thousands of names if you can find them.' He was starting to get animated now. 'It'd be a start. You can then start to cross people off as your investigation progresses. Eventually you'll get a handful of people that occur on both lists.'

Emma nodded. 'And then we can start to investigate those people.' She shook her head. 'But then we've got our second victim. A local GP, who's by all accounts a well loved and respected member of the community. Hard working, mother of three and no reason to be on either list.'

Pete frowned. 'And it's medical so you can't get the names of all her patients and make a third list.'

'It's worse than that. You'd have to factor in everyone who worked at the surgery. And she did other voluntary stuff like running help groups and various community initiatives. The only plus side is that she doesn't seem to have had much of a social life.' She stopped and shook her head. 'I mean, the other two, we can't really run down the drug dealer's contacts. People won't admit to knowing him. It's been a slog trying to build up a picture of his socials. At least the paedophile who's fresh out of prison for a few months has a really restricted social life.'

'I could still line up the three lists if you want,' Pete offered. 'All three victims are local to Bradwick, so that's where to start. If we start with the first two victims, then we can add their addresses to each list. Then, without a warrant and without any confidentiality issues we should be able to get a catchment area for whichever surgery she worked from.'

Emma nodded excitedly. 'It was the medical centre on Logan Road that she worked from. I've already had a brief look, but the problem is that the area for Bradwick High is most of the town, and the one for the surgery fits completely inside it. And there were another three doctors at that surgery, so we'll only have a one in four chance that there is a link.'

'But, it will be a start. If you put the details over to me tomorrow, then I'll be able to make a start.'

'Thanks, babe!' She was still thinking about the conversation she'd had with Rob Haines. 'Do you know anything more about geographical profiling? I mean, we've got the catchment areas, where the GP worked, the car park the dealer was working out of, the address of the paedophile. That's a lot of data points.'

Pete took a deep breath. He ran a hand through his hair. 'OK, on one level, you could go on courses, that run for days and days. Or you could spend a fortune trying to find a geographical profiling analyst who'd run it for you and give you a big report at the end of it.'

Emma squirmed round to look at him. 'I know what you're like. You've thought of an alternative.'

'Well, you could just put a map up in the incident room and stick coloured pins in it. You know, one colour for crime scenes, one for workplaces, one for home addresses. See what leaps out.'

Emma frowned. 'You know what, that does raise a point. Victim one was killed at his workplace, if you want to call it that. Where he dealt from. Two was killed on her way from work to home and then three was killed at home.' She stopped for a second. 'No idea what it means.'

'It means you're working too hard. Are you in tomorrow?'

'Yeah, active investigations don't stop for two days over the weekend.'

'In that case, go to bed now.'

'Now that I like the sound of.'

CHAPTER THIRTY-SIX

The following afternoon Emma had only just finished her lunch of a slightly stale canteen sandwich and yet another cup of coffee. The caffeine was starting to make her feel jittery and she knew she should slow down. But since she'd stood on Benjamin Scott's doorstep yesterday morning, she had been working flat out. Door to door enquiries had been arranged with the uniforms, a deep dive into the victim's past was underway, and a start had been made on downloading available CCTV. And while all of this was going on, forensic reports had been uploaded to the system. That all this had happened over a weekend, with associated overtime, showed how seriously this case was being taken.

Now Emma's boss, DI Michelle Jones had called an update meeting. She strode to the front of the open area and waved at the board. 'Right, we've got to a place we never wanted to be. We now have three victims. It's hard to see any link between them, the ages and gender have a widespread. As do the professions and personal lives. Even the actual crimes have a different feel to them.' She indicated the three photographs. 'Hawsley, the first victim, was almost clinical.

One stab wound to the abdomen, then the blade dragged sideways and left where he fell. Then we have the second victim, Dr Donnelly. She was dragged out of sight, stabbed once, and laid beneath a tree. No evisceration and the body was quite clearly placed. And now we've got Benjamin Scott. A lot more violence here, obviously some sort of fight or something happened before he went back to what he knows – a deep stab wound followed by evisceration. Any thoughts on what this means? Is it a pattern or an escalation?'

There was silence around the room as everyone considered the new information. Finally Nick Dent broke the silence. 'Maybe Ben Scott fought back?' When everyone turned to face him, he continued. 'I mean, look at it this way. Bill Hawsley, he's stoned, it's late in the night, he's just chilling outside his car, smoking a blunt, waiting for the next drug deal. Our killer approaches, maybe from behind or maybe as a potential customer. Either way, he's not on his guard. Before he knows it, he's got a deep stab wound in his abdomen. His blood pressure is dropping, he's in pain, he'll be on the ground. Likewise, our second victim. She's walking home from work and our killer grabs her from behind. Maybe he even stabs her at the same time. But it's the same pattern, he surprises his victim and they're stabbed before they can even react. Neither of them were in any way trained or expecting to defend themselves.'

Emma nodded and picked up the thread. 'But our third victim is going to be paranoid. I can't imagine what his life was like. Living in that dump, knowing that anyone who knew his past would hate him. Being a paedophile makes you someone it's socially acceptable to victimise and bully.'

'Exactly,' Nick said. 'And so, when someone knocks on the door, he's going to be keyed up already. If I were him, I'd half be expecting someone to be pouring petrol through the letterbox. Or something worse. So, this time our killer can't just surprise him.'

'It does look like overkill, even considering that,' Michelle Jones said. 'He could've subdued him with a couple of blows, or stabbed him straight off. But there's a lot of damage. It looks like rage.'

'We'll have to wait for forensics,' Nick said. 'We might get lucky. What if our victim actually injured the killer? That would account for the rage. A kind of swapping of the roles. He goes around there, hoping to kill a victim and suddenly he's the one being attacked.'

There were nods around the room. Michelle said, 'That would explain it, especially if that then angered him and he got carried away. But we have no way of knowing. I like this theory because it explains the three different methodologies, but I think we'll have to leave this open until we get more information.

'Now, I've assigned actions and updated the computer. There'll be a lot of information coming in today. We've still got uniforms doing door-to-door enquiries, and scene of crimes are wrapping as we speak. We've dragged Dani in on a Sunday and she should be finishing up the post-mortem. Emma, could you go over and liaise with her and see what she can tell us?'

EMMA WAS BACK in the morgue. The first time she'd come down here, she'd found it gloomy and depressing. She had succumbed to the stereotype of the department in the basement of the hospital. But as she got to know the pathologist, Dani Price, she started feeling warmer towards the place. Dani expressed a caring attitude towards the dead that ended up on her table. She genuinely cared for those for whom she could carry out a final service.

Now Dani held out an evidence bag to Emma. 'This is your link between all three deaths.' Inside the bag was a large, silver coin. Emma looked at it and saw a third different football team – this time it was Sunderland.

'Well, I hope to God our killer's not trying to complete the set.'

'There's a set?'

'Yeah, it's the centenary of the Football Association. There's a big boxed set that you can get to put them all in. Thirty of the bloody things.'

Dani Price's eyes widened and her face paled. 'And you don't think he's going to do all thirty, do you?'

'We have no idea what he's doing at the moment. There seems to be some vigilante aspect, but I can't imagine he'd kill thirty people.' She sighed and pushed the hair back off her face. 'To be honest we just don't know what the deal with coins is, except that they've turned up at all three scenes.' There was another pause. 'Is there anything else we need to know?'

'Yes, this was a lot messier. The first stab wound was the deepest. He probably knocked on the door, and then rushed in, knife first. But it then looks like Mr Scott here didn't go down quietly. He has some defensive wounds on his arms and bruising on his knuckles. But that first cut would've resulted in some heavy blood loss. I doubt he was able to fight back for any meaningful length of time. Once he had fallen to the floor, then our killer started dragging the knife sideways. He made some in and out, sawing motions. And then, when he had him opened up, he stuffed the coin inside.' She shook her head. 'I'll tell you one more thing for free though. He's no professional. I've had all the training on how to open someone up, look through the organs, but this guy, he wouldn't even make it as a butcher. Horrible work.'

'OK,' Emma grimaced. 'Now we've got three, do we think it's the same weapon?'

Dani Price frowned and thought for a moment. 'It's certainly possible.' She nodded as she recalled the details of both cases. 'In both cases the wounds were caused by a long knife, probably sharp on both sides. And sharp enough to do some real damage.'

'So, like a dagger or stiletto?'

'No, much longer. Based on my estimates and examination of the wound track I'd say you're looking nearer the range 200 to 250 millimetres.'

Emma thought for a minute, trying to imagine the size of the knife. 'That's the length of the blade?'

'Yep.'

'That's almost a small sword, it'd be huge.'

'Well, the wound was deep, so that fits. Once you find the knife, I'd lay good money that it hasn't been cleaned properly. The tech boys will be able to take it apart and find some DNA.'

Emma nodded. 'So, we're looking for a long thin knife, something like a bayonet or a small sword?'

'Yep. And if you find it, then I'm sure we'll be able nail the killer.' She paused, looking uncertain.

'What Dani? Listen if you've got some weird theory, then tell me. It might help us and we don't have to write it up unless it becomes useful.'

'OK. This one was a lot more violent, you already know this, there were multiple stab wounds and abrasions. But if you look really closely, you can see that the final cut where he opened him up is much more ragged than the previous two. There is more tearing and it looks like he was almost sawing to try and get through it. I mean, this guy has obviously never trained even in a butchers or abattoir, but this job is far rougher than the previous two.'

Emma frowned. 'What do you think that means?'

'I have a theory. Maybe the blade was homemade? I don't know the specifics, but it might be that there wasn't enough tempering or hardening on the blade. If I'm right, then it might have been blunted in the initial attacks and not be good enough for the final cut.'

Emma nodded. 'It might even be an improvised weapon or something that's been sharpened?'

'Possibly. 3D printed even? But the wounds point to something with a proper blade down at least one edge.' She shook her head. 'Anyway, whatever caused the wounds, I hope you catch them soon. I don't want any more of the victims in my lab.'

'That's what we all want. Thanks for the information, I have a feeling it'll come in useful.'

CHAPTER THIRTY-SEVEN

Sitting at home watching TV on mute, Rob Haines turned his phone over in his hands. He hadn't realised until now how much he'd become invested in chatting with Amelia. He felt a little guilty, but he knew deep down that he treasured his relationship with his girls. Not that they were girls anymore, they were women now, with their own lives, careers, relationships. He'd done it, he had raised two decent human beings. He had achieved the end goal of parenting, or at least this phase of it.

But that sense of completion, that sense of having been there and done that, did leave a void. He'd done his job too well and now they didn't need him. And he'd filled that gap in his life with Amelia. She had been his chance to do things again, to correct the mistakes that he'd made. Or so he'd thought.

Something about his interview at the police headquarters had been nagging at him. Rather than spend the evening at a loose end he called Emma to pick her brains.

'Rob? This had better be good. We've gone up to three bodies now, it's late on Sunday evening and I'll be back in early tomorrow.'

'Sorry, I forgot what it's like when you're in the middle of an investigation.'

There was a slight pause while Emma assessed the few words that had been spoken. Rob had been through a lot since she'd first met him. And he'd always faced things head on. But now he sounded, for want of a better word, defeated.

'No, I'm sorry,' she said, adopting a softer tone. 'Listen, I think we might finally be getting enough evidence to make some real progress. Anyway, what's up with you? Why did you phone?'

'Oh, nothing really. Just, you know...'

'Rob. Something must have made you call me.'

She decided to turn his tactics on him and keep silent till he spoke.

'You know this mentoring that I've been involved in with a local teenager?'

'Mentoring? Is that what you're calling it? I thought you would've knocked it on the head by now.'

'Well, I'm calling it what it is.' He paused, now unsure about his gut feelings and whether he should trust Emma.

'OK. I'm sorry, that was a low blow. I really shouldn't have said anything.' Now it was her turn to pause. Rob wasn't going to make it easy. 'Listen, my head is spinning and I can't really focus on the phone. Can we do this face to face?'

There was a pause. 'I've got a bad feeling about this whole case. Can I come over there?'

'No, one of my housemates is on earlies.'

'Ah, well Jem has couple of friends over for a bit of a girly chat tonight, so here's out.'

There was another pause, then Emma said, 'Seafront by the all-night shop that sells coffee?'

'Yep, first one there buys the coffee?'

Emma gathered her stuff together and persuaded her car

to start. By the time she was driving down the seafront, she saw Rob's car already parked, nose facing out towards the sea. She parked next to him, then went to join him in his car. She figured she might as well be comfortable if she was going to help Rob.

He handed her a coffee and they settled back, looking out over the water. Lights from the harbour moved on the surface and the whole scene would have been serene if she couldn't remember where she'd found bodies. Somewhere out there were the three dark shapes of the islands in the bay, and she'd attended a body recovery on one of them.

'So, what about your mentoring thing with that girl? What's going on there?' She tried hard to drag herself back to the present.

'Her name is Amelia or Amy. Well, the boys in Bristol, at headquarters, have raked me over the coals. It seems the conversation was flagged up on a computer somewhere. Anyway, now that she's missing, I'm just worried about her is all.'

Emma went silent. Although Rob had only spoken a few sentences, there was a lot for her to unpack. In the end, she went for the big one, the elephant in the room. 'Wait a minute. Why have headquarters called you in? Which department was it? How deep are you in trouble?'

Rob breathed in and sighed loudly. 'It's not me I'm worried about, it's Amy.' He turned around and caught her expression. He wouldn't be allowed to carry on until he'd made some further explanation. 'All right, I'll tell you, but I want it kept quiet. They won some court case with the makers of the messaging app we've been using, StringCan. The specialist grooming unit in Bristol got a list of conversations between older men and younger girls. Obviously someone saw my name and thought they'd have a go at the bent ex-copper who's been talking to a teenage girl. It's all something and nothing. I've got a lawyer and I'm co-operating fully. They'll find nothing because there's nothing to find.'

Emma knew that plenty of times the police could be like a dog with a bone. Just because there was nothing to find didn't meant that they would drop the case. 'Oh my God! Did they arrest you?'

'No, they doorstepped me, tried to strong arm me into giving up my rights. That didn't work, so then I arranged to meet them the next day with my lawyer. Like I said, that side of it is all in hand. It's Amy that I'm worried about.'

'Go on then, I'm not going to be able to dissuade you. What are your concerns?'

'Well, I've already told you what the father is like. I'm worried about how controlling he is, how she doesn't have any access to the internet or her own phone. Can you see where this is heading?'

'No, my brain is foggy and full of this ongoing case. Spell it out, would you?'

'Well, the obvious next step, once they'd spoken to me, would be to go to her parents and arrange to interview her. Apparently she's only thirteen, so they'd need an appropriate adult present. But those adults don't even know that she's got a phone, never mind that she's been messaging me with it.' He paused for a moment. 'I'm just worried that I'm responsible for Amelia going missing. I warned her that the police may try to talk to her parents about her phone. Now, either she got my message and ran or her father found out and did something.'

'Hmm. I do see what you mean.' Emma thought fast. There wasn't a huge amount that she could do about this right away. There was a chance that something had happened. 'What did they say during the interview? Had they been able to talk to Amelia?'

Rob closed his eyes for a moment, reliving the interview. 'No, they sounded quite concerned. I don't think they'd been able to talk to her.'

'And she's already been reported in as a missing person. All the usual things have happened, all uniformed officers have a description, all hospitals have been checked, and the databases have been updated. I've asked to be kept in the loop so I'll know as soon as things change. All that means it's far more likely that she got your warning and ran, than that she came to harm at the hands of her father.'

'Thank you.' Rob fell silent, looking out at the darkness. He shook his head. 'I don't know. My gut tells me that something is going to happen. Might be domestic violence, or underage drinking, or shoplifting. It feels like this investigation in Bristol has set something in motion. I just have no idea what's going to happen next.'

CHAPTER THIRTY-EIGHT

For the first time in his life, ex-DCI Robert Haines was in handcuffs in the back of an unmarked police car. He was being driven at speed up the M5 towards police headquarters in Bristol.

'You could at least take the cuffs off,' Rob said, looking out the window at the landscape speeding past. 'It's not as if I can go anywhere.'

'I see, because you're an ex-cop, you think you get special treatment?' DC Astor practically sneered at him. 'You should remember the regulations regarding the correct transfer of prisoners.'

There was a long, uncomfortable pause. Finally Rob said, 'And what was all that with the arrest and cuffs in front of my wife? I've co-operated fully so far.'

'Listen, you don't get to pull that special treatment ex-cop bullshit on me. Cops like you make all our lives harder. For every one bent cop, there are one or two hundred who are struggling. We get it harder because the public don't trust us, because they figure if one is bent, who knows how many others are? So, no, I don't like you and no, you aren't getting any ex-job special treatment.'

'I wasn't that bad! It's not like I was just lining my own nest or using my badge to stalk women,' Rob protested. 'I kept the town safe and my men happy. I did good.'

For the first time, PC Clovis joined in. 'You just don't get it, do you? Sometimes the ends don't justify the means. And it's not up to us to pick and choose which laws and regulations we follow. It's all or nothing. We have to be better than all of them out there.'

The rest of the journey passed in sullen silence.

Finally, they arrived and Rob passed through the indignity of processing, before having his cuffs removed and being shown to an interview suite. He was numbly aware that he was now on the other side of the table and all the cameras and attention were focused on him.

Once again, DI Peterson took the lead. 'I'll get straight to the point, where is Amelia Bagshaw?'

'I don't know.'

'You are aware that we've searched your house and your office? We'll get to the truth eventually.'

'And that truth is that I don't know where she is and had nothing to do with her disappearance.'

'Oh, but that's not 100% the truth is it?' Ruth Peterson sounded sly. 'I mean, you warned her that we'd be investigating. So, you did have a bearing on her disappearance.'

Rob took a deep breath and tried to calm his anger. A distant part of his brain was telling him that this was an interview strategy – keep correcting him, keep him off balance. But that part was getting harder and harder to listen to after the day he'd just had. 'I had legitimate concerns for her welfare, concerns that I passed on to your team. When it became clear that you weren't going to act on them, I did warn her what was coming.'

'Ah yes, when you tried to interfere with my investigation and protect your relationship with Amelia from further scrutiny.'

'Her father is dangerous.' Rob slapped the table with his hand. 'Oh, I know he looks great on paper, local schoolteacher, active in the community, all that bollocks. But underneath it all, he's one of those people who looks fine until they just snap and we're left picking up the bodies.'

Rob had tried watching modern, American influenced police programs and hated them. Usually he'd have no truck with psychology or profilers. And he sure as hell wasn't going to start categorising people as different kinds of murders. But the words "family annihilator" did cross his mind, not that he'd ever say them out loud.

'You seem quite worked up about Mr Bagshaw. Is that what led you to target Amelia in the first place?'

'Target? Target! How fucking stupid are you? I've given you the transcripts. She came to me. I thought I could help!' He stopped before he said anything he might regret.

'No need to get upset, Rob, we're just trying to get to the truth and find Amelia.'

'In that case, why don't you go through the evidence? You've had me arrested for two hours already. I assume you've searched everything under PACE?' There was no answer so he ploughed on. 'I have never met Amelia. I don't know where she is. You'll find no evidence of her at my house or my office because she was never there! I don't have any allotment sheds or lock-ups! You're going to find nothing because there is nothing to find!'

Ruth Peterson frowned. 'Why did you mention allotment sheds and lock-ups? Is that where you've hidden her?'

'Oh, for fuck's sake! No. I have not hidden her anywhere. I've never met her. When are you going to get that through your head? All the time you're pissing around in here, trying to get me to admit to something that never happened, Amelia is out there somewhere, scared and alone and you're doing fuck all to find her.'

An awkward silence fell over the room. The two officers looked at each other, trying to decide the next approach. Before they could say anything, there was a knock on the door and the solicitor entered.

'Joseph Malone has entered the room,' Ruth Peterson said for the tape.

'Thanks to Mr Haines shouting, I've heard the main gist of things from the corridor. May I ask Detective Inspector Peterson, whether you have found any evidence at all connecting my client to the missing person case of Amelia Bagshaw?'

'Well, we have his communications over the StringCan app.'

Malone waved his hand. 'They were all prior to her going missing. And you've been furnished with full transcripts and access to the messages several days ago. I presume that you've had the chance to review them and find nothing suspicious? Let me be a bit clearer. Following Mr Haines' arrest and the subsequent PACE searches, have you uncovered any further evidence linking my client to Amelia Bagshaw and her disappearance?'

The two police officers looked at each other. Finally Peterson spoke. 'No, to date we have not uncovered any evidence linking your client with Amelia Bagshaw.'

'And I'd assume that you've been very diligent as there's a missing girl and every minute counts. For the tape, DI Peterson nodded. So, it seems that your arrest of my client has served its purpose. You have interviewed him and searched his premises and found nothing that suggests he has any involvement in this matter. Is that correct?'

'We still have the right to hold him for twenty-four hours,' DI Peterson said.

'Of course you do,' Malone said graciously. 'But you've had days to go through the transcripts and hours to conduct searches on my client's property. Do you really think that the next twenty hours are going to magically throw up some new evidence?' There was silence so he continued. 'My client has been nothing but co-operative with you. He owns his home, and has family and his own business in Bradwick. There's no indication whatsoever that he's a flight risk. If you do find anything further, then you can re-arrest him.

'But in the meantime, I'd guess you've found all you're going to find. And my client has been nothing but co-operative with you, so far. And, given your insistence that he's in some way a corrupt officer, despite there being no evidence, it could be viewed as, ah, slightly vindictive on your part.'

'Listen, we have arrested your client on suspicion of child abduction. That is, as I'm sure you're aware, a serious offence. We need to exercise due diligence. If that appears as vindictive, well, I can assure you that it isn't. We have the simple facts that your client was in contact with a teenager, and since we started investigating, that teenage girl has disappeared. We will investigate -' DI Peterson was interrupted by short rap at the door, followed by a young man opening it and leaning into the room. 'DC Bryan has just entered the room.'

Rob Haines and Joseph Malone looked at each other. Rob knew from experience that a DC wouldn't interrupt an interview unless it was urgent. He just hoped that Amelia was all right.

'Sorry, boss, but I've got some new information.'

'Well, can't it wait? Can't you see I'm in the middle of an interview?'

'It is relevant, ma'am.' DC Bryan looked pointedly at Rob Haines. 'If I could have a quick word? Outside?'

DI Peterson rolled her eyes and said, 'Interview suspended at fourteen thirty-seven.' She left the room.

Rob and Joseph looked at each other and Rob shrugged. PC Clovis was still in the room so they didn't really want to say anything. No one could tell if it was good or bad news. Soon one minute turned into five. Obviously the quick word was getting more involved.

Finally, a harassed DI Ruth Peterson swept back into the room. She switched on the tape to briefly announce that the interview was terminated and then turned to Rob Haines. 'Much as it pains me to say so, you're now free to go.'

'May I ask why? Ten minutes you were all set to string me up for child abduction.'

'New information has come to light. It's become clear that Amelia was not abducted.' She paused, sizing up her opponent. 'In fact, she was last seen alive while you were in here conducting a voluntary interview.'

Rob nodded, not trusting himself to say anything at all. He stood up, and with his solicitor, left the room. He couldn't get out of the station fast enough.

CHAPTER THIRTY-NINE

A LARGE PART of being a police officer was knowing who to talk to and when. DC Emma Angel sat at her desk on Monday morning, and drank her coffee. She'd worked straight across the weekend and knew she'd be powering through the day on caffeine. But she hadn't forgotten her late night conversation with Rob Haines, or the favour he'd asked of her.

The first priority was to go through the missing person's report and see what progress had been made. She read the logs of the initial phone call and the interview when they'd called at the house. The language was very careful, but it was clear that something wasn't right. She knew that if anything went wrong then this report would be part of the enquiry, so it was clear that the officers who attended were cautious in what they wrote down.

Emma made the phone call and after being passed around a few times, learned that PC Kate Davis, who'd conducted the initial interview, was currently patrolling the town centre. Emma needed both to get out of the office, and to have a candid conversation to uncover the truth.

Although the weather was still grim, it was good to be out

of the office. She found PC Davis in the pedestrian part of the town centre, working on her own. 'Can I have a quick chat about that missing person report you carried out the interview for on Saturday?'

'Of course, shall we grab a coffee? Have you heard any news?'

'Nothing yet,' Emma said. They walked together to a coffee shop. Emma treated Kate to coffee and a muffin and they sat on the stools so they could keep an eye on the street outside.

'So, why is CID investigating a missing person?'

Emma like the fact that Kate came straight to the point. 'Well, it's come up as incidental to another investigation we've got on at the moment. But when I came to read the report, well, it didn't quite seem to be the whole story.'

Kate looked to each side, then back at Emma. 'What do you mean? I put down everything I needed to in the report. You can check with my sarge, we worked on that together.'

'I'm sorry, I'm tired and that came out all wrong. I'm not accusing you of writing a bad report or anything like that. I just wanted to talk to you like this because it seemed a little odd. Like maybe there were things going on that you didn't want to commit to paper? I thought if I spoke with you I could get a feel for how it went.'

There was a pause. Emma was happy to sip her coffee and wait. Finally, Kate said, 'You're right. I mean, this job you see a lot of weird stuff, it's just what happens. But that was a really weird morning.

'First of all, the mother, Sharon Bagshaw, tried to stop anyone from calling round. Her daughter went off to school on Friday morning, left at ten past three, and then hasn't been seen since. She only calls it in the next morning, and even then it's like it's no big deal. Anyway, she was really nervous, didn't really want to co-operate. Kept on worrying about what everyone would think.'

'And what about the husband? How was he?'

'Thomas Bagshaw? Luckily my sarge dealt with him. If you can believe it, he was in a shed at the end of the garden. Carrying out some sort of woodworking as a hobby. He wasn't happy at being disturbed and again was much more concerned about how it would look like than actually finding his daughter safe and sound. He was absolutely insistent that we didn't put anything out on social media.' She shook her head. 'That's usually the best way to get traction. But he didn't want any publicity. Between you and me, it would have been a really big help. Amelia is a pretty girl, from a middle-class family, the press would've made a big splash.'

Emma nodded without saying anything. She didn't trust herself to say what she really thought about the press and their prejudiced views on which missing children were worth helping.

'I mean, you could ask your boss about the media,' Kate said uncertainly. 'You don't always need the parents' permission.'

'You're right. It is possible, just as it's possible that it might leak out anyway. But, it's a nuclear option. At the moment it's probably best to maintain a good relationship with the family. If we go against their wishes, well, it all becomes much more difficult.' Kate nodded her agreement. 'But we'll bear it in mind, for the future. This chat has been really helpful though. I'm sorry we got off on the wrong foot, this should definitely help us build up a picture of what we're dealing with.'

They said their goodbyes and Emma returned to the station. When she was at her desk, she called up the report, and carried on reading through to the end. Amelia's phone was a big problem; they hadn't managed to get a warrant to trace it, because it was unclear who owned the phone and who the SIM was registered to. The last action was more hopeful though. Officers had gone round to talk to Sara Frost, Amelia's best friend. Initially she'd stuck to her story and claimed to last see Amelia when they left school on the Friday afternoon.

But, when the officers left the Frost home, Sara had rushed out to talk to them. The officers' doubts about talking to a minor without her parents present were recorded. But ultimately they decided that Sara wasn't a suspect and the most important thing was getting Amelia home safely.

Emma read the report and learned that Amelia had stayed Friday night with Sara and had been well equipped when she left Saturday morning. She blew out a big breath of relief. This one piece of information turned the entire case around. Amelia hadn't come to harm at the hands of her father, but rather had decided that living rough was better than being at home.

It wasn't a great result. Emma wasn't sure at this point what a good result would look like. If Amelia was found, there'd be a battle to keep her out of the clutches of her father. But it was a move forward, in a good direction. It was also something that Rob needed to know, to allay his fears that he'd done the wrong thing.

Twenty minutes later, Emma was worried. She was looking at her phone and wondering where the hell Rob had gone. Both his personal and work mobiles were switched off, and his receptionist confirmed he wasn't at the office where his agency was based. She knew that Rob didn't go out in the field, so she was at a loss to explain where he was.

She had one chance left, so she phoned his home landline, amazed that he still had one. The phone barely rang before Jem picked up.

'Hi, it's Emma, I'm after Rob.'

'Emma! Thank God you've phoned. Can you help?'

'Jem, what's wrong?' Emma could hear the panic in the older woman's voice.

'Rob's been arrested. I mean, Rob of all people. Arrested!'

'OK, I can sort it out. Who arrested him and what for?'

'Well, it was some detectives from Bristol and they were saying some nonsense about child abduction or something. I mean, I know he's a bloody fool but how can they think he's abducted a child? It's Rob, you know. He's given his professional life to the police.'

'Jem. It's okay. Well, it's not okay, but I know what's going on. I think I can help here. Listen, it will work out all right.'

'Really? It'll be all right?'

'I think so. Give me half an hour and I'll see what I can do.'

'Emma, don't hang up yet.' There was a pause, as Jem gathered her thoughts. 'I wanted to ask you about Rob.'

'What about him?'

'Well, you're his friend. I wondered what you made of all this with the girl and everything?'

'In what sense? I mean, I trust him totally, I know he wouldn't, well, you know. He just wouldn't.'

'No, it's not that.' She paused again, then the words rushed out. 'It's just that you hear these cases where someone has a bang on the head and suddenly they're taking risks or gambling away the mortgage or even just talking in a funny accent. You know the kind of thing. I'm just worried that this might be the beginning of something.'

Emma was exhausted but she tried to get her thoughts in order. Recently it seemed that defendants were using any excuse from autism to a brain tumour to dodge their responsibility for their actions. She was, like many police, sceptical. 'I don't think it's that bad. When the thing with the faces came up, I did a bit of research into brain injuries. The Rob I know now is the same person as I knew before the injury. I don't think his personality has changed, do you?'

'No. If it's daytime and I'm being rational, he's still my Rob.'

'But I do think this was a reckless, even foolhardy thing to do. It might be worth checking in with his GP or whoever is managing him. I only read a few articles, but it is possible that his impulse control has changed. He might not be thinking through every possible outcome of his actions before he carries them out.'

'That does make sense.' Jem sounded relieved. 'I mean, it's still something I'll have to keep an eye out for, but it's not as bad as I imagined.'

'Listen, I know you're worried sick with Rob arrested and all. But if you let me go and make another phone call I think it can all be fixed.'

Emma hung up and dialled through to the child protection team in Bristol. As she suspected, she got through to another detective constable. They exchanged names and ranks.

'I'm in the CID department here in Bradwick and I'm looking into the missing person case of Amelia Bagshaw. I'm given to understand that you also have an interest in Amelia in connection with a grooming case.'

'Yes. Do you have any new information?'

'I do. It's recently come to light that her best friend hid her on the first night and sent her off on Saturday morning with spare clothes and money.'

'Okay, that does change things.'

'You might want to tell your boss, before he does something that might embarrass him.'

'I can't interrupt her, she's busy interviewing a suspect.'

'But if that interview is for child abduction, then this new information proves that she wasn't abducted. She's just missing. Your boss would want to know that before the interview goes too far.'

'How did you know–'

'I'll let you go now and sort it out,' Emma said briskly before hanging up.

Emma sat and looked at her phone. She'd acted rashly, out of a desire to protect her friend, Rob Haines. Now she had to face the reality of what she'd just done with her boss. Not only her boss, but a former adversary who'd worked for the professional standards department.

No, she thought, she'd done the right thing. When a teenage girl was missing for this length of time, then it was only right that CID get involved. And as they already had her father as a suspect, then it was logical that the case would land with their team. As for warning Bristol, then she'd just put that down to being zealous about the rules. They were meant to co-ordinate with other departments, and that was just what she'd done.

She hoped that the last part of the conversation wasn't ever repeated, but she could simply deny that she'd said it. Or that she didn't precisely recall what had been said.

Either way, she really needed to get to the bottom of what was going on with the Bagshaw family.

CHAPTER FORTY

'Thank God you're here.' Jem was obviously worried as she opened the door to Emma, later that evening. 'Thank you for coming over so quickly, I hope I didn't interrupt anything.' Emma shook her head. 'Maybe you can get some sense out of Rob. He's just sitting in his snug, drinking whisky. I haven't got more than two words at a time out of him. I think this arrest has really shaken him. I mean, he's been through a lot in his career, but to be arrested? And for child abduction? It's the first time he's been on the other side of the table. It's not like anything he's experienced before.'

'It's all right. I hope I was able to fix things with the people in Bristol?'

'Yeah, I don't know what magic you did, but he got home mid-afternoon. Apparently he's been released without charge.' She looked scared and uncertain at the direction her life had taken in the last few days. 'Well, you'd better come in and see what you can do. He said he'll talk to you.'

Emma went in and found Rob sitting in his favourite armchair with a cut crystal glass of whisky. She nodded at the bottle, which was a twenty-year-old single malt. 'Onto the expensive stuff already?'

He gave a weird lopsided smile. 'It has definitely been that kind of day.'

She settled into the chair next to him and poured herself a small measure of the whisky, noticing that it was sealed with a proper cork.

'You want to take that slowly. It's the good stuff. If you're not used to it, put some ice in it.' He gestured to a bowl of ice cubes.

She did as she was told, listening to the crack as they hit the alcohol. She took a small sip and felt the heat on her lips and tongue. She'd drunk whisky before, but mostly cheap blended stuff at parties. This was much smoother and easier to swallow. She was grateful she didn't really like the taste, as it was far too easy to drink. As she sipped slowly Rob relayed the details of his day.

'So...' Emma spoke slowly as she tried to get her head around what Rob was telling her. 'So, you've been arrested for child abduction? Or do they suspect you of grooming a child?'

'That is true. But I don't get what they're playing at. I mean, she contacted me first and they know that. Apparently though, she was last seen alive while I was in there giving a voluntary statement on Saturday morning. So, I think everything will be fine. I haven't done anything wrong, I've co-operated fully and hopefully I've kept a lid on it.'

Emma quickly filled him in on what the latest was in the missing person case. He nodded as he realised how she'd got him out of trouble in Bristol.

'Listen,' Emma said. 'I know you're innocent, I really don't believe that you did anything wrong.' She thought, maybe stupid and ill considered, but not wrong. But she knew better than to actually say anything out loud. 'But you know what cops are like. They have a fixed idea and they'll do anything to prove it's true.'

'Well, let's just hope they don't do that this time.'

Emma nodded her agreement.

'We may have a problem,' Rob said. Emma noticed the use of "we" but again she chose not to say anything. 'The child I've been mentoring, Amelia Bagshaw, I told her that the police were investigating.'

'You did what? I'm surprised that they let you out at all. Perverting the course of justice.'

'I had to.' He took a breath. 'You can see that, can't you?'

'Yeah. I mean, if we're right about the father, then we can't even imagine what would have happened if he'd learned that she had a phone. I do see that.'

'I still think that the Bagshaw family are key to all this,' Rob said.

'I know what you said, but we're going to need some solid evidence. I picked up your tip on the helpline and ran with it. The problem is Michelle Jones. You know better than I do that she's used to sniffing out when things aren't what they appear and I have a feeling she's onto us.'

'You think she knows that tip came from me? How much does she know?'

'Don't panic. If she knew, you'd have more troubles than just Bristol. I think she suspects something, but at the moment, it's giving good results so she's letting it go. But I don't think she's forgiven you yet for slipping through her clutches. The problem with Thomas Bagshaw is that he is a pillar of the community. School teacher, does charity work, happily married with kids. I hate to say it, but it might be easier if he was that weird loner that none of the neighbours knew.'

'Did he intersect with any of the victims?'

'Again, it's a case of yes and no.' Emma paused a minute to gather her thoughts. 'He did teach at the same time as Ben Scott and he was also there at the same time as Bill Hawsley. And he's in the catchment area for the GP surgery. But there's no proof that he had any kind of connection with any of them. I mean, there's a thousand pupils at the school, give or take, and over a hundred staff. We have no information that he had any kind of special interaction with any of our victims. For all we can find out, he might never have even spoken to them.'

Rob ran his hand over his head. He would've run his fingers through his hair, but he'd kept it shaved short since the injury that had ended his career. 'I hate this. We're so close but so far. It's one thing to suspect who the killer might be, but without proof there's no warrant and no charges and no justice.'

'Yeah,' Emma said wearily. 'It's always been that way. There are some cases where you know what happened but you don't ever get to prove it.' She yawned, not bothering to try and hide it. 'I'd love to sit here, drinking expensive whisky and spouting philosophy about how shitty the job is but I've got to try to get some sleep before I get back to it tomorrow.'

CHAPTER FORTY-ONE

DC Emma Angel sat down in the cafe with the teacher from Bradwick High. She looked younger and trendier than Emma expected. Somehow she always imagined teachers to be the same as she'd viewed them when she was a child. They should be older and fustier and wearing frumpy clothes with thick glasses and bad haircuts. But she had to accept that most teachers were now closer to her generation than any other.

She'd gone to Rob's aunt, Bea Matthews, who had been headteacher of Bradwick High for several decades before she retired. Bea had set up this meeting with a teacher who'd been at Bradwick High long enough to have known both Scott and Hawsley. So, Emma thought, revising her opinion, Sandra Green must be at least in her thirties.

'So, Bea said that I might be able to help?'

'We've got an ongoing complex enquiry and it seems that some of the people involved are connected with Bradwick High. I wondered if I could have an informal opinion from you about a few people?' said Emma as they sipped their coffees. She briefly wondered exactly how much time she spent in coffee shops interviewing people.

'I'll see what I can do. Who do you want to know about?'

'Well, let's start with Ben Scott? Do you remember him?'

Sandra chuckled softly. 'We could hardly forget that name! I was an NQT – a newly qualified teacher,' she added when she saw Emma's blank look. 'So, obviously I didn't want to say anything, you know, being new, not just in the school, but in the job. I knew Ben was weird. No one would want to sit next to him in the staff room.' She looked a bit rueful. 'I mean, now, after MeToo and everything, I'd say something. But at the time, we just let him continue and assumed someone else would say something.'

'I've read the report on his arrest. It started with parental complaints and spiralled from there.'

Sandra nodded. 'Yes. A group of the year seven girls got together and five of them persuaded their parents to complain at the same time. The school couldn't ignore it.'

'Right. Did anyone stick out as being particularly upset? Someone who might have held a grudge while he was in prison and wait for him to come out?'

Sandra blew out a breath. 'Not really. I mean, don't get me wrong, he wasn't a popular man. And when he got out, I couldn't believe that he came back here. There'd be a long list of people who didn't like him. Not just one name I could put to the top.'

'OK, so let's move on to William Hawsley.'

'Name doesn't ring a bell.'

'He left four years ago.' Emma corrected herself. 'Well, from what we've got he didn't do much of year ten and was definitely gone by year eleven. So you probably would've seen him five or six years ago.'

Sandra shook her head. 'If he was troubled, then he would've been scooped up by The Centre.' Again, she had to explain. 'It's kind of a catch-all for special needs, troubled children, difficult backgrounds, attendance issues – all that kind of thing. He might have been put into a small provision or a reduced timetable to try to get him back to full time attendance.'

Emma thought about what she knew of Bill Hawsley and imagined that all the efforts would have been wasted on him. Still, she had one more card to play and it was the one she really wanted answered. But she also knew she'd have to be quite careful about how she framed it.

'There's one more name that I wanted to run past you, but it's a bit more delicate. We need to know about someone who still works at Bradwick High.'

'Okay. I'll probably be a bit limited in what I can tell you, but sure, try me.'

'What can you tell me about Thomas Bagshaw?'

'What do you want to know?' Sandra brushed her hair back out of her eyes.

'Just some background really. His name has come up in an investigation, tangentially at best. But we do want to know what kind of a person he is.'

The teacher took a deep breath and blew it out. 'That's one hell of a big question. Well, he's hard working and generous with his time. I take it you know the basics, he's a design and technology teacher. But before they changed all the names he'd be a woodwork teacher. That's what he always wanted to be. And, you know how many hours teachers work? Well, on top of all that, he's the school caretaker.'

'Is that a second job? Is he hard up?'

The teacher shook his head. 'As far as I know, he volunteers. I mean, I know we have a maintenance team and for bigger things we can go to council services. But that takes requisition forms and then it goes onto a job list and sometimes it can take a week or two. If it's a small job, it's just easier to ask Thomas. Any door that sticks, or if a desk is wonky, or a window leaks, just let him know and he fixes it. And that's not all. I heard that he's got a workshop at home. He makes lots of those wooden toys and simple jigsaws and things.'

'And what does he do with them?'

'He goes round selling them at school fetes and boot fairs. Again, he's very generous. He donates all the money to PTA funds. Doesn't even claim expenses. I mean, he could quite easily, you know. Just for the raw materials. That would be reasonable.'

'And the wider Bagshaw family? Sharon and Amelia. What do you know?'

'Well, that's a tricky one. I need to tread carefully on several fronts. Thomas has been a teacher here longer than me and obviously his daughter Amelia is a pupil at the school. So, I'm not entirely sure how much I'll be able to say.'

'Well, nothing you say will be on the record. I don't even need to take notes. I just want to fill in the background.'

'Well, as I said, Thomas Bagshaw is a good teacher. And both his daughters have gone through school.'

'We know very little about Amelia's older sister,' Emma said. It had been mentioned in the missing person report that Amelia might go to stay with her sister, but so far there had been no success in tracing her.

'Yes, Sophie, a few years ahead of Amelia.'

'What do you know about her? We haven't got much information from either parent.'

Sandra sipped her coffee. 'That's surprising. I always get the feeling that Thomas is very protective of his daughters. Maybe she found him too smothering.'

'Was that how Thomas was around his daughters in school then?' Emma asked.

'Listen, it's always going to be awkward when you have a teacher and their child in school. I've seen it a few times. Usually they choose to keep it professional, you know. They don't teach their own kid, try to keep their distance, just act like pupil and teacher if they have to interact while at school.'

'But Thomas Bagshaw didn't do that?'

'No, Amelia and Sophie liked to go down to the far end of the playing fields but Thomas would make sure he was on playground duty and watched them as much as he could.' She paused again, still weighing her words carefully. 'There are also rumours around the classroom. Thomas is very particular about teaching. You should see his technology rooms. All the tools are lined up, everything just so.'

'Well, surely that's what you want, isn't it? Especially in a technology environment.'

'Yes, up to a point. But there's been more than one teaching assistant in tears after he's gone off the deep end because they wouldn't follow his precise instructions. Between that and him following his girls around, I'm just glad that I'm not one of his daughters. Why do you want to know this? Surely you don't think he's involved somehow do you?'

'We don't know. He was teaching here at the same time as Benjamin Scott. And he would've taught William Hawsley. But Hawsley only overlapped with Scott when he was in year seven.'

'Yes, and although Scott was interested in that age range...' she stopped, unsure what to say.

'We know he was interested in girls. And obviously Amelia is too young to have been there at the time.'

'But Sophie was the right age, although we never heard anything about her being a victim of Ben Scott's.

'Right,' Emma said. She suddenly found the whole subject a bit depressing.

'Well, Sandra, thank you for your insights. It's certainly filled in a lot of the background for us.' They left the coffee shop together, Emma heading back to the station to check if there had been any progress in the search for Sophie.

CHAPTER FORTY-TWO

Rob looked at his phone for what must have been the hundredth time. He switched it into standby, then woke it up again. But nothing had changed. The message was still there. Three words but they contained a huge challenge to him, and to all he believed in.

Can we meet?

The first feeling that washed over him was relief. Ever since Rob had found two police officers on his doorstep, he'd been worried about Amelia. He knew that Thomas Bagshaw was dangerous, and his daughter had defied him, broken one of his most important rules. And, while he knew that Amelia was probably safe for now, it was an uncertain safety. It wasn't just the police that were searching for her. Rob was certain that Thomas Bagshaw was currently looking for his missing daughter. And he knew that nothing good would happen if her father found her first.

But she had made contact. She was definitely still alive.

Now he was faced with a dilemma. If he did the right thing, reported it in to the police, then there was a problem. The first action for the missing person team would be to inform the parents that she was still alive and had been found. Which would deliver her straight into the hands of her father. Who would already know that not only had she defied him and got a phone, but she'd also run away from home.

On the other hand, he could keep quiet and manage the situation himself. He'd done enough shady things in his career to last more than his lifetime. He wasn't sure he could square his conscience with the idea of knowing something about a vulnerable missing teenager and not acting on it.

Then his mind swung back the other way. Everything he'd done in his career had been to keep people safe. Either the whole town or individuals, he'd always worked to keep them safe. And if that was the case, then there was only one choice he could make. The safest thing he could do for Amelia was to keep her away from her father.

He was painfully aware that it was a temporary solution. She was only thirteen, so there was no way she could stay on the run for the next three years, then move out. Something would have to be worked out further down the line.

His main hope was that the police would find enough evidence to lock Thomas up before Amelia came home. Which exposed him to the other problem caused by his decision. If he chose to run this on his own, to keep the meeting secret, then he'd be keeping a mother away from her daughter. A woman who was currently living with a vindictive, controlling man.

He shook his head. Whatever he chose, someone would be hurt. So he did the only thing he felt he could and reached for the phone to arrange a meeting.

CHAPTER FORTY-THREE

ROB NERVOUSLY ENTERED the fast-food restaurant and looked around. He had justified his actions to himself so far, but he knew the further he was going, the deeper in trouble he was getting. He had arranged to meet Amelia here at eleven thirty in the morning. His plan, such as it was, was to persuade both Amelia and her mother to move to a domestic violence shelter. He thought the first step would be to talk to Amelia and get her to see that it would be a good idea. Then, he could ask Emma to talk to Sharon and persuade her to go to the shelter so she could be with Amelia. It was a plan full of holes, one of which was getting Amelia's mother alone.

As they'd never met, he was looking for a teenage girl in an orange hoodie. He was grateful because that meant he didn't have to explain his face-blindness to someone he'd never met. He went into the garish plastic restaurant and scanned all the tables. There was only one person in orange, and she was a teenage girl. He suppressed a smile. There was no doubt now that the police were right and she had lied. There was no way she could pass for fifteen. But then again, what teenager hadn't pretended to be older by a couple years? He'd done it himself in pubs and off licences in an age before the internet, smartphones and messaging apps.

He nodded at Amelia and then bought a meal at the counter, upgrading everything to large.

'I'm guessing you're Amelia?' She nodded. 'And I also guessed you'd be hungry.' He sat down facing her. She was in a corner, so he could look over her shoulder at half the car park, and she could see the other half past him. He pushed the tray over to her.

'Thanks.' She pushed her hood back. She had black hair tied back in a ponytail. This was the struggle with Rob's condition. He could see that she had a slightly small nose, hazel eyes and a dimple in her chin. But somehow he couldn't put the pieces together and he certainly couldn't recall those features and assign them to Amelia in his memory.

She took the tray and gave Rob a look that was caught between gratitude and her natural surliness. 'At least you look a bit like the photo on your website. Robert Haines, ex chief inspector of Bradwick police.' She waved her phone in the air. 'Never had one of these before, it's amazing what you can find.'

Rob nodded. 'You do know that there's a missing person's report out on you?'

'So, what are you going to do? Phone me in?'

Rob chewed his bottom lip. 'I should do. Your family is worried about you.'

'My family?' She laughed. 'You can't really mean that, can you? I suppose my dad might be worried about how it'd look, what people would say. But I can't imagine he's too happy about all the fuss. Admitting that he's lost another one of his girls.'

Rob nodded. 'You're right about that. It was your mother who called it in.'

Her eyebrows shot up. 'Oh! I really didn't think she'd ever stand up to him. All I ever get is how much she loves him and that no one should come between a husband and a wife.'

'Well, maybe she does care for you. She is your mother after all.'

She fell silent, considering this fact. 'So it's all my fault? Mum's going to get hell from Dad. And if you make me go back, then it'll be a living nightmare. I can't stay there for years till I'm able to escape.'

Escape, Rob thought, there's that word again. Escape. Amelia was talking as she was in a prison. Before he could figure out how to respond, Amelia was asking him a question.

'So, have you decided what you're going to do yet? Call it in? How much head start will you give me?'

'I still haven't decided. I'm enough of a company man, enough of an ex-copper to report it sooner or later. I get that you don't want to go back, but what's your long game? Have you considered going to a shelter?'

'I don't know. Could I even do that? On my own?'

Rob shook his head. 'Probably not. But I have contacts that could try and talk your mother round. If she goes to a shelter, we can find one where you could stay together.'

'Yeah, I can't see that happening. She's totally brainwashed. Just keeps on banging on about the importance of keeping a marriage going, how I don't understand.'

'Well, you could give us a chance to talk to her. See if it is an idea that will float or not.'

There was a pause as Amelia took a big bite of her burger, then shovelled in some fries. As she ate, Amelia stared out of the window at the car park. 'I just feel like there are no options. Nowhere left to go. Can't stay homeless forever, can't go back.'

Rob saw a flash of yellow and blue over Amelia's shoulder. A police car pulled into the car park. 'They must have got a warrant to track your phone,' he said. 'The police are here, and that's the only way they could get here so quickly. Better keep it off from now on. Only switch it on when you need it.'

She swivelled round to check on the police car that was driving slowly as if they were scanning the car park. When she turned back, her eyes suddenly widened. 'Oh shit! It's worse, my father is out there too. That blue Vauxhall is his car.'

'Do you think the police called him?'

'No, I was stupid.' She looked around. 'This is my favourite Maccy Ds. Whenever he was in a good mood, Dad would take me here. I'm out of here.'

She pushed her seat back, grabbed her burger in its paper and nearly ran to the toilet. Rob twisted around to see what had spooked her. He was just in time to see a man slam the door of a blue Vauxhall shut and start walking purposefully towards the restaurant. He flicked his gaze back to the toilets, but there was no sign of Amelia.

Although it went completely against the grain, Rob decided to leave and run from the police. He chucked his food away, stacked his tray and left. As he did, a man came into the restaurant with his head lowered like a bull about to charge. He looked straight at Rob with narrowed eyes as they passed in the doorway. Rob estimated that he was just under six foot, so he probably had a couple of inches on him. And the stranger had a normal build so Rob probably also outweighed him by a couple of stone. The man, presumably Mr Bagshaw, made a similar calculation. He cut his gaze away from Rob and pushed his way into the restaurant and started scanning the tables. None of the other patrons seemed to have noticed anything.

Outside the restaurant, he saw the police car approaching and driving past his car. He didn't want to draw attention to himself, so he walked around the side of the restaurant and away from the police. It felt alien to be actually fleeing from the police, but he needed time to work out what to do.

He should phone it in. But he didn't want to. He had never run from a fight in his life but he knew he'd get turned inside out by the missing persons team. He'd have to make a statement. He'd have to admit how he knew Amelia. And then, when they'd finished with him, the department in Bristol would start. None of it would look good. He was screwed and he knew it.

As he walked, he tried to be rational. If he was in the police, what would he do? He'd go into the MacDonalds and ask if anyone had seen anything. Then, when they'd established that Amelia had been there, they'd seize CCTV. So, he knew he had, at best, a couple of hours before his world came to an end.

The only option was to get in front of the problem as best he could. If he walked to the police station from here, then he could be making his statement before they even looked at the CCTV. That would make the best of a bad job.

He knew the way, so he allowed his feet to find the route and started to plan what he would say. After walking for nearly ten minutes, he took a short cut through a residential street that came out to a small roundabout with a short row of shops. He saw a man hanging around outside the betting shop. Over twenty years of being a police officer gave him an instinct that made Rob look twice.

But he had forgotten that his natural ability had changed so that he was unable to recognise faces. Sure, the man was just under six foot tall with sandy brown hair. But he couldn't tell much else. He fell back on his usual tricks – the man was wearing smart grey trousers and a dark blue fabric jacket. Rob was sure he'd be able to tell if this man was following him.

Something about the man had spooked him, so he decided to see how it'd play out. He continued on his way, down to a footpath that was a short cut to the main road. In his peripheral vision, the man who'd been waiting and watching outside the betting shop was now moving and on a route parallel with Rob's.

Rob Haines had never taken the taken the time to train in martial arts like Emma Angel and learn fighting skills. But he had over thirty years of policing experience and that counted for a lot. His entire career had been full of people getting physical and him knowing how to deal with them. So, when the stranger got closer, he already knew that an attack was about to happen.

The man tried to barge into Rob but he swung his left arm to block him and pivoted so instead of crashing directly into him, the man rolled off and stumbled to the side, slightly behind Rob. The ex-cop kept swivelling and the two people faced off to each other.

Something dark was in the attacker's right hand and he jabbed forward with it. Rob was expecting it and danced to side as he came closer. He felt a slight tug as the point of the knife slid across his jacket. His opponent had a big advantage because the knife gave him both more reach and the chance to do fatal damage very easily. So there were two things to do, neutralise the extra reach, and then get away.

As soon as the knife was past his body, Rob went against all his instincts and moved forward. It was clumsy and badly done, but Rob managed to step so that his foot was the other side of his attacker's ankle. He then used the only advantage he had, his size, and body checked him. With his balance off, the attacker stumbled and sat down with a thump.

Rob didn't stop or slow down. He simply carried on moving, jumped over the man and ran as fast as he could. He couldn't face off against someone who was both armed and younger than him. He recognised this and ran away.

Rob wished that he could arrest him, get the cuffs on and use his radio to call in support, but those days were gone. He still missed having his kit and the backup. After a few steps, he became aware of a sensation of cold air on his arm. Following that sensation, a burning started in his left arm. He looked down and saw that his jacket was ripped open and there was a long deep gash down the outside of his arm. Now he'd seen it, the pain tripled. Blood was now welling out and starting to drip off his fingers. He felt faint, partly from the pain and partly from the knowledge of how deep the cut was. He'd been lucky and used the outside of his arm to block so none of the major blood vessels had been damaged. So far, the blood was welling up, and running down into his hand. He was lucky that it wasn't spurting out as it would if an artery had been cut.

As he ran, he became aware of a scratch on his side. He looked down, and saw that he'd been nicked by the knife. His shirt was completely ruined but the cut didn't look deep, certainly not as bad as his arm.

Without really thinking what he was doing, his legs were moving towards the main road. The blood was flowing over his hand now and he tried to raise it up to slow the blood but the pain wouldn't go away. He made it to the main road and stopped for a minute to rest. He put out a hand to rest on a lamp post.

He was lucky and was resting right outside a large pharmacy. A matronly woman came out and asked if he was all right. When she saw he wasn't, she steered him into the consultation room. He heard her call out, "Chantelle! Call the ambulance. I'll try to stop the bleeding in here."

Rob put his head back against the wall and let his eyes close.

CHAPTER FORTY-FOUR

EMMA SAT IN THE OFFICE, looking out of the window. This close to Christmas, it was dark by late afternoon, and the window was just a black rectangle, streaked with drops of rain.

After two weeks of making no progress on the case, there was now a sense of urgency in the department. There were three victims that weren't linked, but Emma couldn't shake the feeling that somehow the Bagshaws were at the heart of the case.

Her reverie was disturbed by Michelle Jones calling Suse Berman and John Fletcher into her office. Emma and Nick, left alone, looked at each other, obviously thinking the same thing – that this had a definite sense of being called in to see the headmaster.

They both carried on working, occasionally glancing at their three colleagues through the blinds on the window, trying to figure out what was going on, but there was nothing obvious to give them a hint. About ten minutes into the meeting, they heard Michelle's desk phone ring. She picked it up with a frown, and spoke for less than a minute. Then she opened the door and beckoned Emma into the room. Nick looked around with a slightly panic-stricken air, as if he might be next.

'Emma, come in, I'm just about finished with John.' She paused, and thought for a moment. 'Actually, stay here a moment. I know what police station gossip is like. Let me fill you both in now so at least your get the facts straight.' She called Suse and John back into the open plan office.

'Suse was checking over the socials on our latest murder victim, Ben Scott. Obviously, considering who he was, there was a lot about him online – when he was released, where he might be staying. I'm sure you can imagine without me going into details...' Emma glanced over at Nick, wondering where this was going. 'Anyway, Suse started going through the posts, trying to see if anyone was getting worked up enough to act on the information and kill Mr Scott. Unfortunately she found that several of the posts were shared by John Fletcher.' She paused to glance at the trainee detective constable who awkwardly stared at the ground, as Emma and Nick struggled and failed not to show their shock.

'We have no reason to believe that he had any involvement in the death, and all the sites he shared were reputable news articles, not the more aggressive vigilante ones. For those reasons, rather than suspend him, I've told John to go home now, and when he comes back in the morning he's on desk duty with strict instructions to stay away from the Scott case while I decide what to do next. In the meantime, Emma please come into my office so we can have a word.'

When Emma and Michelle Jones were both seated, Michelle steepled her fingers, deep in thought. Finally she said, 'Have you heard from your friend Rob Haines recently?'

Emma considered the question carefully. She remembered the earlier comment about station gossip, and knew that her boss wouldn't ask a question unless she knew the answer already. 'I have been talking to him recently. He's been mentoring a teenage girl and the child protection team in Bristol have got the wrong end of the stick. I understand he hasn't been charged, but there's been a lot of pressure.'

'And you've taken an interest in the missing persons case of the same girl?'

'Yes,' Emma said, deciding that it was time to lay all the cards on the table and trust her boss. 'Rob has a gut instinct that's telling him that something is up with the whole family, especially the father. It was him who phoned it through to the tip line and that's why I followed it up.' She studied DI Jones' face and saw no reason to stop. 'Anyway, that's why Thomas Bagshaw is a suspect in our murder investigation. Unfortunately, everything is circumstantial at best, although there are tenuous connections between him, his family, and the victims, but I thought it was worth a look. Especially now that his daughter's gone missing.'

There was a long pause as Michelle digested this new information. Finally, she spoke. 'There have been some troubling developments. It may be that Rob is right, I would certainly be a fool to ignore his instincts after so many years in the police. Either way, he remains our best chance to either find this missing girl, or to put away this killer. I want you to stay working with him and get what information you can.'

One question immediately arose in Emma's mind. Before she could consider the wisdom of it, she asked, 'What about conflict of interest? You've just benched John for something far more minor.'

'I don't know John, but I do know you. That drug raid where you and Rob first came to my attention, you made the call. You turned your boss in because you knew he was breaking the rules. I haven't forgotten that. I know that if push comes to shove, then you'll do the same thing again. If Rob Haines is breaking any laws, I expect you to come straight to me with it. But in the meantime, something very odd is going on and it's centred around the Bagshaw family. And Rob probably knows more about it than anyone in this department.'

Emma picked up on a couple of things that her boss had said. 'What exactly has happened, ma'am? What are the developments?'

'First of all, I want to reassure you that Rob is okay, but he is in hospital.' When Emma started to speak, she held up a hand and carried on speaking. 'We got the authorisation through to track the phone that Amelia Bagshaw is using. She powered it on this morning, and was moving around a lot. But then she stayed stationary for a while in the McDonalds out on the industrial estate. So we sent a couple of uniforms over but she bolted and we lost her.' She paused and sighed. 'But, when we went back over the CCTV, we found that she was meeting Rob there. He left the estate and went into a residential area and out of CCTV range. We don't know precisely what happened, but obviously he was attacked, which is why he's now in hospital.'

'Is he okay? What are his injuries?'

'He's been stabbed, but it seems to be superficial.' She considered her next words, staring out at the rain for a moment. 'I know Rob Haines was a rogue officer and left under a cloud. But I won't have someone in Bradwick who's attacking fellow police officers, whether or not they're still serving and however they left.' Michelle paused again. 'What's particularly interesting is that Rob was walking on the shortest route from the restaurant to this station when it happened.'

‘So he might have been about to report it in?’ Emma couldn’t keep the hope out of her voice.

‘Maybe. But he had his phone on him, so he could have called it. He’s not exactly coming across as the good guy here. And we don’t know for definite where he was going or why he left his car at the restaurant. I want you to visit him in hospital, find out what he knows. Don’t worry about formal statements, I’ll get someone from uniform to do the paperwork. You’re there as a friend.’

‘And to report back?’

‘Obviously. This is your job.’

CHAPTER FORTY-FIVE

Emma found Rob in a side cubicle in the A&E department of Bradwick Hospital. He looked absolutely fine to her, although it was odd to see him with his shirt off wearing a hospital smock. Jem was there already, twisting a Hawaiian shirt in her hands. She saw Emma looking and said, 'Oh, this. Yes, Rob needs something short sleeved that buttons up and this was the first thing I found.'

Emma nodded. Before she could say anything, a uniformed officer poked his head through the curtain. 'Oh, I didn't realise that CID were here already,' he said. He was tall and thin, with a mop of dark hair.

'I'm here because I know Rob. Why don't you take the statement now and I'll listen in?'

Jem stood up and put the shirt down. 'It's going to get crowded in here. I saw a Costa in the foyer, so I'll go and find a decent coffee. I'll bring one back for you, Rob.' She leaned over and gave him a peck on the lips before going leaving them to it.

The officer was efficient, asking all the right questions. Rob's answers were comprehensive, but he made it sound as if it was a random attack, possibly a mugging gone wrong. The uniformed officer took a description.

'And, if you want to pop into the station, we can get an e-fit made up. Someone like this is probably a regular mugger, so this'll help us catch him.'

There was an awkward pause. 'I'd rather not, if that's all the same,' Rob said stiffly.

Emma decided to come to the rescue. 'Did you not get a good look at his face?'

'No,' Rob said. 'He was kind of turned away from me as he barged into me. It was all so quick, I honestly didn't see his face at all. It'd just be a waste of time and resources to do an e-fit.'

'Well, if you're sure, sir,' the officer said. There was an awkward pause.

Rob regained his wits first. 'It's all right, she knows as well,' he said to the officer. 'Before I was attacked, I met with Amelia Bagshaw who's currently a missing person. I'm guessing you know, because uniformed officers turned up and spooked her. And you've had enough time now to run down the CCTV and see me buying her a meal.'

'Right you are then, sir. And would you care to tell us why you met with a misper without thinking to inform us in advance? Don't you think her parents have a right to know?'

Rob took a deep breath, partly to gather his thoughts, but mainly so he didn't get too angry at the officer. 'As I'm sure you know, the reason Amelia is missing is because she's scared of her father. So while the parents have a right to know, I was in two minds about whether or not to let her father know where she was.' The officer opened his mouth, but Rob cut him off. 'I didn't contact uniform immediately, because I wanted to see how she was. I wanted to assess the situation before making a decision. Given that you all turned up with a marked car and high-viz jackets, I think that was a good decision. She was already a scared teenager, and seeing the police in the car park made her run.'

'I didn't make the operational decision -'

'I know, son,' Rob cut him off. He'd been a senior detective for years and knew how to intimidate people. 'Write this down. You've got CCTV so you know where she was and when. She looks okay, I fed her a warm meal. There's no sign of injury or coercion. All in all, I'd say she's coping at the moment. We discussed the possibility of getting her and her mother into a shelter away from her father. But I didn't get a chance to find out how she felt about that.'

'Thank you for that, I'll pass it on,' the officer said stiffly. 'About the shelter, has any formal approach been made yet to her mother, or any suitable shelters?'

'No, I thought I'd start with Amelia and see how she felt about it. Getting her mother alone might be harder. And victims of domestic abuse are notoriously difficult to convince that a shelter might be best.'

The officer nodded curtly and left the cubicle. Alone in with Rob, Emma took the opportunity to ask, 'What's the real story? I know you well enough that you're keeping something back.'

'Well, first of all thank you for covering for me.' Rob looked sheepish. 'They've given me some pain killers for the arm. I'm a bit slower than usual.'

'Not slow enough to give half a story to the uniformed officer who just left.'

'You always were sharp.'

'So, enough stalling,' Emma said. 'What are you hiding?'

'Before I tell you, I need something back. I've fucked up and need to know how deeply I'm in trouble.'

Emma closed her eyes and tried to navigate between her

friendship with Rob and her instructions from her boss. 'I don't think there's actually anything they can arrest you for yet,' she said. 'The good news is that you've managed to put the Bagshaws firmly on my DI's radar.'

'Michelle Jones?' Rob asked, the distaste obvious on his face.

'She's not that bad,' Emma said. 'She's not gunning for you just yet. She wants to make sure Amelia is safe and catch this killer. And she thinks you can help with that.'

'That all sounds very noble,' he said. 'But I bet she wouldn't hesitate if there was a chance to nail me into the bargain.'

Emma decided that she'd never bridge the gap between her former and current boss, and it'd be pointless to try.

'I think I know who stabbed me.' Rob looked slightly shifty. 'Or rather, it could be one of two people.'

'You're sure?'

'Well, I can make a logical guess. But I'll never be one hundred percent certain because, well, you know...' He tapped the side of his head. 'One thing I didn't tell that officer is that Amelia thought she saw her father in the car park and that spooked her just before the police showed up.'

'And the reason you withheld this was?'

'I don't know. I have a bad feeling about him. And the fact he showed up at the same time as the police? I can see that he was probably cruising around, checking out Amelia's usual favourite places, saw the police car and decided to turn in. But, on the other hand, it might be more than coincidence.'

Emma nodded slowly. 'Do you think Thomas Bagshaw actually saw you?'

'I think so. We were sitting in a corner, with those big windows on each side so we could keep an eye on the car park. Of course, that meant that anyone could see us. I cleared my table and left pretty smartly as I didn't want to hang around. But when I left, there was an angry man coming in. He could easily have been Amelia's father, storming in there to catch her.' He shrugged.

'And then, later? I mean, I know you can't be sure, but what do you think? Was that the same man who stabbed you?'

'The person who attacked me was the same height and build as her father. The hair and the general build were the same.' He shrugged. 'I don't know. It's not impossible. He had enough time to back to his car and drive round to where I was attacked. It's not like one was a short white guy and the other was a tall Black guy. They were close enough that they could've been the same person.' He paused, deciding how much else to say. 'The problem is that Amelia's father isn't the only one who could've attacked me.'

'You said there were two possibilities. Who's the other one?'

'Do you remember me telling you about Mr Church?' Emma nodded. 'Well, he's no longer a client of the agency. It wasn't exactly what you'd call an amicable parting of the ways.'

'How bad was it? I remember you telling me that you were worried about him and his wife. Do you still think you were enabling him to stalk her?'

'Kind of. The wife, Nancy, spotted Ed while he was carrying out surveillance. She even knew that he'd been sent by her husband and told Ed that she was planning to leave.' He shook his head as he recalled the final scenes. 'Mr Church got aggressive when we told him that it was all over. Started threatening all sorts. Unfortunately Ed told him what Nancy had said. I do still worry about her. He's got a hair trigger temper. I swear he would've swung for me if Ed hadn't been there.'

Emma thought it over. Two ex-police officers in a confined space would be hard to take on. But if he'd seen Rob on his own, and he'd had a knife, he could have tackled him by surprise from behind. It simply confirmed her theory that most bullies were, at heart, cowards. Not the sort to attack someone head on.

'So, this Mr Church could be the one who attacked you?'

'Maybe. I think it's worth warning Ed, just be on the safe side.' He thought for a moment. 'But on balance, I think it's more likely that Mr Bagshaw was the one who attacked me.'

'Why is that?'

'Basic police work. You hear hoof beats, and you think horses, not zebras. Amelia had literally seen him less than twenty minutes before my attack. And he was all riled up because of his daughter and he saw me as a direct threat to his family.'

Emma nodded. 'The timeline makes sense. I mean, you were seen talking to his teenage missing daughter. He might have suspected that you abducted her.'

'Hey! You make me sound like some sort of creep who deserved to get stabbed.'

'Well, you said it, not me!'

There was a brief pause. Before either could fill it, Jem came back into the room and handed Rob his coffee. She caught the look between Rob and Emma. 'What? Still talking shop?'

'Not shop,' Rob said. 'We were talking about Amelia, but Emma still thinks that I look like a creep because I'm trying to help a troubled girl, so she wasn't sure what to say in front of you.'

'Yeah,' Jem said, sounding resigned. 'I think he's an idealistic fool. I mean, I get it. Our children were privileged in the way they grew up with us. And I get that he misses the experience and wants to help those who weren't as privileged. Add in a big helping of both empty nest syndrome, and the end of his job serving the community and you get a stupid decision. I mean, I understand why he did it, but at the end of the day, it doesn't look good.'

CHAPTER FORTY-SIX

THE FOLLOWING DAY, Rob opened his door to find two white women there, both blonde and younger than him, one taller than the other. Emma had called to say she was coming round, so he guessed she was the shorter one, on the left. He frowned at the other woman the one with her blonde hair tied back. She was taller than Emma, but Rob had no idea who she was. He looked at Emma with a question in his eyes.

'Oh, God, yes, sorry. Rob, this is Dani Price, the pathologist.'

'Hi, Dani, sorry. I had a bang on the head and...' he trailed off. 'Yes, Dani. Hi, of course I know you. Come on in!'

'Yes, of course. I've heard about this face blindness but, you know, you read these things in books and papers, but to actually meet someone–' She stopped suddenly, her excitement overtaken by courtesy. 'Oh. I'm sorry. That was tactless of me.'

'You know what's strange,' Rob said. 'As soon as I heard your voice, with your accent, I knew exactly who you were. It was like all of the pieces just fell into place.'

Dani nodded and they went into the kitchen. While Rob made the coffees, Emma asked how he was feeling.

'Tired more than anything. It took forever to get discharged with all the right painkillers and antibiotics. But at least they didn't keep me in and I could sleep in my own bed. Of course, I've got dressings on my arm and side, so it was tricky to get comfortable. Not that I'm ungrateful, it could've been so much worse.' He looked at both women in his kitchen. 'What brings you round here? It's business hours and you haven't brought flowers.'

It was Emma who answered the question. 'We were talking around the case this morning. And we're aware that this is all speculative, but if you believe that Thomas Bagshaw is our killer, and you think he might also be the person who attacked you... '

'... then he was definitely trying to kill me,' Rob finished the sentence for her.

'I wouldn't have been that blunt,' Emma said with a smile. 'But that's the main thrust of it.'

'And you brought the pathologist with you to see if there's any evidence in my arm.' He shook his head. 'It was cleaned out and stitched and the A&E was busy. No evidence was kept.'

'It's not that,' Dani said. 'I've seen the wound profile from the three bodies, so if I could have a look at your arm, I might be able to tell if it was a similar weapon. Or, if not that, I might at least be able to rule it out as a possibility.'

'I don't mean to be rude, Dani, but are you OK to be working on a, well, you know, someone alive?' He was cradling his injured arm in his good one protectively.

Dani laughed. 'Oh yes. I've got my medical degree. Pathology is just my speciality. But I did all the training, rotations through the specialities, all that.' She frowned theatrically. 'It was quite a while ago though. It'll be a nice to work on a live subject for a change! I just hope I haven't forgotten too much.' She winked at Emma. She went over to the kitchen sink and scrubbed her hands. 'Right, if you would lay your arm here on the kitchen table, I'll have a look at it.'

With care, she unpeeled the dressing from his arm and angled her phone-torch so she could see. 'Of course, it's harder because it's been stitched together. Quite neatly, the nurse did a good job. But I can't actually get in there and poke around.' She turned her head the other way and peered closely at the wound. 'Well, it could be the same. It's another long straight cut so that figures. There are no marks at the edges, no puckering or anything, so that's the same. It means that the blade wasn't serrated.' She nodded thoughtfully and said, 'It really easily could be the same. We don't have a deep wound here, so we can't judge the length, but the way it went along the arm, the fact that it's smooth, it all looks as if it's the same weapon.'

'So, let's just follow this train of thought through to its logical conclusion,' suggested Emma. 'Rob, you met Amelia yesterday at McDonald's and she ran when she saw her father in the car park. Then, less than an hour later someone, who has the same physical build, rough age and hair style of her father stabs you.'

Rob nodded. 'That's all pretty much true. But you have to remember there is another possible suspect so it's still only fifty-fifty.' He ignored the look of surprise on Dani's face.

'But Amelia has a theory that her father, Tom Bagshaw is the killer. If all of our reasoning so far is right, then what Dani's just said corroborates that.'

Rob said, with surprising calmness, 'You mean that Tom was trying to kill me, using the same knife that he already used to kill three other people?'

'To be blunt, yes,' Emma said. 'You might have been victim number four.'

Emma sat down at the table and put her chin in her hands. 'There is just one small problem.'

'None of it is admissible in court?' Rob asked.

'None of it is even strong enough to get an arrest warrant.' She held up her hands and started ticking points off on her fingers. 'Amelia identified that man as her father, but we can't get to Amelia as she's still missing.'

'And even if she was here,' Rob said, 'I have no idea if we could get a thirteen-year-old to testify against her own father. We'd have to get deep into social services before we even started the interview with her. And she doesn't have a smoking gun, just some vague suspicions.'

'And then,' Emma said, folding down another finger, 'you can't identify your attacker as the same person who was at the restaurant.'

'If you're looking for problems,' Dani added, 'then the knife isn't strong. I mean, it looks like the same one, but there are no distinctive features. It's not definite proof. The only way you'd get that is if you actually found the weapon. If it had blood on it that could be DNA matched to Rob, and the other victims, and a fingerprint back to this Bagshaw fellow, well, then, you might stand a chance.'

'And without something definitive on the knife, we can't link back from the man who stabbed you to the three other murders.' Emma looked shocked for a moment. 'It's catch twenty-two. If he'd succeeded he'd have left a coin for us to find. But then we wouldn't have you here telling us about the link to Amelia.'

'In all honesty, Emma, we have strong suspicions. My gut tells me that this is the right theory. But we have zero proof.' He shook his head.

Emma laid her head down on the table.

'I know I'm not an active officer anymore. I'm not your boss or anything. But I do know how to play this.' He sighed. 'I don't like Michelle Jones. She nearly brought me down and cost me my pension. But, all that aside, I still think that she is a good cop. You've said this is all on her radar and it sounds like she's willing to let you run with it. Work with her, apply pressure wherever you can on the Bagshaws and I'm sure you'll get the proof you need.'

Emma raised her head and sighed. 'Right then. We'll start off with some deep background. Even a vague hint of a motive would go a long way to helping this case. I'll head back to the office now and we'll see which rocks we can turn over and what's underneath them.'

CHAPTER FORTY-SEVEN

When Emma got home after a frustrating afternoon at the office digging into the Bagshaw family, she wanted nothing more than a quick shower and to fall into bed, but her thoughts wouldn't stop swirling around the murders. It was more likely that the same person had committed the murders and then attacked Rob than it was that two people were going around stabbing people.

And if that was true, then it meant that the killer, Thomas Bagshaw or not, was off balance. Attacking a former police officer in broad daylight wasn't a careful, considered act. To Emma it smacked of desperation. The best thing that CID could do now was to keep up the pressure, force more mistakes and arrest this person as soon as possible. She certainly needed him off the streets before anyone else got hurt.

Since late afternoon, Lukas had been alternating calls and texts. She knew he had a problem, but she couldn't break her concentration on the case. She felt bad, but she'd been deep into work and worrying about Rob. And as much as she excused Lukas for being flaky and unreliable, she also got the same consideration from him when her job demanded a lot of her.

Now, as she was winding down from the day, she reviewed the texts and her answers. She could tell something was up. Something serious. She closed her eyes and leant her head back on the sofa. Florence came in and head butted her leg. With a weary sigh, she got up to feed the cat and sent an apologetic text to Lukas stating that she'd been busy but was free now. She half hoped that he was already asleep.

But her luck wasn't in. As she watched Florence happily eating, her phone beeped again. She put the kettle on before picking it up, guessing that it was going to be a long night. As she spooned coffee into a cup, she saw it was a message from Lukas. He knew it was late but he really wanted to meet up. Something fairly big was wrong.

Glad that she'd made coffee already, Emma added milk and an ice cube to it so she could glug it down before she left again. She was almost dizzy with tiredness, but this was the job she had chosen. She wasn't prepared to either let her job or her friends down.

By the time she'd parked outside Lukas' caravan, the combination of coffee and the cold night air had made her feel more awake. Lukas let her in and they went through to the lounge. He had the gas fire on but instead of warming himself beside it, he was pacing to and fro.

'What's up Lukas? I haven't seen you like this before?'

'It's Violet,' he said simply.

When the silence stretched out, Emma prompted, 'Has she got in trouble with the police again?'

Lukas threw himself onto the sofa and grabbed a tin. He started rolling a cigarette with quick, nervous movements. 'The police started hassling us again. We were in the Winter Gardens, with a few friends, just having a smoke and a drink.

Not like a huge party, just a few of us, you know, with a few tins, just chilling and relaxing.'

Emma had a sinking feeling. This story was starting to sound familiar and she wondered when her friend would ever grow up.

'Anyway, as usual, the police turned up.' He finished rolling his cigarette and wedged it between his lips. 'Actually, it was just a PCSO. But she informed us that we were upsetting the locals. Can you believe that? I mean we're all Bradwick locals.' Emma shot him a look that warned him that she was too tired to put up with all of this nonsense. 'Sorry. Anyway, Violet started arguing back against this PCSO, who decided that she felt threatened and called in the real police. Violet was properly annoyed by this point. The two officers who came to support were those ex-military types, the ones who like throwing their weight around. Anyway, it all got a bit heated, one of the police told Violet to move back, she refused, he reached out towards her and she batted his hand away. Now she's up on a whole host of charges from assault of a police officer to breach of the peace and obviously possession as well.'

'Where is she now?'

'They've said they'll hold her in the cells overnight and put her up to the magistrates in the morning.' He paused, looking lost. 'Are they allowed to do that?'

'Yes, they can. Tomorrow morning the magistrates will hear the charges and make their decision. But given the number and severity of the charges, together with her history, the magistrates might just pass it on to the Crown Court.' Emma wasn't proud of it, but to protect Lukas she had had a quick look through Violet's police record. There was nothing surprising but a long list of arrests without charge and police cautions. With her expert eye, she could see that the police would be running out of patience with Violet.

'Crown Court? That sounds serious.' Lukas' usual laid-back approach had vanished, leaving a scared and worried person behind.

Emma nodded. 'Yes, it really depends on how it all goes with the magistrates and how Violet responds. Magistrates can only issue fines, assign community service or pass sentences up to six months. If they want to sentence Violet for longer than that, then it'll be passed over to Crown Court.'

'No! They can't put her in prison for years! She's not that bad!' He turned to Emma and fixed her with his stare. 'Is there anything you can do? You know, from the inside as it were?'

'Not really. Once the decision has been made to hand it to the CPS, there's not a lot we can do about it. And if the CPS decide to press charges, well,' she shrugged, 'it's like a sausage machine at that point. Move from point A to point B and on to point C.'

'And there's nothing to stop it? Couldn't you like, I don't know, write a reference or something? Be a character witness?'

Emma stopped and took a deep drink of her coffee, to give herself time to arrange her thoughts. 'I'm not sure that would be entirely wise.'

'What, because helping a friend would look bad for your career?'

'Lukas, you know it's not like that.' She took a steadying breath. 'Listen, Violet is one of those people who doesn't respect the police.'

'I thought you didn't respect them? That's what you've always said.'

For some reason, Emma's father came to mind. Short of

having ACAB tattooed across his knuckles he was about as anti-police as it was possible to be. 'I am aware of their shortcomings, but it's also my job. And yes, I did start down this path just to piss off my parents, because I was angry at them. But I've found something I'm good at.' She paused again, trying to figure out what to say to Lukas. 'It's like, Violet needs to give officers a chance. Some of them are bastards and will go out of their way to be a pain. The ones who enjoy throwing their weight around. But there's a hell of a lot more who just want to make sure she makes it home safely when she's had too much to drink. They don't actually want to arrest her and put her through the system.'

'So why do they do it then?'

'Because she doesn't give them a chance. She doesn't wait and see if they're going to be respectful, she just goes in all mouthy and giving them attitude and then wonders why they're hard on her. You've no idea what it's like, especially for uniformed beat officers. They get so much crap, all day, every day. If she just started off being a bit nice, things would go better for her. Even the drunks who are crying and emotional but apologetic are all right to deal with. But someone who's decided you're the enemy before you even open your mouth? They're the problem.'

Lukas nodded slowly. 'Well, I did want to get her to calm down a bit. Settle down. Maybe turn down some party invites. Maybe this is the wake-up call she needs and now I could start to steer her onto a better course.'

'You've got this to deal with first,' Emma said. 'And I won't go into bat for her. Those officers, the ones she swore at, they're the same people who are on the end of a radio when I call for backup. Now, I don't think that they'll deliberately leave me hanging, but there we all depend on each other and cover each other. If I was seen, even remotely, to be on the side of someone who's been aggressive to fellow officers. No, I can't really do it.'

'I already worry enough about you. I don't want you in more danger.'

There was a pause, more comfortable this time.

'Lukas, are you sure she's right for you?'

'Who, Violet?' He stopped and gave the question proper consideration. 'I think she is. It's not like other times, you know. It feels different. Maybe I'm getting older. Maybe it's being back in touch with your parents and the old crowd. I don't know. But I'm feeling ready to settle down. Not totally conform and get an office job and all that crap, but maybe see if there's something more than getting off my head every weekend.'

'And Violet's the one you want to do that with?'

Lukas nodded. 'I think she is.'

He collapsed back into the sofa. He briefly lifted his head up to sweep his hair out of his eyes and light a cigarette.

Emma was torn. She wanted to say that Violet had brought it on herself. She'd never warmed to his girlfriend. Violet had been given enough warnings by Emma, and to no avail. What stung most was that Emma knew she could've kept her out of trouble, if she'd only listened. There was nothing more frustrating to her than someone she could help but who wouldn't allow her to.

'Listen, there are things you can do, even at this stage. I know it's late but you need to pack her a bag. Her smartest clothes and whatever she needs to look good, make-up and so on. First impressions do matter and if you get to the station early, they might let you give her a change of clothes.' She paused, still unsure if she approved of Lukas and Violet's relationship. But whatever she thought, it looked like it was there for the duration. 'And if you can clear it with your work, being there all day will mean a lot to her. A friendly face in the gallery, someone to take her home.' Emma wondered if Violet would be remanded or released on bail, but decided that Lukas had enough on his plate at the moment. 'Anyway, you've got a lot to do and I need to get to bed. Are you OK? You know what to do?'

Lukas nodded. As Emma suspected once he had an idea what was happening and had something to do he was calmer. She just hoped that tomorrow brought some good news even if she didn't know what that would look like.

CHAPTER FORTY-EIGHT

'So, Emma what did Dani make of Rob's injuries? Do we have a match?' Michelle's attitude was all business as she sat opposite Emma in her office.

'It definitely doesn't rule anything out, but it's not conclusive enough to get a warrant either,' Emma said. She desperately wanted to rub her eyes, but kept herself professional. Her late-night visit to pat Lukas back into shape had taken its toll. This morning she had relied heavily on concealer beneath her eyes and strong coffee.

'Why do I feel there's more to this than you're saying?' Michelle asked, indicating the sheaf of paper in Emma's hand.

Emma sighed and held up the folded-up sheets. She'd known this moment was coming, it had been inevitable since she'd persuaded Rob to hand them over. It was nearly the smoking gun, and it didn't matter how much Rob might be embarrassed by it. 'I've got some of the transcripts of Rob's conversations with Amelia.' She saw the look on her boss's face. 'He is co-operating fully with the guys in Bristol, so he downloaded them and printed them out. He gave me a copy. Have a look at the sections I highlighted.'

There was a brief silence while Michelle read through the sheets.

Finally Emma said, 'So, as you can see, the day after the first murder, Thomas Bagshaw was in an unnaturally good mood. Not that notable, but exactly the same thing happened after the second murder.'

'Interesting but not convincing. It could be circumstantial.'

'Yes, but it does show one thing. Thomas Bagshaw has a connection to Bradwick High, we know that. So, at the very least, we know he's happy when one of his former pupils is killed. I mean, that in itself is concerning. But then, the death of a GP who worked in his area is also a cause of celebration? I think it's gets more suspicious. And then the day we think Ben Scott was killed, he locked Amelia and her mother in the house all day.'

'Okay, you've convinced me. What did your background research on the Bagshaw family turn up?'

'On the surface, the father is a great guy. Works as a Design and Technology teacher in Bradwick High. Does loads to help out around the school, kind of like an unofficial handyman or caretaker. But he doesn't claim any extra salary for it. And it gets better because he also makes wooden toys which he sells for charity. Again, he doesn't even claim expenses.'

'So, an all-round saint then,' Michelle said sarcastically. 'Did you find out what he was hiding?'

'Well, it's weird. In a way, everything that he does that would ordinarily be good, he somehow makes into a problem.'

'What do you mean?'

'For a start he's really organised, everything has to be in its place.'

Michelle nodded. 'Well, that's how you want a DT

teacher to be isn't it? You can't have tools going missing in a school.'

'Yeah, but he takes it so far that at least two teaching assistants have been reduced to tears by his attitude. He's a bully. But he's also useful to the school, so it's been kept quiet. The assistants have been moved sideways and nothing has been said or done. It's the same with his own daughters. He works in their school, but he doesn't leave them alone. Even at break time he's watching them. Up to a point he looks like an attentive parent, but then you factor in that he doesn't allow Amelia to own a mobile phone or use the internet, and add into the mix that he tends to bully people, and the picture becomes a lot less rosy.' She paused and shook her head. 'I can't quite put my finger on it, but something's wrong.'

'Daughters?' Michelle said in surprise.

'Yes, that's something else I've come across,' Emma said. 'Amelia has an older sister, Sophie. She'd be twenty now.'

'Really? So why have we only been looking at Amelia so far?'

'Because Sophie seems to have disappeared. Missing persons have done all the standard checks, revenue, benefits, register of electors, and there are no records of her. Wherever she's gone, she's not leaving a record. She hasn't been arrested either. And she doesn't have a driving license. Obviously it's ongoing, but unless she wants to be found, I don't think she will be.'

'Well, this does add to the overall picture of Thomas Bagshaw – one daughter has dropped off the radar, the other one flagging up concerns to a complete stranger. We've all known the abusers who can front it out in public. They have the perfectly created facade to hide the crap they get up to behind closed doors. Do you think that's what we've got here?'

'I think it is', Emma agreed sombrely.

Michelle thought for a moment. 'So what are the next steps here? With regard to Sophie, without an address we'd never get a warrant for the banks.'

'The most likely outcome is that she's left the country or done a very thorough job on changing her name.'

'If she's still alive.'

'Well, let's just hope that isn't the outcome. The main thing is that it's yet another black mark against the family.'

'That's true.'

'I'd really like to talk to Thomas Bagshaw and just get a general feel,' Emma suggested.

'We still haven't got enough to pull him in yet,' Michelle said.

'That wasn't what I was thinking. The misper case is still active so I could go round there. Show a bit of CID presence after the case has been open for five days. I can just frame it as a routine follow up on a concerning case.'

'OK, but be careful. We've got him in our sights for three murders and an assault. Don't go taking risks. Do you want to take someone with you?'

Emma thought briefly. John was on desk duty, and Nick was out chasing up CCTV and getting a feel for the area that Amelia had last been seen in. Suse was in the office, but Emma didn't want to turn up with a sergeant just yet. She'd prefer to keep everything low key and see how it played out.

'The Liaison Officer should still be there, so I won't be alone. I'll go in there, drink a cup of tea, chat to both parents and see what the lay of the land is. Meeting the wife should provide useful intel too. If there's anything funny going on, then it'll be the wife who gives it away. I'll know what I'm looking for, so if there's anything that leaps out then I'll just note it down, keep it to myself and get out of there to call it in.' She paused. 'And, if we're right, he seems to act in order to protect his family. So, I'll do my best to be submissive and non-threatening. I promise I won't challenge him, try to separate him from his wife or anything like that. I'll literally just have a look around and leave.'

'I've reviewed your record, DC Angel,' said Michelle, sternly. 'I know that you can act rashly. I would advise you very strongly at this time to follow my orders. If you're right, then this a dangerous man. Make sure that you do what you said – gather information, keep a poker face and get out of there alive.'

'Yes, ma'am.'

CHAPTER FORTY-NINE

THE CLOSER AMELIA got to her house, the worse her nerves became. Streets that used to be familiar, part of her usual route to school, were now dangerous.

But she'd spent days hiding away. She'd thought that the best thing in her life would be to be free of her father. When she'd first run away from home, she thought that she'd achieved that. But she'd found herself trapped.

She'd got the keys to one of the self-catering houses that Sara's mother cleaned for. But while it was freedom from her father, she still wasn't free. She was aware that she shouldn't be in the house, so every day she had to clean the shower, clear the washing up, make sure that she hadn't left a trace. And her money hadn't lasted as long as she'd hoped. She'd bought a few ready meals, but then had to resort to stealing bits and pieces from supermarkets. She was grateful for the meal that Rob had bought her even if the meeting had nearly ended in disaster.

Even though her father wasn't there in the house with her controlling her day-to-day actions, she still felt his presence every time she left. She imagined that he was out looking for her. She knew that she'd been reported as missing and that the police were after her as well.

Now boredom had driven her out of the house. She'd decided that she was done waiting to see what would happen next. It was time to make things happen instead.

So she was approaching her family home. She knew that her father would be at work. And Wednesday morning was when her mother did the big grocery shop.

She had been watching her own front door for ten minutes now, and there had been no movement. She couldn't risk being seen, so she'd arrived after she'd guessed that her mum had gone.

Finally, she moved from one corner to the next, naturally staying close to parked cars, ready to duck if she saw anything. But nothing happened until she was standing at her own front door. There was a car behind her and she was primed and ready to duck behind it if she needed to. She banged loudly on the door and pressed the bell, thinking how weird it was to be doing this at her own home.

Before the noise had died away she scurried towards the parked car and crouched down, looking out over the bonnet.

The whole street was quiet. None of her neighbours were alerted by her making a noise. Somehow the silence seemed ominous, as if the whole street was waiting for something to happen.

Nothing did. Her leg began to cramp and she straightened up without thinking about the risk. She looked up and down the road, but nothing moved. It was a quiet residential street at ten past eleven on a Wednesday morning.

Feeling as if she was out of her body and floating along the path, she approached the gate to the back garden. It was locked but she knew the trick. She hooked her foot under the bottom edge of the wooden gate and gave a jiggle. She could feel the wood cut into the top of her foot. While she was kicking the bottom, she jerked the top sharply. The latch came up and the door swung open.

Amelia was through the gate and down the side of the house before she could worry about being seen. Everything in the back garden looked different. Nothing had moved or changed, but she felt that she was trespassing in her own home. She didn't know any details of the murders, but if her father was guilty, then the evidence would be in the shed. Her plan was simple; she'd photograph everything and send it to Rob Haines. He was an ex-police officer, so he'd be able to sort through them and figure out what was useful.

She put her hand on the back door into the kitchen and prayed. Then she pressed down and the handle turned. It was unlocked. She opened the door quietly and leaned into the kitchen. To the right of the door was a rack of keys. Third from the left was her father's workshop key. It lived there unless he was using it. In theory any member of the family could have reached up and taken it at any time. But it hung there as a symbol of his power. The key was there, within reach, but forbidden.

But now Amelia felt outside of the family, outside of the normal rules. She took advantage of that feeling and took the key.

Amelia actually paused for a moment before entering The Shed, the inner sanctum of her father's world. Pushing herself forward, she went in. The space seemed smaller on the inside because it was crowded with machinery that she couldn't identify. The air smelled warm and woody. She could identify pine and a host of other natural smells. But she wasn't there to look at woodworking machines.

She walked toward the back end of the building. Here was a more traditional workbench with a vice and a board of tools hanging on the wall. And a laptop. Amelia spent a moment looking around with wide eyes, before she got her new phone out and selected the camera app to start taking pictures.

After what seemed like an eternity, but was probably no more than five minutes, she decided that she had taken enough pictures. She felt a sense of dread, that her father would come home in the middle of the day, or that something else unspecified but awful would happen. She couldn't bear to be in there any longer, surrounded by things that reminded her of her father. She ran away, through the door and into the garden.

She locked the shed door and was halfway to across the lawn when she saw someone on the patio. It took her a second to process what she was seeing. Her mother was standing there gaping at her daughter.

'Amelia? Is that really you?' Sharon clearly wasn't sure what she was seeing. 'What are you doing here? I mean, back? Were you in his shed?'

'I don't know. Mum, please don't tell him that you've seen me.'

'You're not staying then?'

'No, I can't come back, not now that he knows about my phone.'

'So it's true then? We didn't believe the police when they came round with some strange story about how some dirty old man was trying to groom you. Your father sent them off with a flea in their ear. Told them that no girl of his would be so stupid.' She paused, obviously trying to figure out what to say next. 'But then you didn't come home and we had to go back to the police to report you missing.' She sobbed and held a hand to her face. 'And now we don't know what to think. But don't worry about all of that. We need you home. You've no idea what it's like. It's so quiet, it's like we've got no purpose.'

'But can't you see? If I stay here now,' Amelia said through gritted teeth, 'he'll be all nice and smiles while all the fuss dies down. And then a few weeks later, he'll punish me.'

'But he told you not to have a phone and you just had to be stubborn and find a way around him. And you know what he's like. You know, and you did it anyway! Why shouldn't you be punished?'

There was a pause as mother and daughter stared at each other. 'Well, what are you going to do then?' Sharon asked. 'That was always your problem, you never think things through. You just act.'

Amelia tried to focus through the worry that her father might arrive home without warning. Time was running out. And although she didn't want to admit it, her mother had a point. She didn't have a long-term plan. 'Just give me a week,' she said, pulling a reasonable sounding period out of the air. She had no idea how long Rob would need once he got the photos but at least it sounded like she knew what she was doing.

'A week? Well, where are you staying? Are you safe and warm? Enough food?'

'Yes, I've got somewhere. Not on the street. I'm safe.' And bored. And scared to leave the house. 'Could you give me some money though?' She looked like the child she was, embarrassed that she wasn't as grown up as she hoped. 'Didn't know how much it'd cost to, you know, live and eat and all that.'

Sharon reached behind her, into the kitchen and grabbed her handbag. 'I've only got thirty quid.' She held the notes out. 'But you really will come back? In a week?'

'Yes,' Amelia said sadly and took the money in exchange

for the workshop key. 'Promise you won't tell anyone that you've seen me?'

Sharon looked unhappy with the idea of lying to either her husband or the police.

'Please, Mum. Please. This is important.'

'Maybe, I don't know.'

Amelia knew that this was as good as she was going to get. Half running, she left the garden by the side path, careful to close the gate behind her.

CHAPTER FIFTY

Rob gently rubbed his arm through the bandage. Not only was it still sore and achy, but it was also starting to itch. He thought over the conversation with Dani and Emma. Had he narrowly avoided the killer that they'd all been trying to catch?

He felt frustrated, and not just by the injury on his arm. He felt useless, on the outside of the case. He also felt that he was missing something.

He went back to his transcripts and idly leafed through them, hoping that something would leap out at him from the mass of teenage angst and adult advice.

He stopped at a page that caught his eye. It was from just after Amelia had first suggested that her father might be the killer. They'd discussed his pattern of behaviour, that he acted oddly the night before each murder, and the morning after he'd been much happier and the mood in the family had been lighter. He had asked Amelia to message him if her father ever repeated the pattern.

He had failed to follow up on that. But now, he had time to go back over the transcripts and see if there was any further evidence of this pattern. His eye was caught by the day that Tom had locked Amelia and Sharon in the house and forbidden them to go out, and arrived back home late in the evening. And on the following morning he had been in a happy, almost gleeful mood.

Looking back over the conversation, Rob wondered how he had missed it. Then he remembered that Amelia had sent the message the day before he'd been doorstepped by two officers and when his nightmare had begun.

He pulled his laptop over to check the news sites and see how this connected with the discovery of the third body. At first, he was disappointed. The body was discovered when Ben Scott failed to attend a probation morning. The first news report was at the same time that Rob was being interviewed in Bristol. It didn't correlate at all.

He let his eyes drift over the article. Something had caught his attention, but he didn't know what. He went back and very carefully read each sentence, forcing his damaged brain to concentrate and read the whole article.

When he was done, he sat back and closed his eyes. He had the sense that pieces of the case were moving in his head, rearranging into new positions. The body had lain undiscovered for several days. Which moved Thomas Bagshaw right back into the frame.

He reached for his phone and rang Emma's number, but it went straight to voicemail. He was owed a favour, so he called Dani Price instead.

'You know how I let you poke around my arm this morning? How I didn't complain or anything?'

Dani sighed. 'What do you want, Rob?'

'Do you have an accurate time of death for Benjamin Scott?'

There was a pause. Rob was certain that Dani was considering her options. Rob was no longer a serving officer and she shouldn't be helping him. On the other hand, there wasn't much value in the information she was being asked for.

'We're giving a rough time of sometime on Wednesday night. Quite late, he'd started digesting his evening meal. Let's say, between ten pm through to three or four am the next morning, depending on when he ate and how fast his metabolism was. Does that help any?'

'It really does, Dani. Thank you! I've got to make some more phone calls now.'

Before he called in the cavalry, Rob made sure he had his facts straight. Previously they'd assumed that Thomas Bagshaw had been a nasty piece of work who'd been cheered up by the untimely death of people he knew. But this new information changed that.

While the body of Ben Scott had been lying in his hallway, Thomas Bagshaw had been celebrating. At that point, no one apart from the victim and the killer knew what had happened. Rob had the proof that he needed.

He tried Emma again but it still went straight to voicemail. Before he decided what to do next, he switched on his work mobile to see if Amelia had resurfaced.

It came up with a notification that chilled him. All thoughts of a potential murderer forgotten, he stared at his phone as if it were an angry rattlesnake.

CHAPTER FIFTY-ONE

Even though it was cold, Emma stopped at the kerb and looked at the house before going further. There was no reason whatsoever that anyone would pick it out from its neighbours. It was a nice house, in a good area. Semidetached, neat lawn, well weeded flowerbeds. Once she started looking at it, however, Emma found it a little creepy. No sign of the wheelie bins, nothing out of place. Even the curtains in the windows were neatly tied back. It had as much soul as a show house.

She shivered and zipped her coat up. It was a cold, dry day and overcast with it. Although it wasn't yet four in the afternoon it was already starting to get dark. She wished the winter solstice would come around and the days would start getting longer.

Nothing for it, she thought. It's time to see how the Bagshaws live their lives. She went up the path and rang the doorbell. There was no answer. Nothing happened. But years of experience told her that the house was not empty.

She rang again, then banged on the door. There was silence. No dog barked, no TV played, but she could feel that someone was waiting for her to go away. She frowned. Where was the Family Liaison Officer?

The door was blue, solid wood, and only had three small windows in a fan at the top. They were filled with wavy glass and there was no way she could see through them. She bent down and opened the letterbox. Hopefully she'd see something suspicious to justify making a forced entrance.

'Mrs Bagshaw? Mr Bagshaw? Hello? Is there anyone there?'

Inside she saw a neat hallway, with freshly polished furniture against the walls. She straightened up and banged on the door again, then leant on the doorbell.

She raised her voice. 'Hello! I'm just here to have a chat about your daughter.'

She jumped when the sash window in a bay window to her right shot up. A nervous looking woman, thin with dark shoulder length hair, leant on the sill. 'My daughter? Amelia? Have you found her?'

'No, we haven't found her yet. I'm Detective Constable Angel. Emma. I'm just carrying out a routine case review as it's several days since you filed a missing person report. You must be Sharon Bagshaw?' The other woman nodded. Emma paused, looking at the window and the door. 'Could I come in? We shouldn't really be discussing this on the doorstep.'

'Err, yes. No. You can't come in.'

'Can't?'

Emma could see the emotions battling across Sharon's face. She was obviously scared, but also hopeful and desperate for information about her daughter. Eventually she reached a decision of sorts. 'No. I've lost the front door key.' She laughed, but it was a harsh, brittle, sound. 'Silly me. I shouldn't be trusted really. Anyway, I was just looking for it. But the house is a bit of a mess, so I need to tidy up and find the key.' She nodded as if she was trying to convince herself.

Emma frowned. Nothing she had seen so far indicated any sign of a mess anywhere on the property. 'I could help,' she said simply.

'Help?' the concept was lost on her.

'Yeah, I could help you look. And we could chat while we looked. What do you think?'

'But the door is locked and I don't have the key. I don't see how you could help.'

'Well, that sill doesn't look too high. How about you step back and I climb in?'

They had reached a standoff. Emma knew that often the best way forward was to take action. She stepped across to the window, very careful not to tread on any plants. When she rested her hands on the sill, Sharon stepped back to let her in.

Soon, Emma was inside the house. It didn't look like a mess. In fact, it looked like a photographer for a glossy magazine was about to arrive.

'Like I say, I'm sorry about the mess. I was in the middle of cleaning, so I just need to finish up and put things away. Tom will be home soon, so I need to get everything straight.'

As she talked, she walked through to the kitchen. Emma followed, marvelling at how the whole house was immaculate. Sharon put away a dish cloth after wiping the surface. She looked at the floor and tutted.

'Mud! I knew you shouldn't have come in through the window. Don't worry about it though, I've got just the thing.' She went through a door at the other end of the kitchen and returned with a small caddy and a tiny hand held hoover. 'Won't take me a moment.'

Emma watched in amazement as her footprints vanished with a series of quick wipes and short sharp bursts of the hoover. When it was all done and everything put away, Sharon came back into the kitchen. 'Right then. What have you found out about Amelia?'

'It's not so much what we've found out. You'd be amazed how many times in cases like this you come back to the parents after a few days and they'll remember some crucial detail.' Emma looked around. 'I thought that the Family Liaison Officer would be here?'

'No,' Sharon said dreamily. 'No, Tom had a row with her. Chucked her out on her ear.'

Emma nodded, adding another item to her list of concerns about Thomas Bagshaw. 'So, has anything new occurred to you since we last spoke?'

'No, not really,' Sharon seemed distracted. 'So there's no news?'

'No. Are you all right? You seem worried about something.'

'It's just that Tom will be home soon. And I ought to get the place ready. It'd be good if you could go before he gets here.' Her eyes flicked to a clock on the wall.

'It really would be better if I could talk to both of you. It would help find Amelia. And I wouldn't have to climb out of the window!'

Sharon nodded. 'He has got his own key. I suppose that would be okay.'

'Have you got in touch with Sophie? Amelia's sister? She might have gone there. Often children are closer to their brothers or sisters, especially if they've run away from their parents.'

Sharon shook her head. 'We asked. Sophie would've told us anyway.' She paused as if weighing up her next words carefully. 'Can you not say things like that? Like "running away from her parents". She's just confused. She doesn't want to run away from us. We're a perfect family. I mean we have our moments, who doesn't, but we're all right. It's not our fault. We can't have people thinking that she's run away.'

Emma was just processing this when both women heard the key in the lock. They looked at each other as if they'd just been caught out doing something wrong. Thomas Bagshaw was home.

CHAPTER FIFTY-TWO

'Rob! My God, it's been a long time since you were in this place. How's it going?'

'Martin, Hi! Good to see you again. Yeah, it's not so bad. Feels weird to be this side of the desk, I can tell you.'

'Well, I hope that when my time comes, I look as well as you do.' There was a short pause. 'Anyway, what can I do for you?'

'Could you give DC Emma Angel a bell for me? I'd like to have a word and she's not answering her mobile.'

'Of course.' Martin pushed a book across the desk. 'While I'm calling, would you mind filling out the visitor's book and I'll get you a pass? I know it seems a bit silly as you worked here for years but...' he shrugged, a gesture which said, those are the rules and I can't change them.

Feeling slightly weird, Rob filled out the book while the sergeant made the call. Hanging up, Martin frowned. 'CID appear to be rather busy. Most of them are out on calls.'

'Who's left up there?'

'A trainee detective constable, John Fletcher. A bit flash, but I think his heart's in the right place. He's adamant that he can't leave his desk. I wouldn't let an ordinary visitor wander around the station, but I think I can trust you.'

'I'm sure I still remember the way,' Rob joked. 'That name doesn't ring a bell, he must be new.'

'Well, he's the only one in CID so you'll recognise him. Wear this visitor pass and he's expecting you.'

Feeling awkward, as if it wasn't real, Rob moved through the corridors that had been his workplace for many years. He knew he didn't belong but he also felt immediately at home. Entering the CID offices, he found that the desk sergeant hadn't been exaggerating; no one was there apart from one young lad he took to be John Fletcher.

The young man rose to his feet and extended a hand to Rob. 'I'm DC, well, trainee DC John Fletcher,' he said. 'And you must be Rob Haines.' The pause and awkwardness told Rob that John was completely aware of his past and probably his present problems as well.

'Nice to meet you,' Rob said. He shook his hand and gave him a cursory glance but couldn't be bothered expending the energy to try and memorise him for later reference.

'So, what brings you back to CID? Nostalgia?'

'No, not really. I was actually looking for Emma. She's not answering her mobile.'

'She's out working on the case at the moment.' John looked theatrically around the department open plan area. 'Same for Nick Dent. DI Jones is out at the Church shooting-'

'Wait, there's been a shooting at a church?'

'No, it's the surname. Husband and wife. Looks like husband killed her and topped himself. Anyway, it was the boss's turn as Bronze Commander so she had to go. Took Suse as her sergeant. Which leaves me minding the shop.' There was an edge of bitterness to his voice and Rob wondered what

John had done to upset his boss. 'Can you wait or was it something I could help with?'

Rob barely heard a word after "surname". He was reviewing every decision that he had ever made in the handling of the Church case and whether it could have led to this deadly outcome. But he knew two things. There was no way of knowing what effect he could have had on the actions of Sean Church. And he also knew that it didn't matter, he would always carry the blame.

'Rob? Are you listening?' John was annoyed that his complaining hadn't been given attention.

'Sorry, yes. Just a bit taken by surprise.' He mentally gave himself a shake. He still hesitated though. He knew that he was probably already the source of department gossip and was reluctant to add to that. But on the other hand he needed to know what was on his phone. His instinct told him it had to be now.

'I can make a guess that it's something important,' John said. When Rob frowned, he continued. 'You can't get hold of Emma, and whatever you want with her must be official. You know the way the job is. If you'd have waited a few hours, she would've phoned you back at the end of her shift. So, whatever is going on, it's urgent enough to get you off your sofa and come down here.' He paused and shrugged. 'I know that I'm a trainee detective constable, basically the lowest rung on the CID ladder. And you've never met me before today. But I can help. And if it's delicate, I know when to keep my mouth shut.'

That was enough to convince Rob. He pulled a chair over from another desk and sat down next to John, putting his phone on the desk next to the mouse, and looking at it as if it was an unexploded bomb. 'That's your phone,' John said, to break the tension.

Rob took a deep breath. 'How much about Thomas Bagshaw has made it officially onto the system?'

John frowned and turned to his screen. He typed and clicked his way through several screens, before stopping to read a page of text. 'It says here that some info came through an anonymous tip. Looks like Emma's been putting a lot of effort in to looking into it. There's a fair amount of detail up here, she's gone into some deep background.'

'Yeah. I was the anonymous source.' John tried hard not to look surprised. 'I've got into a StringCan conversation with the daughter. Getting the inside track on the family.'

'The daughter?' John asked. 'Not the thirteen-year-old girl who's a misper?'

Rob nodded. 'The very same.' He paused. 'I don't know how efficient the rumour mill is, but let me save you some time. Yes, I have been arrested by the funny squad down in Bristol, and I've been released without charge. Yes, I'm a man in my fifties talking over the internet to a teenage girl. No, I am not a paedo, I've got two grown up daughters of my own and thought I could be a father figure. Does that clear everything up?'

John blinked several times in rapid succession. He went silent as he processed what he'd just been told. 'How does your conversation with Amelia Bagshaw relate to her going missing and Thomas becoming a suspect?'

Rob warmed to the young officer. He'd got straight to the heart of the problem. He quickly outlined the situation between Amelia and her father, and that he'd warned her that the police were about to interview her parents.

John glanced nervously at the phone on his desk. 'Wow! That's a lot to take in. So where are we at today? What's so urgent that you've come in here?'

Rob pointed to his phone. 'Even while she was missing, I

was still messaging Amelia. I was trying to figure out where she was staying, help her in any way I could.' He held up a finger. 'And, I've always kept it fatherly. Never strayed into anything remotely dodgy – nothing about sex or boyfriends or anything like that. And then today I get a message, with photos attached to it.'

'Ah. And what's on these photos?'

'Well, that's the big question, now, isn't it?'

'You mean, you haven't opened them?'

'No, that's what I'm here for.' John looked confused. 'I'll unlock the phone. And we'll view the photos together. You can check them over, give it to your tech boys, I don't care. But if she's sent me anything dodgy, even a hint of cleavage or underwear, I want it on record that I didn't solicit anything, and I don't want to see it.'

John nodded slowly. 'You know that doesn't really count, don't you? I mean, either you're in possession of indecent images or you're not. It's like running through a red light, it's a black or white offence. Your intent doesn't really come into it.' He spoke with the assurance of someone who'd been hitting the books ready for his new job.

'Yeah, I get that,' Rob said sadly. 'But I'm hoping that, if it ever comes down to it, this will play better in court. It's not like I'm hiding under my sheets at home at one in the morning with my phone. Anyway, let's hope it's not that. But whatever it is, it might be important as she's never sent pictures before.'

'Well, if you're sure.' John paused, clearly trying to find the right thing to say. 'You're right about the rumours in this place. I've heard plenty about you, when you worked here and how you left. But I've always made my own mind up about things and I hate gossip. My gut tells me that you're not the bad guy here. It's not an easy situation. All that being said, if this does go tits up, I'll go into court for you.

That's all I can do.' He took out his pocket book and made notes.

'Is that necessary?' Rob asked.

'Yes. Definitely. I'm just noting down when you came in the office and what we've discussed, just broad terms. Like you said, this might end up in court.'

Rob nodded, unlocked the phone and opened the StringCan app. He tapped on the screen, then swiped through several photos. John leaned in so that their heads were nearly touching. Rob looked at them with growing confusion. They seemed to be random pictures of the inside of a workshop. He could see lathes and drills, covered in a fine layer of sawdust, along with a workbench and cupboards full of tools. One of the photos suddenly caused John to gasp. He looked at Rob and reached for the phone. Rob nodded, so John took the phone and zoomed in, frowning. Then, with a quick double tap, he continued scrolling. When he got to the last picture, he sat back in his chair, stunned.

'Fuck.' He sounded calm and deadpan but his eyes gave him away. He was panicking at such a deep level that everything else appeared calm.

'What? What is it?' Rob was frantic.

'It's serious,' John said. 'I mean, there's obviously no child porn, so you're clear on that front. But I have to make a phone call right now. And I need to send these photos to myself so I can upload them onto the system.'

Rob nodded, and John set to work. He dialled on his desk phone, then put it onto speaker while he worked on Rob's phone. As with his daughters, Rob was envious of the ease with which young people navigated technology.

'Ma'am, it's John Fletcher.'

'John. I'm right in the middle of a major incident. If you've called up to whinge about being on desk duty, you'd better hope your uniform is ironed because you'll be wearing it tomorrow.'

'No, it's not that, ma'am, I've got Rob Haines here–'

'Rob Haines is back in the office? I hope you're not listening to what he's saying–'

'Ma'am with all due respect, shut up and let me speak!' There was a chilled silence on the line. John knew that his next few words would make or break his CID career. 'Where is Emma Angel right now?'

'She's gone round to make routine enquiries with the family of that missing girl, Amelia Bagshaw.'

'Shit. Rob's got concrete evidence that Thomas Bagshaw is the killer. And we can't raise her on her personal mobile. I'm on the desk phone, so I'll try her work mobile from my mobile. Ma'am, while I'm doing that, could you get someone to try her Airwave?'

'I'll do it myself,' Michelle said. Any hint of annoyance was quickly overridden by concern for a fellow officer.

A tense few seconds passed in the office and at the other end of the line.

'No contact,' Michelle said.

'Straight to voicemail,' John confirmed. 'I'm sending over pictures now. Are you still with the firearms unit?'

'Yes, why?'

'Any chance they could help? I think it's serious.'

'I've got a murder-suicide here. Two bodies, no other suspects, firearm secured. There's a mountain of paperwork and forensic work to do, but the unit could move to another incident.' There was a dangerous pause. 'If I deem it necessary.'

John was already sending the photos. Again there was a pause as his DI absorbed the new information. When she had, she rattled off the address for Thomas Bagshaw and told John to get whoever he could find down there, instructed to approach with caution. She'd handle the firearms unit herself.

'I think that covers everything,' DI Jones said. 'And John?'

'Yes, ma'am.'

'Don't ever talk to me like that again. I don't care how many officers are at risk.' She couldn't slam her mobile down, but Rob imagined there was an angry stab at the red button.

Rob took his mobile back and went through the photos again, trying to see what had caused all the panic. The one that John had zoomed in on was of a set of collectible football coins with three missing. That triggered a memory of something Emma had said, but he couldn't quite recall it. Then he came to the last one which was a photo of a laptop, showing its internet search history. His eyes weren't as good as John's, so he zoomed in to read the text. Thomas Bagshaw had been searching around one phrase that made his blood run cold.

"Glock 9mm".

CHAPTER FIFTY-THREE

'Sharon, why's the window in the front room open? We are paying to heat this place, you know?' Thomas Bagshaw went into the kitchen and his attitude changed immediately. 'Oh, I didn't see that we had company. I don't believe I've had the pleasure?'

'Detective Constable Emma Angel. I'm here for a quick case review about Amelia. And no, before you ask, we don't have any news yet.' She paused, assessing the best thing to say. 'Sorry about the window, Sharon here didn't have a key, so I was going to help her look. And we needed to talk, but then you came home.'

'Oh yes.' He dropped his voice even though Sharon could still hear him. 'She gets anxious. Has her moments. She's got something from the doctor to help. But sometimes she gets forgetful.' He moved to a kitchen drawer. 'We always keep the spare key in here.' He pulled it open and rattled around noisily in the drawer until he produced a key with a flourish. 'It was here all along,' he said, shaking his head.

Emma noticed that during this speech, somehow Sharon had become smaller. She seemed to occupy less space in the room and she'd gone quiet. She kept her head and her eyes down. She wasn't ignoring her husband, just waiting to be called on.

'Anyway,' Thomas rallied the conversation away from domestic matters. 'You said you were here about Amelia. I honestly don't know why Sharon bothered the police about it. I'm sure it's something and nothing. Teenage girls, you must know what they can be like.'

'Yes, but she's only thirteen and she's been away for nearly a week now. We are obviously concerned.'

'Right, yes. Well, why don't you go through to the sitting room with Sharon and I'll put the kettle on and rustle up some biscuits. Tea or coffee?'

'Tea please. Milk, no sugar.'

The two women went through and perched on sofas, looking at each other over a coffee table. 'So, I was asking you about Sophie. You say she hasn't seen Amelia?'

'That's right. We've always been close as a family. That's why I reported it. I can't imagine that she'd run off, I'm worried that something would've happened.'

'Well, we've made extensive enquiries, and we haven't found any evidence that she's been in an accident or that anything untoward has happened to her.'

Thomas came into the room bearing a tray with their drinks and a plate of biscuits. 'See, what did I tell you? You're worrying over nothing. She's probably staying round a friend's house or something. You're sure you haven't forgotten about a school trip?'

Sharon shook her head.

'Well, I'm sure she'll come home soon with her tail between her legs.' He took a big sip from his mug. 'Nothing beats that moment when the tea is just the right temperature.'

He took another gulp and Emma followed suit. He might be behaving weirdly, but Thomas Bagshaw was right.

'How was Amelia on the day she went missing?' Emma asked, keen to get the conversation back on track.

'I'm not sure I like the direction you're going with this,' Tom said. 'It sounds to me like you're blaming us, blaming me. This family is always happy. I mean, look at this house. I work hard to give us a good life. So, to answer your question, Amelia was fine on the day she disappeared.'

'Not moody, or worried about anything?' Emma asked. 'I mean, it doesn't have to be a family thing. You know what girls that age are like. She could've fallen out with friends, had a teacher who didn't like her, a subject she was struggling with, could be anything.'

Thomas frowned. 'Well, no, she was no different. She's always been good at school, her teachers all like her, her grades are good. I've always brought my children up well.'

Emma nodded and took another sip of her tea.

'Okay, so we may have had a sighting of Amelia. We sent officers round to check, but she'd already left the area. We were told she was at the McDonalds on that big estate outside town, the one with the cinema and the bowling alley.'

While she was speaking, Emma tried to pay close attention to Thomas Bagshaw. She saw a brief narrowing of his eyes at the mention of the sighting but she couldn't be sure if he already knew about it or not.

'I know the one you mean,' Thomas said easily. His mask was back on and he was talking smoothly and easily. 'It was the place we went whenever we fancied a treat. It makes sense if she was spotted there, it's somewhere she knows.' He paused for a second and frowned. 'Was there anything else that you wanted?'

'Earlier, I was asking about your other daughter Sophie.

Do you know if Amelia might have gone there?' Emma tried to look at both of them, but Sharon kept her head down. 'Has she been in contact?'

This time Emma caught the merest hint of a shadow across Tom's face before it disappeared. 'No. I mean, we were worried as you'd obviously be, and we've been in daily contact with Sophie, you know, making sure she's all right.'

Emma frowned. Something didn't ring true. Why was Thomas worried about Sophie? Did he really think that someone was targeting his family? 'Why would you be concerned about...' Emma frowned, trying to remember the older sister's name. She was suddenly exhausted. For the last few weeks, she'd been bashing her head against this case. Now she was chasing down a missing person's case alongside worrying about Rob, following his assault. And there was Lukas and his wholly unsuitable girlfriend who was in trouble. She knew she hadn't been sleeping, but usually she thrived on stress. She drank the rest of her tea, hoping it would wake her up a bit and ploughed on. 'Sophie!' She'd remembered the sister's name, but now couldn't keep up with the thread of what she'd been asking. Something about Sophie.

'Are you all right, Emma?' Thomas moved from his armchair, and loomed close to her. 'You look tired. Give me your phone and radio, and I'll get your colleagues.' Without asking, he took her Airwave and phone. Emma tried to stop him, but her limbs felt too heavy to move.

CHAPTER FIFTY-FOUR

Detective Inspector Michelle Jones turned to the head of the firearms unit. He was a short stocky man who was only a couple of inches taller than her. But he exuded a confidence and command far in excess of his rank.

'Harry, what's the situation here? How close are you to finishing up?'

'Well, we've got the weapon secured, we've searched the house and found no further victims. It looks like a murder-suicide, but we'll have to leave that to you lot to determine eventually.'

'I need you to deploy to the other side of Bradwick.'

It was the nature of his job to make quick decisions. 'Is it important? I mean, we need to tidy up here and do the paperwork, but we can redeploy immediately. We've had no shots fired at this incident, so we can go with a full-strength team. What's the situation?'

'I sent an officer in to interview a suspect. At the time we thought there was a remote possibility that he was dangerous. But, since she left the station, we've had new information.

He's now number one suspect in multiple murders and he's been Googling Glock handguns.'

'A fellow officer? You should've said. That's a whole other thing.' He turned to his second in command, whistled and made a circling motion with one hand. Immediately the team rallied, packing bags, stowing kit in car boots and getting ready to leave. 'There's nothing more to do here except admin. Are you going to come with us?'

Michelle nodded. 'It won't be popular but I'll leave my sergeant here as a link to CID. We'll have to get the uniforms to secure the scene and manage the pathologist, scene of crime etc.'

'We're all sorted then. Send me the address and follow on.'

'Okay. We have no contact with officer concerned, but her Airwave is still at the premises. We'll have silent approach and we'll establish a base one street away so we can assess the situation on the ground.'

'WHAT'S THE DEAL THEN, MA'AM?' Harry asked. He had that kind of ruggedness that Michelle immediately pegged as ex-soldier. They stood on the corner of a quiet residential road, casually looking down the road.

'On the right there, number thirty-eight. Still no contact from the officer and we've had someone quietly keeping an eye, no one's been in or out. Nothing on her Airwave, but it's still location pinging so we assume she's on the premises.'

'Right. Seems clear enough. What's our involvement?'

'We've obvious concerns because of his search history and that he's the chief suspect in the recent string of murders in Bradwick.'

'Right. But they were stabbings, weren't they?'

'Yes, but he's a design and technology teacher. He might be working up to a gun. He'd certainly have the ability to re-activate a deactivated weapon. Or make a firearm from scratch. Or even make an improvised explosive device. We can't really take anything off the table.'

'Right you are, ma'am. We'll deploy to cover the front. Have you scouted the whole property yet?'

'We believe there's an alley that runs down the back, and comes out on that side street over there. There's likely to be a gate from the back garden through to that alley. And there's a large out-building in the back garden. Again, we're watching both ends of that alley.'

'Very good. I'll have two of my men to replace those the two officers at each end of the alley with the rest of the team at the front of the property.'

'The control room has activated passive listening on the Airwave. Apparently our officer is still in there but we're not sure of the situation.'

'We'll be standing by if you need anything.'

CHAPTER FIFTY-FIVE

'I KNOW WHY YOU'RE HERE,' Thomas said, with a sneer. 'Not that bullshit about the missing person. That's a rookie mistake, sending out a detective for a simple missing person case. No, I know the real reason, you're keeping tabs on me, because you've seen my search history. I must be getting close to the truth about vaccines.'

'Vaccines? What have they got to do with anything?' Emma was struggling to keep up with this conversation. Her thoughts were slow and sluggish. She wondered if Amelia had received her childhood vaccinations but it wasn't something that was ever recorded in a missing persons case.

'Yes! I mean, obviously, not that someone from the government walked into your station and told you to come here.' He leapt up and started pacing. 'But I know how it works. I'm on forums, on the internet, stuff that they don't want you to know. Someone from the BMA would've gone onto the Home Office, who'd have got your chief constable and it would have gone down the chain. I almost feel sorry for you. Almost. You're just a pawn in their machine. Dancing to their tune.' He started stabbing his finger at Emma.

'Me?' Emma tried to gather her wits in vain. 'Why would anyone send me here to talk about your daughter? I'm just trying to do my job and find your daughter.'

'Ah! You see! That's your mistake. I know you're lying. You don't want to find my daughter. No! That's not the plan at all. I'm making waves, starting to tell people the truth. First you disappeared Sophie, now you've come for Amelia. It's all pressure trying to make me be quiet. Well, I won't -'

'Thomas Bagshaw, this is the police. We know you're in there. Please allow our officer to leave, then come out with your hands in view.'

The voice was artificially amplified and echoed throughout the room. It made Emma's head throb but it did penetrate the layers of fog that she was fighting through. She realised in a burst of clarity that she was in a murderer's house, without her phone or radio. She had to leave.

'Thomas, what have you done?' Sharon asked quietly, as if the police on the street outside could hear.

'Nothing,' he snapped back at her. He stood up and started pacing to and fro, focussing his tirade on Sharon. 'You know what it's like. They're always out to get me for something. It's always the same. The poor white man, in his own country can't avoid being harassed by the fascist government. Besides which, never mind me, what have you done? It was you who invited the police into our own home.'

'Me?' Sharon momentarily forgot to be afraid of her husband.

'Yes, you. And your two bastard daughters. Bloody Sophie declaring she wants nothing more to do with the family and now sodding Amelia's run off. Have you any idea what that looks like to the neighbours? To my work colleagues? To everyone? We must be a laughing stock, just because you can't control your own children.'

Emma had got as far as the door to the hall, and rested her cheek against the wooden door frame.

'Oi! You! Did I say that you could leave? Fuck's sake! I'm surrounded by women who won't do what they're fucking told! Pretty little thing like you should be at home with the babies anyway.'

Emma tried to push him away but instead stumbled into him, making him take a couple of steps back. Relying on muscle memory from years of training she pivoted away from him and staggered for the hallway. She felt tired and dizzy and collapsed against the front door, reaching up and scrabbling for the handle.

CHAPTER FIFTY-SIX

Rob stood on the dark street in the cold drizzle. He'd lost count of how many hours he'd spent standing on streets like this over the years. Always standing outside while some drama played out inside an ordinary house. This time the ordinary house he was look at presumably contained Thomas Bagshaw, his wife Sharon, and Emma Angel – the players in the unfolding drama.

He'd started his career standing on these streets in uniform, keeping out the onlookers, letting in the vast array of professionals who needed to be in. And he had worked his way up the system, becoming someone whose name was recorded on a clipboard before the police tape was lifted for him.

Now, he'd come full circle and was outside the cordon again. He was an onlooker, a ghoul, straining to see what was happening. Ex Detective Inspector Robert Haines. He rolled the words around in his head, trying to get a feel for them. It sounded all very fancy, but it was very simple. He wasn't police, he was a civilian, no longer on the inside.

He smiled quietly to himself as he remembered that he

still had enough natural authority to find this address. He remembered the look on John Fletcher's face when he'd barked out that his friend was in danger and he needed to know where she was. Fletcher had been conditioned by his short years in the police and had provided the information Rob needed.

He clenched his jaw to stop a gasp escaping. With searing clarity he saw that he'd been reminiscing to avoid thinking about the elephant in the room. Sean Church. As an aside to all the drama unfolding around the Bagshaw family, Fletcher had mentioned that there'd been a murder-suicide. It was the way the police were, they saw too much tragedy to be emotional about it. Fletcher had said that the husband had come home, shot his wife, then turned the gun on himself. Simple, open and shut case, that obscured all the pain that led up to that incident and would follow after it.

What it also meant was that Robert Haines Investigations had a murderer as a client. No, Rob decided, he wouldn't hide behind niceties, he had shared a room with a murderer and given him information on his victim. As an officer, he'd obviously been close enough to death, both ordinary and violent. But this was the first time as a civilian he'd genuinely shouldered some of the blame. Of course, with hindsight, there were plenty of times in his policing days that he could have acted differently, could have done something to prevent a tragedy.

There was a big difference between going back over his professional decisions and seeing how he could have done things differently, and this situation. The Church case was clear. He had a bad feeling about the man, but he'd allowed the charade to continue. He'd done his bidding and followed his wife, given him photos and details. Fundamentally, he had enabled a stalker. Worse than that, he'd been found out and had probably given her the impetus to leave her husband. Which, Liz Baker had said, was often the one thing that pushed an abusive husband over the line to becoming a murderer.

Rob shook his head and took off his woolly hat to rub a hand over his head. He focused again on the anonymous house down the road. Nothing appeared to be happening. There had been no gunshots. But he couldn't help but worry that the Church case was being replayed here. Could there really be two similar murders on the same day in the same town?

No, he reminded himself, this was different. With the murder suicide at the Church home, everything had taken place behind closed doors. The first the police had known about it was when the gunshots had been reported in. This time, they were here before any violence had taken place. It was obviously concerning that Emma was in there with no contact. But on the other side of the equation, there was a whole armed response team, together with senior officers, paramedics and negotiation teams.

He just hoped it would be enough this time.

CHAPTER FIFTY-SEVEN

'Guv, the front door. Something's happening.' Nick Dent pointed at the house.

Michelle could have told him that it was bloody obvious because, like everyone else, her attention had been fixed on the house. But instead she said, 'Thank you.'

Very slowly the door opened inwards and the figure of DC Emma Angel lurched out. It was immediately obvious that something was wrong. She missed a step down, and took two or three more correcting steps ever more wildly until she careered off the path and fell onto the lawn. She lay there, not moving.

Michelle immediately rushed over to where two paramedics were waiting. 'We have an officer down. Go, now!' She pointed to the lawn.

The two paramedics looked at each other nervously. The older of the pair was a man in his late forties or early fifties. He was heavy set and jowly with his hair just starting to grey. His younger companion was a woman with a thin face and a ring through her eyebrow. She looked at the other paramedic, wondering what to do. He took the lead and said, 'Have we got clearance from Gold Command? Or at the very least, do firearms say that it's safe?'

'This isn't time for protocol! My officer is injured on the lawn. Surely you have a duty to help her?'

'I'm very sorry ma'am, but we can't walk in front of firearms officers without clearance.'

By now they'd walked up to the perimeter that had been set up around the house. Michelle approached the leader of the firearms unit. 'The paramedics won't attend to the officer unless you give clearance.'

'No, ma'am.'

She looked at his implacable face as he scanned the building. 'You're not going to give it, are you?'

'No, ma'am.'

'Well, in that case, I'll go over there. I know first aid. I can at least check that she's breathing.'

'I'm afraid that I can't let you do that.'

The officers looked at each other in uneasy standoff. In one sense, Michelle outranked the Authorised Firearms Officer. She was the highest-ranking officer there, and assigned as Bronze Command, the link between the situation on the ground and the control room back at the station. But, in this very limited case, he was in charge of his firearms team and he could tell her what to do. Neither of them were happy with the situation.

'My main role here is to minimise casualties,' he said kindly. 'We can't see inside the house, but the door is open and there are at least two windows with line of fire on the lawn. I'm just trying to protect you and the paramedics. I appreciate your loyalty to your officer, but she wouldn't want you to get shot for her. And I definitely won't put medical personnel at risk. Trust me, we have protocols for situations like this. It'll work out.'

The discussion was cut short when the door was pulled all the way open with a bang. Thomas Bagshaw stood on the top step of the path and glared at everyone with wild eyes. In his right hand was a pistol that he waved unsteadily across the crowd.

EMMA LAY ON THE LAWN, where she had fallen. She could see the blades of grass, feel the damp seeping in through her clothes. The ground was cold beneath her cheek, a contrast to the hot and stuffy house. She felt awful, her head was swimming and she felt slightly sick. She was so tired. Tired enough to just lie there and take a rest for a moment.

Lights snapped on, throwing the grass into sharp relief. She rolled over and saw the house bathed in unnatural bright white light. Standing on the doorstep, madly waving a gun around was Thomas Bagshaw. His eyes were wide and his lips drawn back showing his teeth. He looked like an actor on a stage. Emma closed her eyes for a moment. She could still see the lights, making everything red through her eyelids. She didn't have the strength to raise an arm to block it out.

'Mr Bagshaw. This is the police. We have armed officers surrounding you. Please lay the gun down on the ground and place your hands behind your head.'

Dimly, in her confused brain, the thought "first warning" floated. They had called in the Armed Response Team and given him one warning. What did it mean?

'Stay back! I'll shoot someone. Maybe this woman police officer lying on my lawn.'

Woman officer? Emma suddenly realised that she was being talked about. She ought to get up, get involved, make a change. She put a hand on the ground and tried to lever herself upright. But her hand slipped on the wet grass and she rolled over again. She lay there for a moment, just to get her breath back, so she thought. Looking straight up, she could see a fine rain had started. Each drop shone in the bright lights as it floated gently down. She was woken from her reverie by another shout from the armed officer.

'Mr Bagshaw! This is your second warning. Put the gun down and your hands behind your head.'

An uneasy calm spread over the entire scene. Emma felt calm and light, as if she could float way from it all. Away from the blades of grass that were each distinctly outlined in the harsh lights that had been brought to the scene. She could see her own breath forming clouds. Somewhere beyond the grass, beyond the lights on their tripods, a crowd had formed. Someone had run some police tape which kept them back. As in every police incident, there was always a group of onlookers, ready and waiting to gawp at someone else's misfortune.

Thomas Bagshaw had also noticed the crowd. He was scanning them, his gun subconsciously following his eyes as he went to and fro across the line of faces. 'You!' he bellowed. 'You're the pervert who abducted my Amelia. You think you can take my child away from me? I can see you.'

In the crowd, Rob Haines was frozen. He realised too late that he was standing under a street lamp. He had thought that with the bright lights he wouldn't be identifiable, but now Bagshaw had called him out. He felt all his training leave him as the man on the doorstep brought both hands up and levelled the gun in his direction.

Rob knew he should drop to the floor or dodge. But if he

dodged either left or right, then he'd be hiding behind someone. He had always faced problems head on and didn't intend to start hiding now. He locked eyes with Thomas and tried to decide if he was really a threat. Was he looking at someone who was about to pull the trigger, or was he all bluster?

He couldn't tell. Thomas's eyes were red rimmed. But Rob noticed that they were moving, first to him, then off to either side, presumably at the armed officers. If those eyes ever stayed on him, then Rob would move. He knew from his time at the top of CID that all sorts of conversations would be going on right now. Gold Command would be in touch with the head of the firearms unit. Any minute now, either Thomas Bagshaw would surrender or the authorisation would come through.

'Mr Bagshaw. This is your final warning. We don't want to fire, but we have to act to protect the public. Lay down your weapon now.'

Instead, Thomas Bagshaw spread his legs slightly and brought his left hand up to support his right. But now the gun moved from side to side, first aiming at one of the AFOs and then at another, before wavering back to Rob. Without warning there were four cracks, in two neat pairs. The crowd gasped and pulled back. The noises of the shots echoed around the buildings.

Emma heard the gunshots and recognised they came from two directions. She propped herself up on one elbow and saw Tom lying sprawled against the door frame. Blood was soaking his shirt, from two bullet wounds on each side. The gun was laying by his side.

She saw boots and black trousers rush past her. Some stayed back at a safe distance while one officer approached. First he secured the gun, then he leant over Thomas

Bagshaw's body for a second before standing up and shaking his head.

Then, once this ritual had been completed, all hell broke loose. Emma was aware of being crowded by paramedics, and of Rob and Michelle hovering just behind them. Once again, a wave of tiredness crashed over her. This time she could see no benefit in staying awake.

CHAPTER FIFTY-EIGHT

'HEY, EMMA, HOW ARE YOU FEELING?' Michelle Jones asked as she walked into the room and approached Emma's bed. Emma was immediately taken aback with the warmth which was a definite contrast to both her previous boss and her previous dealings with this one.

'Not too bad, all things considered. The nurses say that they were told by the police that they found Diazepam in the house and it had been added to my tea. So that's what they're treating me for? Is that right?'

'Yes, in a cupboard next to the kettle. Together with a pestle and mortar to grind it up. My guess is that his widow will end up in here being treated for dependency, even though she didn't know that she was taking it. But you probably had an overdose.'

'Widow? I mean, I thought I heard gunshots, but... oh. That's a whole new thing.' She paused for a minute, then gathered her thoughts. 'Sorry. Whole head is full of cotton wool. I'm just so damned tired. And not just tired, I can't follow any train of thought. So, Thomas Bagshaw was our killer then? Why did he do it?'

'Yes. We've found a treasure trove of evidence. An initial assessment suggests that he was obsessed with protecting the family. Their eldest daughter, Sophie moved out and cut off all contact, that seems to have been the initial trigger. She made contact with us after she saw the reports on the news. Hell of a way to find out that your father has been shot by police, but we couldn't get in contact with her. Anyway, it was probably that lack of control over the women in his life, the feeling that they were in some way escaping from him that finally tipped him over the edge.'

'I can see the drug dealer and the paedophile as targets if he wanted to protect his family. I mean, wasn't one at school with Sophie and the other a teacher there? But where does the family GP fit in?'

'Poor woman. She was just doing her job. She could see how dysfunctional the family was and kept trying to set up a meeting with Amelia or Sharon on their own. She'd done counselling training courses, and was connected with women's shelters so she would have tried to support them and provide a route out of their situation. We'll probably never know how he found out, but once again, Thomas perceived that as a threat to his control over the family unit.' An awkward silence fell between the two women. Emma was struggling to follow the conversation and felt more than a little awkward at lying in bed in a hospital robe having a conversation with her boss.

After a few seconds, Michelle brightened a bit. 'I know it's a bit gruesome, but do you want to see some evidence?' She was already looking through her bag. She brought out a see through plastic bag with a gun in it.

'Woah! What are you doing? You can't bring that in here.'

'Relax, it's what Thomas Bagshaw was pointing at the

ARU. You remember he was a caretaker and a design and technology teacher?'

'He made that? Was it a replica that he re-activated?'

'No. More than anything, he loved working with wood. He made toys for children, ran woodwork classes at the school. We've even found designs for the wooden knives that he used in the murders and then burnt afterwards. The techs are going through the ashes in the bottom of his burner. Feel the weight of that.' She passed the bag over to Emma.

'It's really light.' She frowned. 'This is really made from wood?'

'Yeah. He made it based on pictures from the internet. Carved out of one single block of wood, then painted.'

'Damn! He was good. It's metallic paint, and everything.' She shook her head. 'No one's going to blame the ARU members who fired the shots. It was dark and this would pass muster in broad daylight.'

'That's the point, isn't it,' Michelle said. 'It's about control. He realised that he had lost his grip on his family, so ultimately he forced the armed officers into killing him.'

'One last act of control.' Emma shook her head and passed back the evidence bag.

'Yeah, this is going to end up in a museum somewhere, once the inquest and internal enquiry are over.'

Emma dragged something else up from her sluggish memory. 'Wait a minute. You said that you thought the knives used in the attack were made of wood?'

'Yeah, his internet search history was a treasure trove of nasty. Apparently there's some South American hardwood that can be fire hardened and hold a sharp edge as well as a steel knife. Obviously it won't last for years and years like a metal one, but if you want to stab someone once and then burn the evidence.'

'Gold star to Dani then,' Emma said. 'She thought it might be an improvised weapon, maybe 3D printed. She was close.'

'Yep,' Michelle said, then frowned. 'Are you up to a visitor? You can say no if you're too tired.'

'Who is it?'

'Sophie Bagshaw wants to meet you. Don't worry though, I'll stay in the room. And as I said, you can always say no.'

'I'd like to hear what she has to say. But before you call her in, could you do me a favour?'

'Of course, what do you need?'

'My friend, Lukas, his girlfriend, Anna Violet Blackton, was meant to go up before the magistrates...' Emma frowned and tried to remember. She looked out the window. 'I think it was yesterday? It's Thursday today isn't it?' Michelle nodded. 'Yes. So could you find out what happened?'

'Yes, I'll do that while you're chatting with Sophie. Don't worry, I'll keep an ear on the conversation too.'

Michelle summoned Sophie into the room, then leant on the doorframe and started talking quietly into her phone.

Sophie came fully into the room and perched on the edge of a visitor's chair. Emma quickly appraised her and decided that she was possibly a bit younger than her, probably late teens or early twenties.

'Hi,' Emma said and then let the silence hang between them.

'Hi. I came here to say sorry.'

'What do you think you need to apologise for?' Emma asked kindly.

'Well, all of it. All the murders and what happened to you. It's all my fault.'

Emma blinked a few times and tried to clear her head. She was still struggling to put her thoughts together. 'Sorry.

I've still got some lingering drugs in my system. Why do you think that?'

'It was me, I started it. I set my father on this course. Without me, it wouldn't have happened. And I should have known better. I'm the oldest sister. I've had the longest to know what to do and what not to do. How not to set him off. So, it's all my fault.'

'That's not the case. I've known people like your father and they always do what they want when they want. You're not responsible.'

'Yeah, but I did start it off. I was just silly really. Bill Hawsley was always tagging me in stuff on social media. I don't think I was anything special, he just carpet bombed anyone female with a pulse. That would've been fine, I could've stayed hidden in the crowd. But one time he posted was a video, it was silly really and I put a reaction on it, just a ha-ha. Nothing really. But it was a mistake. It was one more definite connection between us and my father must've seen it. He spent whole evenings on the internet, and I'm sure he was looking for me.' She stopped to gather her thoughts, then saw that Emma was confused. 'I knew my father was poison from a young age. I mean, when you're growing up you think your parents are infallible gods and then at some point they mess up and you realise what they're like. Well, with my family it happened earlier than most and I realised my family was more fucked up than most. So, I made a plan. As soon as I was old enough, I got a room in a shared house. And once I moved out, I ghosted my own family. It felt weird, kind of liberating and scary all at the same time. I changed my phone number, made sure I didn't tell anyone where I was living. I haven't registered for anything. Apart from clicking on one stupid link on Facebook.' She paused for breath. 'That's the thing about my dad, he never bloody forgets. So he must've seen when I clicked. I mean, after that, I deleted my account and started a new one. But I'm telling you. Twenty-four hours after I clicked on that video, William was dead.

Emma's head swam. She was trying to take in all the details of this poor girl's life and how they related to anything. In all the confusion she picked out on salient fact. 'You said your family. What about your mother or your sister? Why did you cut them off?'

'Well, my mother was the original doormat. She either cowered or grovelled. Let him carry on with it all. Enabled him. And Amelia.' She shook her head. 'I was going to come back for her. Figure out an escape plan. I don't know. I was just trying to get myself sorted and then figure out how to rescue her. I felt bad about leaving her behind.'

Emma took a deep breath. She tried to get her thoughts in order, but it was still a struggle. 'Right, you listen to me. I don't want to be harsh, but this is not your fault. I've dealt with men like your father before. And I don't want to say bad things about him, he still was your father.'

'No, it's fine. I had completely cut him out of my life.' Tears started rolling down her face, completely silently at first. Then, she started having hitching breaths and sobs. Eventually she blew her nose and flipped open a compact mirror to touch up her eyes. Finally with red rimmed eyes she looked up at Emma. 'Obviously, I'm not fine. I mean, I worked out years ago that I was raised by a monster. But, you know, he did raise me. And it wasn't all bad. We had some good times as well. I just, I don't know. I spent my whole childhood trying to work out what he was thinking. And I never did manage. I mean, as soon as I thought I knew, he went off and did something crazy and I was back to square one.'

'Well, if it helps, we think he had some weird urge to protect his family. But you have to understand something.

Whatever he was thinking, it was warped and distorted. And he made his own decisions. There's no way anyone rational would look at you clicking like on a link from someone you haven't spoken to in five years and leap straight from there to murder. If it hadn't been you clicking on a link, it would've been something else. I mean, if you look at it like that, then it's not rational behaviour, is it?'

She shook her head and sniffed again. 'No, I suppose not.'

There was a pause. A thought occurred to Emma and she voiced it before she had a chance to consider if it was a good idea. 'At every crime scene...' Emma still had enough of her wits about her to edit as she spoke. 'A football coin was left. It's what led us to link all the murders together. I wondered if they might have meant something to your father?'

'Football coins?'

'Yes. Commemorative coins that were handed out by petrol stations for some anniversary or something.'

Sophie frowned. 'He was always buying stuff from car boot fairs. Never anything good, just cheap seventies rubbish.' She paused again and thought. 'You know what I was saying earlier about my childhood? About how I tried to figure him out, predict his moods? Do you know what I've realised in the weeks since I left home? You can't figure him out. He's not as bright as he appears. All through my childhood, he did these random things that seem to have some meaning. But they don't. He just does them because they look clever. And because it's another way to control us, to have us all trying to figure out his motives when he probably doesn't have one.

'To be honest, he probably found a website with a list of serial killers and thought it was something he could do. Leave something behind or take a trophy. But without the meaning behind it. Trust me, you'll go mad if you try to find the meaning behind it all.'

Emma nodded. 'We had ideas in the incident room about symbolism and serial killers. But it never went anywhere.'

'And it won't,' Sophie said. 'He wasn't deep. He was a shallow mix of meanness and ideas he got from the internet. He was on lots of forums full of conspiracy theories, but I don't think he ever got that deep into anything.'

The two women lapsed into silence again.

'Anyway,' Sophie said, 'I just wanted to say -'

'No need. You've got nothing to apologise for. You survived and that's the main thing.'

Sophie nodded, unable to say anything. Eventually she said, 'Well, thanks, hope you get better soon.' She left with a nod to Michelle Jones who was still in the doorway.

Michelle came over and sat in the visitor's chair. She glanced at the door, checking that Sophie had left. 'That's the problem, isn't it? It's never just one person like Thomas Bagshaw. Everything he touched ends up damaged.'

The silence hung between the two women for a moment.

'Oh yes,' Michelle said. 'I did make some phone calls. Your friend's girlfriend is off to the crown court. Possession, breach of the peace and assault on a police officer.' She gave Emma a long hard look.

Emma held up her hands. 'I never liked her. Lukas is all right, I've known him since we were kids. But his new girlfriend...' Emma left it hanging. 'Well, let's just say I wasn't her biggest fan.'

Michelle nodded and there was another moment of bonding between the two women, over the universal feeling of disapproving of a friend's new partner. 'Anyway, all that aside, she's out on bail waiting for a date. She has to stay in Bradwick and report into the police station once a week.'

Emma nodded and thanked Michelle. She made a mental note to check in with Lukas when she was able to.

'I've got one more thing to tell you before I leave you in peace,' Michelle said. 'While you were in with the Bagshaws, we were attending a murder suicide on the other side of town. My new trainee detective constable told me that Rob Haines knew the victims and was involved somehow.' She looked, just for a moment, uncertain. But she rallied and continued. 'Anyway, you might want to have a chat with him.'

'Ma'am?'

'He'll probably take responsibility for it. Or try to.'

Emma nodded. They didn't need to say it out loud. They both knew how corrosive that could be. Emma was also digesting the fact that Michelle, in some way, cared about what happened to Rob Haines.

She realised that the silence had stretched out, but she couldn't think of a thing to say.

Finally Michelle said, 'I can see I've tired you out too much. I'll go before I get told off by the nurses.'

Alone at last, Emma thought about the people in her life. Lukas and Violet, Rob and Michelle, Sophie and Amelia, even Amelia and Rob. She tried to figure out how they were all connected but they kept swirling around until she realised she was asleep.

WOOTENSHIRE

THE WAY to Hell is the fourth Angel & Haines novel and is set in the fictional county of Wootenshire which is in the UK, just south of Bristol and north of Somerset. It is the first instance of a new concept in writing - a Shared World where many authors can write stories in different genres but all set in the same world.

Please visit www.wootenshire.co.uk for more details.

ACKNOWLEDGEMENTS

Thank you for reading this book, especially if we've never met. As a writer, selling my books to strangers, is the best feeling. (Obviously, if you're friends or family, thank you for supporting me!) This book took me longer than usual to write, so I'm happy to see it out in the world. As well as my readers, I have other people to thank who turn a first draft into a published book.

The beautiful cover was designed by the talented team at Ebook Launch. Thank you to my wife Ellie who has always supported me and believed in my work, and has now become my editor. Rosie Schoening, Sam Scriven and Anne Miller checked over the text for accuracy and typos. All surviving mistakes are mine.

Please consider leaving a review on Amazon. You can also sign up for my newsletter and learn about my other books by visiting my website GrahamHMiller.com.

Printed in Dunstable, United Kingdom

66261870R00198